The town
with anticip
dedication o
sheriff turns up murdered, a strange warning carved into
his chest, Mayor Palin Majere sends for the one man who
might solve the crime and restore calm to the troubled
citizens: Gerard uth Mondar.

Saving Solace
Douglas W. Clark

The Alien Sea
Lucien Soulban
(August 2006)

SAVING
SOLACE

DOUGLAS W. CLARK

Champions
SAVING SOLACE

©2006 Wizards of the Coast, Inc.

Published by Wizards of the Coast, Inc. Dragonlance, Wizards of the Coast, and their respective logos are trademarks of Wizards of the Coast, Inc., in the U.S.A. and other countries.

Printed in the U.S.A.

Cover art by Victoria Frances
Map by Sean Macdonald
First Printing: January 2006
Library of Congress Catalog Card Number: 2005928109

9 8 7 6 5 4 3 2 1

US ISBN: 0-7869-3977-X
UK ISBN: 978-0-7869-3977-0
620-95459740-001-EN

U.S., CANADA,
ASIA, PACIFIC, & LATIN AMERICA
Wizards of the Coast, Inc.
P.O. Box 707
Renton, WA 98057-0707
+1-800-324-6496

EUROPEAN HEADQUARTERS
Hasbro UK Ltd
Caswell Way
Newport, Gwent NP9 0YH
GREAT BRITAIN
Save this address for your records.

Visit our web site at www.wizards.com

This book is dedicated with love to

JACKIE MILZ CLARK
*for a boundless supply of
encouragement over the years.
Thank you for all you've given me.*

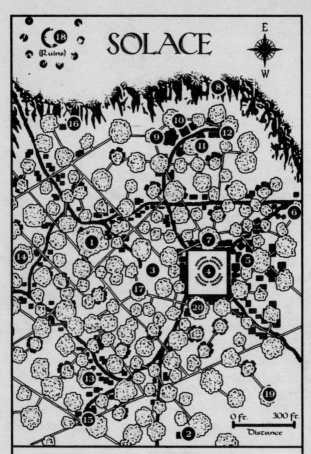

SOLACE

E
W

18 (Ruins)

1. Inn of the Last Home
2. Last Heroes Tomb
3. Fable Park
4. Town Square
5. The Blacksmith Shop
6. The Trough
7. Stephen's Grocery
8. Kerik's Caverns
9. Temple of Mishakal
10. Temple of Majere
11. Shrine of Zeboim
12. Temple of Chemosh
13. Fiddler's Inn
14. Harrin's Supplies
15. Hylar House Tavern
16. Prison House
17. City Guard Headquarters
18. Academy of Sorcery
19. Raven's Mageware
20. Merchants' Guild Hall

0 ft.   300 ft.
Distance

CHAPTER

1

Tom Osterman gripped the reins impatiently but made himself keep them slack, letting the lead horse set the pace as the team, a pair of massive draft animals, pulled the old farm wagon toward Solace. The wagon, heavily laden with potatoes, carrots, beats, and freshly ground flour, rattled and jolted over the rutted road. To the right, the rising sun had cleared most of the trees, and the day was already warm and tangy with pine resin. Somewhere a meadowlark sang its clear, lilting notes.

"I don't care what you say," Tom's wife, Sophie, went on, continuing an argument that had occupied the pair since leaving Jutlin Wykirk's mill down on Solace Stream. "I don't like him. He's such an . . . an. . . ." She searched for a word that sufficiently expressed her distaste. "An *odd* sort," she concluded at last. "Always going on about outsiders who've been making their way into Solace these days—kender, elves, and whatnot. Even a couple of minotaurs he claims to have spotted." She thought for a moment.

1

"Well, maybe the minotaurs I can understand, though I've never seen one myself. But I've heard things about the horned race, and I know I wouldn't care to have any direct dealings with one."

"Ah, he's a good sort," Tom said.

"Who?" she asked, having lost her own train of thought.

"Jutlin," Tom said, flicking his eyes at her—like all of his movements, a tight, intense action. "He's a mite peculiar, I admit, and he does carry on about outside influences, but he's basically all right."

Sophie sniffed, her mouth pursed disapprovingly.

"I rather like the few elves I've met," Tom continued. "Such fine fellows. A bit on the proud side, perhaps, but basically a good sort."

"Oh, that's the trouble with you, Tom Osterman. You think everyone is a good sort."

"Well, weren't you just criticizing Jutlin for *not* thinking everyone is a good sort?"

"Don't you go getting all logical on me!" She stared straight ahead for a moment. "Besides, even you have to admit Solace has changed since they've all been pouring in," she added.

"Well, of course it has. I never denied that."

"There you go, then."

Tom wasn't sure where he went, except to market, but he knew better than to argue.

Around them the woodlands opened out, giving way to fields as they approached the outskirts of town, although they were still far enough away that much of the land stood untilled. Tom hauled back on the reins, and the wagon lumbered to a stop. The lead horse stood patiently waiting for the next command while the other horse began contentedly munching grass along the side of the road.

"Look, there it is," Tom cried, indicating a field to the left of the road with a sweep of his arm. "That's the one I was talking about." He jumped to his feet and surveyed the land as if he could see it more clearly from the vantage of his modest height. The lead horse, evidently mistaking his arm gesture as a command, started forward again, jolting the wagon. Tom sat down abruptly. "Whoa!"

Sophie rolled her eyes. "Yes, I see it."

"Well, what do you think? Wouldn't it be the perfect place to start expanding the farm?"

"What I think is that we'd better get going if we want to get to market in time. You know all the best deals are made early."

Tom stood up again and sprang down from the wagon. "Ah, we've got time."

"Tom, where are you going?"

"To get the proper feel for the land, you've got to walk it." He motioned to her. "Come on."

She didn't budge. "We've talked about this before, and I still say we can't afford to spend the coin."

"Just walk it with me," Tom pleaded.

She rolled her eyes again but stood. Tom grinned and helped her down. "Come on," he said again and, taking her hand, pulled her with him into the field. She plodded after him, unwilling to be hurried. "Isn't it a great piece of land?" he asked. He let go of her hand and crouched, scooping up the loose, black earth. The rich odor of it rose to his nostrils, and he inhaled deeply. "That's good soil. We could grow anything in that."

"We already do, in the fields we have," she reminded

him. "People already say we sell the best produce in Solace." She studied the sun, now angling higher beyond the other side of the road. Her mouth was set in a grim line. "That is, when we make it to market in time."

"Ah, why can't you see the beauty of this?"

She spun on him. "Because I've seen the 'beauty' of too many of your schemes as it is, Tom Osterman! I've seen how hard we both have to work taking care of the land we already farm."

He shrugged. "We'll hire more help."

"Spend more coin?" She stalked back to the wagon. "I'm not even in favor of spending what it would cost to buy the land, and already you're wanting to hire extra hands."

Tom scowled, staring off toward the far edge of the field. "What's that?"

"I said I don't want to spend the coin."

"No, that." Tom pointed to where crows were flocking around what looked like a small earthen mound.

Her gaze followed in the direction he was pointing. She pursed her lips. "I don't know. A pile of dirt maybe. What difference does it make?" She again headed for the wagon.

Tom didn't move. "That's not a pile of dirt."

"Tom, we don't have time to waste on any of your wild ideas. We've got to get these goods to market."

But he was already bounding across the field, his attention fixed on the crows that cawed and feuded as if contending for something. By the time Tom was thirty yards away, he had a pretty good idea what that something was, although he kept hoping he was wrong. But the closer he got, the more his certainty grew.

It was a body.

Not just any body, he saw when he drew up to it, scattering crows as he windmilled his arms and shouted.

It was the body of Graylord Joyner, sheriff of Solace.

A blue-black line of coagulated blood stood out against the sheriff's throat, and the ground around him was stained the same dark color where that blood had spilled out upon the earth. The air here reeked of blood, drowning out the fertile, loamy smell of the field. Tom held his breath against the stench and stooped for a closer look.

The sheriff's shirt had been torn open and into the flesh of his chest was carved a word: *Morgoth*. Tom shook his head in incomprehension.

"Tom, what is it?" Sophie called from the wagon.

He said nothing, thinking what to do. Already the crows were gathering again, flocking closer. He couldn't leave Joyner's body to their predations.

"Tom?" Sophie called again.

He grabbed the body under the arms and heaved. The gash in the sheriff's throat burbled grotesquely as Tom dragged the body toward the wagon. Tom fought down the urge to gag. The sheriff had been a huge man, and although vigorous, Tom was a man of relatively slight stature. Dragging Joyner across the uneven terrain proved hard work and soon had Tom breathing heavily and sweating. Sophie came and stood beside him. "Oh," she said, staring at the body.

"Sophie, wait in the wagon!"

Instead, she leaned down and grabbed one of Joyner's arms. "Don't you even think to be ordering me about, Tom Osterman. I'm your wife, and I'm going to help."

They each took an arm and between the two of them hauled the body to the wagon. Loading it into the bed proved harder, but eventually they managed, flopping the dead man in among the vegetables and flour.

"Here," Sophie said, handing Tom a lap blanket from under the wagon seat. "Wrap him in this so he doesn't get blood on any of the produce."

"I think all his blood ran out already back there," Tom said. Nevertheless, he covered the sheriff and tucked the blanket hem under the body, as much out of respect for the dead man as to prevent any further blood from getting on anything.

They made the rest of the journey in unaccustomed silence. When they reached town, it was still early enough that few people were up and about, and their progress through the streets went disregarded except for an occasional hallo from passersby. They returned the greetings with grim nods, and if anyone found them unusually taciturn this day, it was dismissed with a shrug. People had their own affairs to consider, and the peculiarities of farm folk held little interest to the citizens of Solace.

Tom made his way to a quiet side street that housed the shop of Argyle Hulsey, a local healer Tom and Sophie had once consulted about their apparent infertility. Although Mistress Hulsey had been unable to help them conceive, hers was the only place Tom could think of to go now on this graver occasion. Outside the shop, he helped Sophie dismount. "Go find the mayor," he whispered. "The healer's servant will help me get the body inside."

She slipped off down the street as Tom knocked softly on the shop door.

Palin Majere, mayor of Solace, bent over the body laid out on a worktable in the healer's shop and examined the word gouged into its chest. The smell of pungent herbs and potions almost cloaked the scent of death that clung to Sheriff Joyner's corpse. "What do you make of it?" Palin asked.

"Morgoth?" asked the grizzled, one-armed deputy, Sir Vercleese uth Rothgaard. "It sounds like a word out of the ancient elven tongue." He shook his head. "Not that that helps us much. I don't know the word nor the tongue."

Palin glanced at Argyle Hulsey, but she too shook her head before turning back to her mortar and pestle. "It can't have a very friendly meaning," Palin said, "since it looks as though the sheriff was murdered."

"He was a good man," said Sir Vercleese solemnly. "Didn't have enemies to speak of."

"No." Palin studied the body again. "Well, we'll give him a proper burial, of course, but we'll have to start looking for a new sheriff right away." He parted the curtains just enough to peek out the window to where the town now bustled with activity. The new Temple of Mishakal was scheduled to be dedicated in a few tendays, and Solace was full of visiting dignitaries, pilgrims, and other less savory folk, on top of the immigrants and refugees who already had the town stuffed to overflowing. "This is not a good time to be without a sheriff," Palin muttered.

The corners of Vercleese's mouth quirked down, and his brow furrowed for the briefest instant, immediately replaced by the mask of studied detachment that settled again upon his face. Had Palin not been watching the man, he would have missed the expression entirely.

The former knight's dignity had been slighted.

"I'm sorry, Sir Vercleese," Palin said softly. "It's not that you wouldn't do a fine job—"

Vercleese waved him off with his one hand. "I understand, sir. You need a younger, able-bodied man in the job. And I agree." He paused then added, "Did you have someone in mind?"

"I just might at that," Palin said thoughtfully, rubbing his chin. "But I'll need a message delivered to Southern Ergoth. Will you carry it for me?"

If possible, Vercleese stood straighter, and his chest swelled. "It would be my honor, Your Lordship. I'll leave at once."

"Good. It'll take you a few days to get there, then a few days coming back, with I don't know how much time required in between. All the while, Solace will be at a disadvantage."

"I'll make good time," the old warrior said stiffly.

Palin clapped him on the shoulder. "I know you will."

An hour later, Vercleese mounted his horse and slipped out of town unnoticed. He would follow Solace Stream down to the White-Rage River, which would take him to New Ports. From there, he would seek passage to Southern Ergoth. His departure was accomplished, Palin assured himself, with the utmost prudence. Argyle Hulsey's discretion in the matter could be relied upon. No one in town need be any the wiser for at least several days.

◆ ◆ ◆ ◆

"Sheriff Joyner was murdered?" repeated an incredulous man in the crowd that had gathered around the Ostermans' booth in the marketplace.

Tom Osterman, still unloading vegetables from the wagon and arranging them enticingly on the crude wooden counter, nodded. "That's what I said."

There was considerable jostling in the crowd as people strained to hear the Ostermans' news. Tom glanced at Sophie, who frowned in apparent disapproval that people had come to hear the gossip rather than to buy the produce. "Got some mighty fine beets," Tom called out, seeking to shift the topic of discussion. "And the potatoes are especially good this year."

"And what did you say was carved on the sheriff's chest?" another voice demanded.

Tom blew out an exasperated breath. "*Morgoth,* I think it was. Anybody know what it means?"

There was a general shaking of heads, and no one spoke for a moment.

"What do you say, folks? We have some of the best produce in Solace here," Tom said, trying again. He held up a bunch of plump, sweet-looking carrots in one hand, a fresh onion in the other, and gazed questioningly at the crowd.

It seemed the populace of Solace grew more diverse with each trip he and Sophie made into town. Humans still numbered in the majority, but among the milling crowd today were several dwarves—from sober representatives out of Thorbardin to the merest gully dwarf—a cluster of smoke-stained gnomes deep in discussion, an elf or two, a kender with purloined carrot tops peeking out of several of his innumerable pouches, and a couple of well-armed draconians, hissing in that sibilant tongue of theirs and shunned by the rest of the crowd. Across the marketplace there was even a minotaur—a huge, fur-covered man with the head of a bull and great, curving horns—breasting his way through the crowd toward the Ostermans' booth.

Beside him, Tom heard Sophie gasp at the minotaur's approach.

It was now midmorning, and the marketplace was teeming. There was a rich variety of booths, selling swords and knives, silks and satins, and all manner of foodstuffs. The aroma of roasting meat floated above the crowd. The tunes played by musicians competed with the shrill noise of the sword maker's grinding wheel and the bidding of customers.

Not everybody was on their best behavior. Tom watched a fight break out a few booths over as two tinkers competed for the same repair job. They wrestled one another to the ground and rolled about underfoot, at which point the woman seeking to have her pot mended shook her head in disgust and walked away, presumably to find another vendor.

The minotaur reached the Ostermans' booth and addressed Sophie. "Some of those beets and carrots, if you would be so good," he said in a rumbling voice that seemed more command than request. Sophie gulped and hastened to comply.

Tom's attention was distracted by a scuffle that broke out in front of his own booth. "No need to push," Tom said, stepping between a tough-looking human and two elves. "There's plenty of produce here to go around."

"They know what it means," the tough-looking man said, pointing to the elves.

10

"What *what* means?" Tom asked.

"Morgoth," the tough said. "Tell 'em." He elbowed one of the elves, who scowled down at the ruffian as though the human were beneath contempt.

"Sir elf, can you enlighten us?" Tom asked as others drew closer, listening.

For a moment, it looked as though the elf—tall, thin, and haughty as were all of his kind, his features sharp and his dark hair only partially covering his pointed ears—would disdain to reply. Then he frowned and said, *"Beware.* It means *beware."* With that, he and his companion turned and strode off.

A chill went down Tom's spine, and for a moment all was silent before his booth. Even the minotaur had paused to listen. Then the crowd broke into a multitude of languages and voices, each person striving to make himself heard above the commotion. "Beware" sprang from tongue to tongue, leaping like a squirrel darting though the trees. Beware, beware! But beware of what?

No one seemed to know the answer to that.

CHAPTER

2

Gerard uth Mondar straightened his jerkin, already worn with military precision, and ran a hand through his short-cropped hair in an attempt to smooth it into place. The attempt was useless, he knew, for his hair would stand up in straw-yellow, unruly tufts despite his best efforts, which was why he kept it cut short. As for his face, well, there was nothing to be done about that either. The scars he had borne since childhood illness ravaged his face were still there. Along his jaw, his dark brown beard grew in patchy and splotchy. The only reason he kept the beard was to help hide the scars. Between hairline and beard reigned a nose that was permanently askew from a fight in his youth, while to each side of it sat the startlingly blue eyes that were Gerard's best feature.

Gerard had come to accept that his was an ugly face, and regrets or what-ifs were pointless. But he wished he could look a trifle more presentable on this particular occasion, as he confronted his father, Mondar uth Alfric.

He paced his sparsely furnished chamber in the palatial family residence on Southern Ergoth, where, a fortnight ago, he had come after resigning his commission in the Knights of Solamnia. Since then, his father had refused to see him, furious over Gerard's action, but now Gerard's father had requested his presence in the chamber where Mondar directed the sprawling shipbuilding and repair business that had made the family wealthy.

Gerard's boot heels clicked on the parquet floor, five paces across, five paces back, as exactingly measured as if he were still serving on guard duty somewhere. The footsteps echoed off the hard, unornamented plaster walls. He stopped, took a deep breath, and was about to leave his room when a servant appeared at the door. "Yes?" Gerard said.

"Excuse me, sir. A messenger has arrived for you."

Gerard frowned, wondering at this puzzling news. "Show him in," he said, determining to deal with this matter quickly, then get on with his own audience in his father's chambers.

The servant ushered an aging, one-armed man into the room. The stranger bore himself with the rigid, erect discipline of a career soldier. "Sir Vercleese uth Rothgaard," the servant announced, then bowed and disappeared.

"Sir Vercleese," Gerard said without much warmth. "A Knight of Solamnia, I presume."

"Formerly," the older man said. "I am no longer of that honorable line."

"You and me both," Gerard muttered with a grunt.

He hadn't meant the remark for Vercleese's ears, but the man nonetheless responded, "Yes, but I

13

retired honorably after serving out my full debt to the
Measure."

Gerard scowled. Was the older man implying that he
knew Gerard had left the knighthood by other means,
and that he disapproved?

"You have a message for me?" Gerard asked coolly.

"Ah." Vercleese reached into a pouch he carried and
produced a sealed scroll. Gerard noted the seal, realizing that the message came from Palin in Solace. He
tossed the scroll on the cot that served him for a bed.

Vercleese cocked an eyebrow, saying nothing.

"I'll read it in good time," Gerard growled. "Right
now, I have another matter to attend to." He rang for a
servant and when one appeared said, "Take Sir Vercleese
to a spare room. See that he is given refreshment and a
chance to rest from his journey. He'll be staying with us
a few days."

"Thank you for your offer of hospitality, but I'll be
returning to Solace, where I am needed, by the end of
the day," Vercleese said stiffly.

Gerard nodded, rankled by the man's unspoken censure. "As you wish."

He waited until the old man was gone, merely
glancing at the sealed scroll before gathering his
resolve one last time. He strode down the ornate
corridors, the walls hung with rich tapestries, deep
rugs thickly strewn upon the floors. Mondar went
to considerable lengths to ensure that visitors to the
residence came away impressed by the family's wealth
and social status.

At Mondar's door, Gerard paused, straightened the
seam of his jerkin needlessly, and knocked. "Come in,"
Mondar's voice rumbled.

Gerard took a deep breath and entered. "You wished to see me, sir?" Already he felt his jaw stick out defiantly, and he made an effort to adopt a more relaxed visage.

Behind his desk, Mondar uth Alfric looked up as if he had been deeply engrossed in whatever production report lay before him. He still sported the flowing mustache (full despite having turned almost white) that marked the pride of a Solamnic Knight. The man's frame, however, was no longer that of a youthful knight, for he had gone to fat after too many years of sitting behind a desk, running one of the most successful shipbuilding and repair businesses, first in Palanthas, and now in Southern Ergoth.

Mondar was already red-faced—not a good sign— but he made an effort to speak calmly. "I summoned you to talk about your precipitous decision," he said.

Gerard stiffened. He'd known this confrontation was coming, of course. It had been brewing since he arrived home a few days earlier, conspicuously shorn of the armor of a Solamnic Knight.

"I didn't feel it was precipitous," he said. "I had plenty of opportunity to reflect on it beforehand."

His father's face turned redder, and he huffed through his mustache.

"You can't change my mind," Gerard went on as evenly as he could manage. "Besides, it's already done."

Mondar uth Alfric's face went from red to purple. Veins stood out in his forehead. His mouth opened and closed, seeking words that wouldn't form, and for a moment there was silence in the room, the hub of Mondar's business empire, which dominated the eastern wing of the palatial residence and commanded an imperious view of the mountainside down to the port city of Daltigoth, with its shipyards and docks, and the sparkling bay beyond. Outside the huge windows, open to the summer breeze, a wren sang liltingly.

Not for the first time, Gerard considered the man before him and wondered if this was how he would look some day. But no, Mondar had once been a handsome man, and he still bore those traces; Gerard knew he was anything but handsome. Gerard had inherited the older man's medium height and earlier build, but little else. He would never look much like his father.

The older man's voice rose ominously. "Do you have any idea how much coin I paid the knighthood to get you admitted, or how much more I shelled out to keep you in a safe billet during the war?"

"Yes, Father, I do."

"And that means nothing to you?"

"It means that for eight years, I diligently followed the course you set out for me. And that during most of the war, I was kept away from serving any real function other than to brew tarbean tea for the generals and to guard a tomb in Solace no one was interested in desecrating. That was all your plan for me, Father, not mine. I never wanted to be a knight, not from the day before my knighting when I realized I was on the wrong path. I only followed the knighthood because you wanted me to."

"And now you're throwing all that away? I won't allow it."

"You're too late. As I said, it's already done."

"Well, undo it."

"That's impossible."

"A suitable sum in the right hands, that would make amends."

"You don't understand. I'm not going back. Whether you could buy my way back into the knighthood or not has nothing to do with the matter. I'm through with the knights."

Mondar's face took on a shrewd, conniving look that Gerard recognized as the face of the successful businessman entering into negotiation. "And what made you decide this so abruptly?"

Gerard sighed. He really should try to explain. He owed his father at least that much. "The knights are full of false expectations . . . and compromises . . . even corruption."

His father looked incredulous. "And you're an idealistic idiot, if you think you know better how to change the world."

"No." Gerard tugged on his beard in a gesture of agitation. "But I know their way isn't for me. I'm sorry, sir, but I'm not going back."

Mondar's voice grew low and menacing. "You will if you expect to remain a son of mine."

Gerard stiffened. "You must do as you see fit."

Mondar huffed for several moments, his mustache fluttering with each exhaled breath, too outraged for speech. "You dare to defy me?" he demanded at last.

"I'm not trying to defy you, sir. I'm only informing you of my decision. I thought it my responsibility as your son."

"Then you're no longer my son!" Mondar was bellowing now.

Gerard stood straight, despite the severity of the blow. "If that is your wish."

"My wish? It's my command!" Mondar jabbed his finger at the door. "Out! I want you out of this house by nightfall. I won't suffer an ungrateful son. From this time forward, you are no kin of mine!"

Gerard didn't trust himself to answer further. Instead, he bowed stiffly to his father and started for the door.

"See how far those lofty ideals of yours will get you!" Mondar roared at his departing back.

Gerard walked fixedly erect from the room, summoning his military training to keep his steps measured and assured. But once out of the room and with the door slammed shut by his father behind him, his shoulders sagged.

His mother must have been listening outside her husband's study, or perhaps she was inspired by a mother's unerring sense of danger to her child, for she met Gerard in the corridor, crying and flinging her arms around him. "What happened?" she asked, surely knowing the answer to her own question. "Did you two have a disagreement?"

Gerard snorted at the understatement of the word, then wrapped her in an embrace, not wishing to seem disrespectful or give offense. As he did so, he was struck by how much smaller and frailer his mother felt to him now than when he was growing up. He stroked her hair, noticing for the first time how gray it had turned. And when had she taken to wearing it done up in a severe bun, instead of hanging down like a younger woman's? Even her face, once beautiful and young, had become lined and wrinkled. "I'm leaving, Mother," he said gently. "I'm going away."

She trembled in his arms. "You did have a falling out, didn't you? I'll go to him; maybe I can smooth things over."

Gerard restrained her, holding her firmly in his grasp. "No, Mother. In a way, he's right. He and I can't live under the same roof anymore. It's time for me to leave."

"But where will you go?" Her voice quavered.

Gerard frowned, recalling the message from Palin. "I don't know, Mother. Perhaps I'll go to Solace for a while. Palin Majere has written to me, and I might bear my reply in person."

"Palin? What did he write you about?"

He eased himself from her arms. "I honestly don't know, but whatever it is, I think I'll pay him a visit. At least until I can figure out what else to do." He smiled at her to soften the blow of his leaving home and returned to his room, where he carefully slit the wax seal on Palin's message.

By evening, Gerard and Vercleese had ridden from Gerard's family estate down to Daltigoth. Gerard used his family connections to book passage for them aboard *The Merwitch*, leaving with the evening tide bound for New Ports in Newsea. That would put them at the mouth of the White-Rage River, where the pair intended to continue, riding overland to Solace.

The first two days at sea were hot and clear, with a stiff breeze blowing across their stern and filling the sails. Canvas snapped purposefully and rigging creaked with the sound of authority as *The Merwitch* made good headway toward the Straits of Schallsea. Gerard and Vercleese were at leisure to roam the deck, staring for hours toward the distant horizon in the pensive manner of seafarers from time immemorial. When not thus engaged, Gerard, filled with bright hopes and confident of his ability to fulfill the job of sheriff that Palin was offering him, reflected on fellow passengers and crew, enlightening Vercleese with his observations.

"That one, Sir Vercleese," Gerard said, pointing to a small fellow playing bones with the sailors, "is obviously a light-fingered kender." Gerard scowled. "Wretched little fellows, I assure you. Watch your purse around him. I wouldn't trust him as far as I could throw him."

"Mm," Vercleese said noncommittally, although he gave Gerard a peculiar look.

Gerard turned and pointed to an elegantly clad young woman wearing a fur-lined cape despite the warm weather. "Now that one. Did you see all the luggage she had brought aboard? Clearly on her way to a ceremonial occasion. Note the easy smile she has for the sailors and her fellow passengers, as well as her carefree nature. I'll warrant she's betrothed and on her way to a new life somewhere."

Vercleese looked from the woman to Gerard and back again, his brow furrowing in some unspoken observation of his own. Meanwhile, the woman smilingly accepted an invitation from the captain to accompany him to his cabin.

"How nice," Gerard said. "The captain has asked her to have tea with him." He turned and indicated a figure in the opposite direction, standing at the rail, his features lost in the folds and cowl of a dun-colored robe. "Now there's an intriguing fellow," Gerard whispered. "Strange color for a robe. Sooty, wouldn't you say? The color, I mean. I mark him as a cleric of some sort. Probably one of those in-between clerics, neither dark nor light, that abound these days. Still choosing their gods, I suppose. Harrumph! I know the type, mark me well. Still rooted to earthly concerns. Did you see when he boarded? He had more luggage than the lady getting married. Boxes and crates and all sorts of packages.

"Shhh! He's looking daggers at us." Gerard turned back to the sea and pretended to be absorbed in the horizon. "Clerics!" he hissed under his breath. "Worse than mages, some of them." From the corner of his eye, he noted Vercleese studying him sharply, although the old knight still said nothing.

Once within the Straits of Schallsea, the weather turned and the sea grew rough. Huge swells bore passengers and crew up to towering crests, then plunged them down into troughs where it seemed they would never rise from the watery depths again. The deck was awash; the gunwales ran with water. Rain slashed down so fiercely it was hard to distinguish it from the waves that crashed upon them. His stomach churning, Gerard rose that night to find that Vercleese had already abandoned his hammock. Gerard fought his way onto the pitching deck, where he discovered the old man hanging perilously over the railing, holding on by his one hand and feeding the fishes his dinner from the evening before.

"Oh, gods, why was I ever fool enough to leave home?" Vercleese wailed between bouts of retching. "Please let the sea just take me and get this torment over with!"

Gerard hung onto the old knight's belt for answer

and remained there with him, saying nothing, for a long time. Several times, it was his grip alone that kept the two of them from being washed out to sea.

Mealtimes became haphazard as the cook tried to contend with the weather, although few of those aboard, crewmen and passengers alike, had much appetite. After several days of this, *The Merwitch* wallowed her way through the heavy swells of Newsea and reached the relative calm of New Ports. Rain continued to pelt down, but at least the waves diminished sufficiently to allow them to disembark. Gerard eased his horse, Thunderbolt, a handsome bay, down the gangplank and onto the dock. Vercleese followed miserably with his own nag, which promptly slumped to the ground and died, as if it had merely been waiting for solid earth beneath its hooves once more before yielding up its spirit. Vercleese sank to his knees in the mud, although whether in despair over losing his horse or from gratitude for being returned safely to land, Gerard wasn't sure.

"Come on," he said after a few moments, clasping the old knight's shoulder. "Let's get you another horse. Mine can't bear the both of us all the way."

They soon had Vercleese mounted again, on a raw, lean roan of uncertain temperament that was all they were able to acquire on short notice. The rain continued unabated and had turned the earth into a sea of mud. Nevertheless, Gerard climbed into Thunderbolt's saddle, and they headed for Que-Teh on the first leg of the over-land journey to Solace.

CHAPTER

3

They made for Que-Teh following a road that paralleled first the White-Rage River, then Solace Stream. With the rain continuing to fall unhindered around them, they saw little of the countryside through which they traveled, as they were each huddled as far within their cloaks as possible in a vain attempt to keep from getting drenched. Objects, whether trees and rocks in the wilds or buildings in the towns, loomed out of the gloom as they approached, then receded again into invisibility just as abruptly when they had passed.

Occasionally on the road, they passed signs of outlawry—the remnants of a trade caravan, its wagons overturned and burned; a clearing where a battle had raged, the bodies of one side or other left to rot. Twice, Gerard thought he heard skittering among the trees around them, but though he braced for an attack, none came. It could have been elves watching for the patrols of Samuval, the outlaw chieftain whose rogues roamed these parts, he reflected sourly. He glanced over at Vercleese, whose sharp eyes missed little.

At Que-Teh they crossed Solace Stream to Gateway, arriving there in the afternoon. Gerard and Vercleese took counsel, concluded the rain appeared to be lessening, and decided not to stay in Gateway for the night but to push on toward Solace. They proceeded up South Pass, skirting the northeastern edge of Darken Wood, to the bridge at the south end of Crystalmir Lake, where a mill sat alongside Solace Stream. There they turned north for the last couple of miles into Solace proper, just as night was setting in.

The rain had by then returned full force.

Wet, bedraggled, and weary, they finally entered the town, its vallenwoods majestic and its bridge-walks graceful even in the downpour. They came in on the road past The Trough, a disreputable tavern that had been on the outskirts of town the last time Gerard was in Solace, the year before. Now, the sprawling community had engulfed The Trough, making it look even more dilapidated by contrast with the stylish new buildings that seemed to be going up everywhere at ground level, and the new bridge-walks that extended the town's reach overhead. Even in the rain, Solace swarmed with life, with the music of troubadours announcing a party happening somewhere in the tree-tops above, and carriages, wagons, and riders filling the streets below. Several of the wagons, piled high with family belongings, announced new arrivals to town.

Vercleese shook his head, sending raindrops flying. "I've been gone barely two tendays, and already the town's grown beyond where I left it. I'm telling you, boy, don't rest in one spot any too long or they'll erect a building around you."

Gerard peered around in amazement, feeling a pang

of nostalgia for the Solace of old, scarcely recognizable in its current state. He halted Thunderbolt to let a group of women cross the street, their passage sheltered under cloaks held aloft by a couple of gallant young men. Everyone seemed to be going somewhere, as if all the citizens were streaming to a festival.

"Is some kind of celebration going on?" he asked Vercleese.

The old knight again shook his head. "Get used to it. This is just the way Solace is these days." He looked about grimly, as if the town offended his ascetic sensibilities, which it probably did, Gerard realized.

Vercleese pointed down the road, toward the center of town. "The Inn of the Last Home is down that way, if they have any rooms left. I'll see you at the mayor's office first thing tomorrow, all right?"

Gerard nodded, remembering the way to the inn from the many times he had visited Caramon there, wondering if the place would still feel the same. Or would it too have changed beyond recognition?

He felt a sudden impulse to visit the Tomb of the Last Heroes before heading to the inn, to pay his respects to the final resting place of Caramon Majere and those other representatives of what seemed from Gerard's vantage point to have been a nobler time. Even the kender Tas was commemorated there, although of course his remains lay elsewhere. Gerard spurred Thunderbolt into starting forward again.

By the time he reached the center of town, more of the older, beautiful side of Solace became evident. Here, the buildings were primarily constructed in the high safety of the trees and linked by a series of suspended walkways. Stairways spiraled around the trunks of a few of the trees, allowing access to the graceful, arboreal community overhead. Only a few buildings stood on the ground, and those only through necessity. One of these earthbound structures was the blacksmith's shop on the south side of the town square. Next to it, Gerard found a large, new stable erected, the smaller one at the base of the tree housing the Inn of the Last Home evidently having been outgrown by the expanding community. Gerard noted this change with approval, for it placed the horses near the smithy where they would be shod. He reined in and swung wearily from the saddle.

A young boy hurried from the stable to meet him.

"What's your name?" Gerard asked, handing him the reins.

"Baird, sir."

"Well, Baird, I put a high value on this horse and want to be sure he's treated right."

Baird nodded solemnly.

Gerard withdrew a coin from his purse and pressed it into the boy's palm. "Will you see to it he gets a good rubdown and a portion of oats with his feed?"

"Oh, yes, sir!"

"Good, because I'm counting on you, young Baird."

The boy grinned up at him and led Thunderbolt inside.

Gerard made his way through the crowded streets toward the Tomb of the Last Heroes, where he had spent so many hours on guard duty during the war. As he drew nearer, the passersby dwindled, and soon he found himself standing in front of the structure, alone except for the omnipresent guards. The tomb hadn't changed much, except that the ornate marble and obsidian structure was perhaps a little more riddled with places where kender had chiseled off bits and flecks of the structure as souvenirs, almost sacred relics, despite the fence that now surrounded the building. Gerard suppressed a shudder as he recalled the swarms of kender that used to gather at the tomb for Midyear Day. It was unbelievable how so many of them managed to sneak past the locked fence and gate to apply their chisels to the structure's elegant surface.

Gerard observed the two Solamnic Knights who formed the honor guard for the tomb as they marched back and forth before the gate: one hundred paces over, one hundred paces back, salute each other, salute the tomb, then do it all over again. How the days of this repetitive duty mounted up beyond seeming endurance, he recalled. A strange ball of heat formed in Gerard's belly as he followed the two guards with his eyes. He recognized it as a deep-seated resentment toward the knighthood; among its many solemn failures was the thriving existence of that freebooter, Captain Samuval (who nowadays preferred the grand title of Baron to the less pretentious but more serviceable Captain), who had occupied parts of Qualinesti since the war.

Baron Samuval's mercenary troops ravaged the countryside at will, and though Gerard had tried to get the Solamnic Knights to work to oust Samuval, the knights had other priorities. One priority, Gerard thought contemptuously, his eyes following the two knights, was guarding old tombs. Vercleese had told him that Samuval's men even passed through Solace now and then.

Standing before the colonnaded facade of the tomb

in the rain brought back so many painful memories, reminders that Gerard had spent much of the war stuck in this place because his father's wealth and influence in the knighthood had bought him a safe billet. How Gerard had longed to see action, to test himself in the upholding of an honored tradition. Instead he had paced before this tomb, one hundred paces across, one hundred back, salute, and repeat the process, until he felt he would die of shame and boredom. So much for his father's much-vaunted honor!

The steady marching of the guards lulled Gerard into a familiar state of semiconsciousness, that detached awareness that had enabled him to endure so many days of mind-numbing duty here. And in this state, he could almost hear Caramon's voice: "Come, lad, have some of Otik's spiced potatoes. You hardly eat enough to keep meat on those bones of yours!"

"I eat enough to keep mind and body functioning. That is all food should be for," Gerard said aloud under his breath, feeling his mouth pull up into a crooked smile.

Caramon would have snorted and pushed the heaping plate of potatoes closer, always hoping to tempt Gerard into eating his fill. "Obviously you've never tasted Otik's potatoes, if you can hold such an opinion of food as that. Here, try some. There's more on the stove."

But Gerard had never taken to Otik's famous potatoes. Now he wished he had given into Caramon's good-natured invitation, if only to satisfy the only person who had befriended him the entire time he had been stationed in this town. Now Palin, Caramon's son, had befriended him.

"They need you here, lad," Caramon's voice sounded in his head. "They need you."

"I hope you're right, Caramon," Gerard mumbled. "I hope you're right."

One of the guards, who was passing in front of Gerard at just that moment, cast him a disapproving look, as though to say he would keep his eye on anyone who went around talking to himself. Gerard ignored the man, returning to awareness of the everyday world around him. Then he turned and headed back toward the Inn of the Last Home, slogging through the rain, oblivious to the bustle of people of all races around him. At the vallenwood tree that held the inn nestled among its branches, he began the long ascent up the winding stairway. Already, with evening scarcely begun, sounds of merriment reached his ears from the inn overhead.

He must have been mounting the steps rather slowly, lost in thought, for suddenly Gerard was pushed aside from behind. "Out of the way," hissed a voice that made Gerard's hair rise. To his astonishment, two draconians—stout-bodied, reptilian creatures with leathery wings, long snouts, scales, and lizard tails—shoved past him. A few steps ahead, the first of the pair threw a parting shot over his shoulder. "Next time, don't get in the way of your betters, or it'll go worse for you."

Gerard stood unmoving, stunned. Draconians? In the Inn of the Last Home? He thought to call out a warning to the inn's patrons overhead, to let them know of the draconians' imminent attack, but the noise from the inn would have drowned out any warning he could give. Instead, he bolted up the stairs after the pair, frantically trying to decide whether to draw a weapon.

He burst into the inn, out of breath, startled to find the noise of merriment had not let up at the appearance of the new arrivals. In fact, the two draconians were just seating themselves at a table with another of their kind. A half dozen Qualinesti elves, now enduring bitter exile, stared with unbridled hostility at the lizard-men from one corner of the room, but otherwise little attention was being paid to the strange creatures. In fact, it appeared from scowling looks on the faces of the inn's other patrons that the elves were regarded more suspiciously than the draconians. Gerard's head swam. Evidently, more things had changed in Solace than he'd thought.

Even though it was still early, the inn was packed. Gerard managed to grab an empty seat when a rugged-looking man in badly stitched deer-hide clothes got up and shambled from the room. He looked about for a serving maid to order some dinner, but Laura Majere spotted him. "Why, if it isn't Gerard uth Mondar," she said jovially. "And still with a face that would curdle milk! I heard from that brother of mine that you were planning to pay us a visit."

Gerard nodded, tight-lipped. It was hard to take offense at Laura's easy familiarity. "He wants me to be the new sheriff," he said.

"Does he? Well, you'll be good at it, I warrant. You've certainly got the discipline."

Gerard smiled. "I was wondering if you've got a room for the night."

"A room!" She waved to indicate the crowded inn. "I've been turning folks away all afternoon, and the evening's just getting started. These days, there's hardly a spare room to be found anywhere in Solace." She eyed his wet, shivering form and dropped her voice to a whisper. "But for you, I got something nice in the attic. A bit on the cozy side, I'm afraid, but it's the best I can do."

"Thank you," Gerard said, sincerely grateful. Now that he was here, he almost felt at home. He was glad to be in out of the rain.

"Now, what say we get some dinner in you?" Laura continued. "That and the warmth of the fire will take the chill from your bones."

"I'd like some stew if you have any."

"Stew? Nonsense! What you need is some of our spicy potatoes. They'll warm you right up."

Gerard tried to insist that what he really wanted was just some mild stew and a mug of tarbean tea, for spicy food tended to disagree with him. But before he could make his case, Laura had wheeled away and hurried off to the kitchen. Moments later, a pretty, dark-haired serving maid appeared at his side, plunking a mug of ale in front of him.

"Uh, I didn't order that," he said, as she started off toward another table.

"Mistress Laura said you were to have it," the girl said. "Said I shouldn't take no for an answer. First one's on the house!" She hurried away.

Gerard stared glumly at the ale, another item for which the inn was renowned. But Gerard wasn't much of a drinking man. He didn't like hard drink, nor, for that matter, did it much like him. Then again, he was thirsty, and there didn't seem to be any other options. He took a sip and repressed a grimace. He imagined horse piss might taste much like this.

The serving maid was soon back with a heaping platter of spiced potatoes. She set it in front of Gerard, who looked at it almost dolefully. She stood by expectantly.

"Um, did you need something?" Gerard asked after a few moments, toying with a fork of potatoes without actually putting any food in his mouth.

"I'm to see that you eat. Mistress Laura says you need the benefit of good nourishment."

"I'm quite capable of eating without help, thank you," Gerard said as politely as possible, though he was beginning to get irritated.

Still, the girl didn't budge.

Backed into a corner now and unwilling to offend Laura, Gerard nibbled tentatively at the potatoes, then quickly washed the bite down with a hearty gulp of ale. The potatoes really were spicy! Already, he could feel his stomach rumble. He managed a weak grin for the serving maid, who, fortunately, looked satisfied and went away.

Meanwhile, from their corner the exiled elves launched into a patriotic song, just loudly enough for everyone to hear. Tension filled the room. The three draconians glared at the elves, then sniggered, causing the elves to sing even more loudly and fiercely. When the song ended, one of the elves stood and, with a pointed look at the draconians, began to recite:

"There was a draconian, a Baaz,
Who fought his own kind because—"

The draconians fell silent, glowering at the elves.

" *'Though many obey us,*
Our births still betray us,
And we live against all nature's laws.' "

The whole party of elves joined in the last line, their voices full of merriment but their eyes full of hate as they stared at the draconians. One of the draconians—a Baaz, Gerard noticed—started to rise, but a claw from one of his companions stopped him. "Relax," said the companion, speaking loudly enough for the room to hear, "we still have their homeland."

The three burst into laughter so harsh it made Gerard flinch.

In their corner, the elves' jaw muscles stiffened, and their hands drifted toward their weapons under the table. However, one of them nudged the others and the elves resumed singing, louder than before. All other noise in the room had stopped by now. Gerard watched the three draconians turn purplish with rage under their various shades of green, and they began breathing in short, ragged bursts. Slowly the three lizard-men reached for the hilts of their swords.

"Then Arrowswift, noble warrior,
Flung back his chair and rose,
Leaped into terrible battle,
Fought against scaly foes.

"Around him soon bled the dying
Filling the air with groans,
As Arrowswift turned draconians
To nothing but piles of stones."

There was uneasy scuffling around the room, and Gerard noticed that other hands half-hidden by tables were also deftly seeking out weapons. The dark-haired serving maid was frozen near a table where a man had been flirting with her, midway between the draconians and the elves—right in the line of trouble.

Desperately, Gerard tried to think of what he should do or say. The only thing that came to mind, almost unbidden, was a silly, nonsense song he had learned from his nurse as a child. He leaped to his feet.

> *"I loved my cousin Kate,*
> *But waited much too late;*
> *She married Uncle Nate,*
> *And now has thirteen kids.*
> *Sing hey for the life of a fool!*
>
> *"The first they named Poor Pete,*
> *For his brains grew incomplete;*
> *He uses them for feet,*
> *Which won't do as he bids.*
> *Sing hey for the life of a fool!"*

The elves fell silent, looking at one another in amazement at this strange human who had stood up in their midst to sing a nonsense song. They were clearly dumbfounded. The draconians, too, turned squinting, distrustful eyes on Gerard.

> *"The second, name of Wort,*
> *Was not the brightest sort;*
> *They say he ran athwart*
> *Six armless invalids.*
> *Sing hey for the life of a fool!"*

Gerard, who knew his tuneless singing could be bettered by the bellowing of any run-of-the-mill bull moose, even a very old and sick one, nevertheless belted out the words, grinning broadly, all while motioning to the other patrons in the room, encouraging them to join in. Hesitantly, the patrons did join in, and soon the entire room, except for the elves and draconians, were singing and swaying to the silly song. The draconians glared about them a moment longer, then gave Gerard a particularly baleful glare. "Bah!" the one who had jostled him upon entering cried, downing the rest of his drink and rising from the table. "Let us find somewhere less . . . congenial," he said and led his fellows from the inn. Gerard fell silent, listening to the clumping sounds of draconian feet descending the stairs. Slowly, the elves rose, grumbling, and also left.

The room relaxed. The dark-haired serving maid came over to Gerard's table, looking relieved and as though she wanted to thank him. Gerard waved it off, embarrassed. He made a mental note to ask someone her name. "These potatoes are, um, fine, miss," he said, though he still hadn't had more than one bite. "But perhaps you could take these back and bring me a bowl of that fine porridge I remember from before. Something really bland, with neither milk nor honey." When she hesitated, he smiled, trying to sweeten his words.

She glanced at his mug, still nearly full of ale, then at the scarcely touched platter of potatoes. Her expression darkened. Without a word, she indignantly grabbed up the platter and swept away. Moments later, everyone in the inn was treated to the sound of Laura swearing like a war-hardened veteran in the kitchen.

CHAPTER

4

When Laura had said the space available for Gerard in the attic was "cozy," he discovered what she really meant was that it was cramped—extremely cramped. It was tight even for a dwarf used to short beds and close confinement underground. After a night spent with his knees up around his chin and his toes dangling over the end of the bed, Gerard woke to find sunlight streaming in through the attic's tiny window and the sound of birds singing all around him in the tree boughs.

There were other sounds mixed with the birdsongs: the steady ring of hammer on anvil from the smithy, pleasantly filtered by distance and the intervening trees; the tinkling of bells tolling out the rites at one of the temples or shrines; and the rumble of coaches and wagons through the streets.

Added to the sounds were the smells: rain-swept leaves of the vallenwood trees now warmed by the sun, more spiced potatoes being prepared for the day's patrons in Laura's kitchen downstairs, breads and rolls fresh from the oven at some nearby bakery, and the meat pies of a street vendor who was calling out his wares in a singsong voice.

Solace was awake for the day. It was hard not to be cheerful on such a glorious morning, but Gerard managed. He felt optimistic, perhaps, but not quite cheerful.

He stood, banging his head on a roof beam, and stretched as best he could to work the kinks out of his neck and back. Then he dressed and descended to the inn's main room. After a breakfast of plain, unsalted oatmeal—a breakfast personally served to him by a scowling Laura—he headed for Palin's house, high among the trees. Already, the bridge-walk was teeming with people. Several times Gerard stepped out of the way of approaching groups: businessmen deep in discussions about goods delivered and accounts due, well-dressed burghers and fashionable aristocrats newly transplanted from Palanthas and out for a stroll, and riffraff skulking about on who knew what kind of errands. A couple of dwarves passed by, their expressions locked in fiercely maintained attitudes of unconcern at finding themselves so high above the earth.

Scarcely had Gerard gone fifty yards on his way when his attention was caught by a voice ringing out on the street below.

"Good morning, Solace! It's matins on a beautiful, sunny day and—oops, almost stepped in that puddle—if you're not up yet, you should be, because lots promises to be happening today!"

Gerard frowned, perplexed, and leaned out over the bridge-walk's railing to see a kender emerge from a side street, wandering through town and shouting at the top of his voice. Others on the bridge-walk and the street below paused to listen as well, although no one seemed to find the creature's uproar out of the ordinary.

"Mistress Corinne Nestor's favorite hen hatched a two-headed chicken yesterday," the kender went on loudly, "and Jason and Grace Clabber had another row in the early morning about his staying out late drinking at The Trough the night before. With the town's only constabulary still away on secret business at the time of the argument, no one was available to break it up before the whole area was awakened. Nearby residents vowed that Sir Vercleese uth Rothgaard has much to answer for, being unavailable at the time to ensure the neighborhood's tranquility.

"Meanwhile, Solace's new sheriff Gerard uth Mondar arrived last night with the aforesaid Sir Vercleese and endured a largely sleepless night on a bed several sizes too short for him—oh, hello, Sheriff!" This last he directed to Gerard himself as the kender passed from beneath the bridge-walk where Gerard watched. The kender nodded and continued on his way, unperturbed. "But the big, big news remains the recent arrival of a special envoy of clerics for the upcoming temple dedication. . . ."

The kender headed down another street, his voice gradually trailing away behind him. Gerard shook his head in disbelief. Around him, people resumed their own affairs without a second thought for the kender's odd behavior. The changes in Solace continued to amaze Gerard. He went on his way lost in thought.

At Palin's doorstep, Vercleese was waiting for him. The old knight nodded a greeting and reached up with his one hand to knock. When the door opened to admit them, Vercleese stepped aside. Gerard paused in the act of stepping over the threshold. "Aren't you coming in as well?"

"You two have business to discuss. I'll wait out here."

Inside, Gerard greeted Palin awkwardly, studying the former mage. Palin was grayer now than he had been during the war, and his once-emaciated frame now carried a little extra weight. There were worry ridges across his forehead, but his face bore laugh lines as well. Most striking, however, was the nimble agility of his fingers, shattered when he had been tortured for information he refused to divulge, then magically restored at the end of the war. After welcoming Gerard, Palin smiled at his old acquaintance, the expression dancing in his eyes.

Evidently, life as Solace's mayor agreed with him.

Gerard returned Palin's friendly gaze guardedly. They had not been close, exactly. Rather, they had been comrades during the war, both fighting for the same ends. That seemed a tenuous link between them nowadays, in the bustling atmosphere of peacetime Solace.

"Please, sit down," Palin said, gesturing toward a chair. "Make yourself comfortable."

Gerard glanced across the cozy parlor. A colorful knitted throw rug lay folded and draped over the back of a comfortable-looking stuffed chair, one of a pair of such chairs drawn near a fireplace. A sturdy leather hassock rested in front of the second chair. A little wooden table between the two chairs offered a convenient place on which to set a book or mug.

Gerard sat, feeling oddly ill at ease in the warm intimacy of the room, so different from the cool, aloof austerity of his parents' home. This comfy room attested to a loving relationship between Palin and Usha unknown to him, and that brought a pang of longing.

He turned his attention to the artwork on the walls. The paintings varied from a portrait of Caramon over the mantel to interesting still lifes and landscapes elsewhere around the room, all of them done in the unmistakably vivid style of Usha Majere. Caramon in his portrait appeared ready to smile, as if he would at any moment call for a plate of spiced potatoes, while the strawberries in another picture left Gerard with the impulse to pluck one up and dip it in the painted bowl of cream, so lifelike was the image.

Palin took the other seat. "So, I hear you've left the knighthood," he said evenly.

Gerard peered at him closely, wondering if he meant this as an accusation. "How did you find out?"

Palin crooked a smile. "I still have sources in the wider world. Tell me, do you miss it?"

Gerard held his gaze. "You tell me, do you miss the magic?"

Palin raised his long, slender hands before his face, slowly extending his fingers as though he still couldn't believe they had been healed. "Sometimes," he said softly. Then he dropped his hands and looked back at Gerard. "But I find the modest duties of mayor surprisingly satisfying," he said with a smile.

Gerard didn't fully believe him.

A moment of silence lengthened between them, growing uncomfortable. Finally, Palin interrupted the awkwardness. "I'm glad you came. Glad you answered my summons."

Gerard nodded.

"So you'll take the job?"

"Why me?" Gerard countered. "Why not someone local?"

"Because I think you're the right man."

"Why?"

"Well, your record during the war, for one thing. You're courageous, resourceful, and, uh, well. . . ."

"Yes, and what?"

"Not likely to be encumbered by—how shall I put it?—misplaced feelings of obligation toward one group or another that might affect your ability to handle matters in a fair and balanced manner."

Gerard went cold. "You mean, I have no friends in town."

Palin's face flamed. "That's not what I meant."

"What happened to the previous sheriff? Vercleese tells me he was mysteriously murdered. Does that mean I, too, will be at risk?"

Palin hesitated, staring at Gerard from across the small table that separated the chairs.

Just then Usha entered the room, and the question was forgotten. Golden-eyed and silver-haired—not the silver of age, but of agelessness—she was still as fresh-faced and beautiful as a maiden half her age or younger. Gerard leaped to his feet and drew in a sharp breath, caught off guard as he always was by the sight of her. He felt unaccountably clumsy in her presence.

Palin stood as well and smiled, the tolerant, bemused expression of a man who recognized the effect his wife had on all men and women, and who wasn't threatened by it. Gerard wondered how long it had taken Palin to achieve that measure of acceptance. It wasn't a state a man might come to easily, he thought.

Usha was busy heating water. "Please sit," she said, motioning Gerard back to his chair. "Tea will be ready in a moment."

"Oh, no, don't bother," Gerard stammered.

"Nonsense," Palin said, urging him to sit. "You wouldn't deny my wife the opportunity to play hostess, now would you?"

Gerard sat. The truth was he would not have denied this woman anything, so disarming was her beauty. Yet he realized hers was not a beauty that aroused jealousy or caused a man to glance in sideways distrust at his neighbors, but simply the visible aspect of someone upon whom the gods appeared to have bestowed all that was perfect in a woman. Usha was maiden, mother, and revered elder, all in one.

Palin took his seat again with a deep sigh that bespoke contentment with his lot.

"You really don't miss it, do you?" Gerard blurted with sudden amazement.

"Miss what?"

"The travel, the excitement." Gerard felt his face go hot with embarrassment at having spoken perhaps too indiscreetly. "The magic."

Palin considered. "Travel is just another word for bad food and worse accommodations. Excitement is anything that disrupts the tranquility I have come to treasure. And the magic?" He pursed his lips in thought then laughed as if his musings startled him. "No, I don't really miss it. All those years of desperately seeking the next spell, the next magical artifact, of dreading the loss of magic in the world, and now instead I have this." He gestured with his long, graceful fingers, fingers once shattered and now fully restored. Their motion took

in Usha and the surrounding room and, indeed, all of
Solace. "I think it's a fair trade, don't you?"

Gerard nodded, although he couldn't imagine feeling
satisfied at being stuck permanently in Solace. Yet at
the moment, this room did feel very inviting.

"Besides," Palin went on, "we have plenty of excitement here, as you will see. More than anyone needs."
He peered at Gerard closely. "Look, you will take the
job, right?"

"I wouldn't be staying long," Gerard said, unwilling
to create a false impression. "I could help out until this
temple dedication I've been hearing about, but after
that I'll have to be moving on and you'll need to find
someone else . . . uh, more permanent."

"Oh, of course," Palin said quickly. "If you can stay
only a short while, then I understand."

"So what is this temple dedication all about?"
Gerard asked, eager to shift the conversation.

"I'll take you over there in a little bit and show you
around. But right now, let's have some tea and talk."
He gestured to where Usha was pouring three mugs
with steaming tarbean tea, filling the room with its
welcoming aroma. She handed them each a mug and
took the third one herself, gracefully seating herself on
the hassock.

They talked of old times for a while, catching up
on news of companions and heroes from the war.
"You may even see some familiar faces here for the
dedication," Palin finished with a wink in Gerard's
direction.

Usha smiled knowingly but said nothing.

Gerard shrugged. He didn't want to play guess-the-
secret. "Do you think the sheriff's murder had anything

to do with the dedication?" Gerard said, adopting a businesslike tone.

"That's what worries me," Palin said. "There are different factions in town. Some welcome outsiders, some welcome trouble, some just want to be left alone. You'll find as sheriff that your job is to mediate between these groups and get along with all of them. Sheriff Joyner was good at that, very good at his job. Everyone liked him. I can't fathom who had a grudge against him. Oh, the occasional outlaw he caught, maybe, but someone who hated him enough to kill him? It seems so unlikely." He shook his head.

"What about Baron Samuval?" Gerard asked.

Palin paused for a drink of tea then went on. "Oh, Samuval's been quiet lately. Believe it or not, he steered clear of Sheriff Joyner. Still, that's a possibility, though I hate to admit it. Somehow he'll have to be investigated. And there are other possibilities too . . . but I'll leave that to you and your deputy. I'm no detective."

"Hmm, my deputy seems like a good man."

"Yes, he is a good man. He'll help you get started around town. Oh, and here, you'll want to wear this." Palin finished his tea, set the mug on the little table, reached into his embroidered jacket, and produced a bronze octagonal medallion that filled his palm. Attached to one edge was a loop of green and gold sash. On the uppermost face of the medallion, Gerard saw engraved a majestic vallenwood tree and around it the words, "To Protect the Peace and Promote Prosperity."

"What's that?" Gerard asked warily.

"The medallion of office. You should wear it now that you're sheriff."

Gerard shook his head. "I'd feel funny, wearing a medallion, being only a temporary sheriff."

Palin thrust it toward him. "Still, you'll need it to denote your authority."

Gerard put it on gingerly, feeling the burden of office descend upon his shoulders.

"Now," Palin said with enthusiasm, as if he had just won some contest of wills, "the first thing to do is for you to get around, introduce yourself to people. Get comfortable with folks. Long-time citizens of Solace have been skittish since the sheriff's murder, what with all the newcomers and strangers about."

Gerard drained his own mug and set it beside Palin's. Palin slapped his knees. "You ready for a look at the temple?"

"Uh, of course." Gerard stood up. The medallion felt clumsy against his chest. He nodded to Usha. "Thank you for the tea."

She gave him a smile that warmed him to his toes, making him forget his misgivings. "You're welcome here anytime, Gerard."

Outside, Vercleese was still waiting. "Sir Vercleese, you should have come in," said Gerard.

"I didn't want to disturb two old friends," the old knight said gruffly.

Palin put a hand gently on Vercleese's shoulder. "Next time, come in and join us." Then, as the old knight looked uncomfortable, Palin led the way in the direction of the mountains along a gently curving road that featured several temples and shrines on the eastern edge of town. After several minutes he stopped in front of a large, new structure, which Gerard thought looked vaguely familiar. Stone steps led up to a porch where six marble columns flanked the great double doors of an entryway. The pitched roof of the main structure was pierced by a large, domed tower in the center of the building, while three smaller domed towers rose one on each side of the main building and one at the rear. The building was evidently in the final stages of construction, for scaffolding still stood in several places, giving the army of workmen access to the walls. Men on the scaffolding were shouting and calling for materials, which others on the ground hurried to provide. Several men were dressing blocks of stone, their chisels ringing as they tapped expertly with wooden mallets. A group of laborers mixed mortar to cement the stones in place.

"That's the new temple," Palin said. "Recognize it?"

"Of course, it bears a distinct resemblance to the Temple of Mishakal in Xak Tsaroth!" Gerard exclaimed. "I've read descriptions of the ruins." He turned to Palin. "This is built to the same plans?"

"Only smaller," Palin said, nodding again.

Gerard pursed his lips, lowering his voice. "Look, I'll do my best, Palin. . . ."

"Of course," Palin said a little too heartily, clapping him on the shoulder. "Of course."

Once the temple was dedicated, Gerard would be off to . . . well, he'd be on his way somewhere else. Until then, but only until then, he would do his best to be sheriff of Solace.

CHAPTER

5

Gerard strolled along the bridge-walks, accompanied by Vercleese. The walkways were more crowded than ever as people poured out into the fresh air and sunshine, and frequently Gerard had to turn his shoulders in order to edge past groups headed in the other direction. Down on the street, drivers of carts and wagons shouted at passersby to move out of the way so they could get through. Traffic remained snarled, though few people seemed to care, so festive was the overall mood.

Even Gerard found it impossible to resist the gaiety in the air. Vercleese greeted people as they passed. "Good morning, Master and Mistress Tucker," Vercleese said to one couple, lowering his voice to tell Gerard as the pair smiled and moved past, "Bartholomew Tucker is the leading wine merchant in town, and is said to have his eye on running for town council when the opportunity arises. He'd be a good man for the post if he gets elected." The grizzled knight nodded to an elegantly dressed, middle-aged woman.

"Lady Drebble," he said. She barely acknowledged the greeting. When they were safely out of earshot, Vercleese informed Gerard, "Marguerite Drebble is a relative newcomer in town, a widow who claims the right to the title of Lady, although no one seems to know anything about her family connections. Still, we mostly humor her, as she seems harmless enough. That boy of hers, on the other hand." Vercleese rolled his eyes. "Nyland Drebble hasn't got the sense the gods gave a kender."

Often, the two stopped for more formal introductions, as Gerard was introduced to some of the citizens he'd be protecting. "Ah, Brynn," Vercleese boomed at one tall, extremely thin man with a dreamy air about him and a face dusted with fine white flour. "How's the bread business?"

The man pulled himself from whatever reverie gripped him and smiled wanly. "Rising, Sir Vercleese, always rising."

Vercleese laughed at what had obviously become a standard joke between them. It was probably the bread from Brynn's bakery that Gerard had smelled from his room earlier.

Vercleese indicated Gerard. "Brynn Ragulf here is our leading local baker," the deputy said for Gerard's benefit. "He's descended from a long line of bakers. Isn't that right, Brynn?"

The baker's smile took on a more brittle, stretched appearance. "Nobody knows dough like a Ragulf." But oddly, he didn't sound happy about the boast.

"Brynn's a good man," Vercleese whispered to Gerard when they were on their way again, "but he doesn't like being a baker. Hates it, in fact. Loathes bread, you see.

He thinks it's a deep, dark secret nobody knows about him, though everyone in town's well aware of it. Just don't ever get him onto the subject of adventure; he'll talk your arm off. He's a real arm-chair adventurer." Vercleese grinned wickedly, glancing at his stump of an arm. "Take it from me. That man dreams night and day of traveling to exotic places and doing bold things. He's especially keen on a seafaring life, although he's never so much as seen a ship." The knight shuddered, apparently recollecting his own recent high seas trip. "He doesn't know how lucky he is.

"Brynn's wife, on the other hand, is a stoic, practical woman who knows little of his dreaming and cares even less. She just shakes her head over his constant state of distraction, which isn't good for business—he can forget an entire bread order if she doesn't remind him—and sees to the practical running of the shop. When she is laid up in childbirth—a frequent state, as Brynn seems as fertile as the yeast he employs, fathering six children so far and another one 'in the oven,' as he will tell you with some dismay—the bookkeeping goes to the dogs, and everyone in town knows not to count on getting any of their orders right. So the whole of Solace's bread-eating routine is geared around Molly Ragulf's pregnancies!"

As they walked, Gerard noticed that everyone seemed to know Vercleese, and most clearly liked him. Just appearing in the knight's company recommended him to citizens.

"Come on, there's someone else I think you should meet," Vercleese said, heading down one of the stairways to ground level. "This one's a bit of an enigma around town, as no one seems to know just who he is or where he came from." The knight led Gerard to the smithy in the center of town, where a brawny man scowled as he pounded a red-hot coulter into shape, his hammer blows falling heavily. "Torren, I'd like you to meet Gerard uth Mondar, our new sheriff," Vercleese announced between blows. "Gerard, this is Torren Soljack."

The smith glared at Gerard with fierce, squinting eyes. "The new sheriff, huh?"

Those eyes were like a pair of furnaces, Gerard thought, their fires barely banked behind drooping lids. Gerard forced a smile. "That's right, at least temporarily."

"Just for a while?"

"Until the temple dedication, when the mayor will have had time to seek a more permanent replacement. As you know, the previous sheriff was recently, uh, murdered."

Gerard couldn't be certain, but it looked as though the fiery intensity of the smith's gaze flared a little at this statement. "Don't imagine you'll have much to do before the dedication."

"Except we intend to find Sheriff Joyner's murderer," Vercleese said. "He was a friend of mine, and a loyal friend of Solace's, too. That's a double debt to be repaid."

"Debt, yes," Torren muttered darkly and resumed hammering. "By all means, justice must be rendered."

Gerard wandered about the shop, stopping to look at a half dozen unfinished swords leaning against a wall. He liked the man's handiwork. "I could use a good sword," he said to Torren, picking one up and testing the feel of it. "How long would it take to finish this?"

"Come back in a couple of days," Torren growled without looking up. "I can have it for you then."

Gerard nodded, and he and Vercleese left the smithy. "That man's hiding something," Gerard said in a low voice as they walked away.

"Yes, but what?" Vercleese agreed. "He's an angry, frustrated man whose every hammer blow is a declaration of some inner turbulence. And you should see him eat!" The old knight grimaced. "He gulps his food as if using it to stuff something terrible back down inside him. He's a good smith, but he intimidates most people, and they don't come to his shop with cracked or broken implements to be repaired until absolutely necessary. No one has learned what plagues the man so."

Vercleese led Gerard across the Town Square. "Where are we headed now?" Gerard asked.

"There's someone else you should meet. Ah, here we go," he said as they reached another stairway into a stately vallenwood. The foot of these stairs, Gerard noticed, was flanked by two members of the town guard, obviously on duty. They nodded briefly to acknowledge Vercleese but only stared at Gerard, remaining at attention. Vercleese started up the stairs and Gerard followed. At the top of the stairway was a functional-looking building with a distinctly military flavor. Vercleese ushered Gerard inside, where a tall, lanky man of middle years sat at a desk.

"Gerard, meet Blair Windholm, sergeant of the town guard. He and his small regiment will be among those under your command. Blair, this is Gerard uth Mondar, the new sheriff."

Blair bounded to his feet and stood rigidly erect. "Sir, it's an honor to meet you."

"At ease," Gerard said, taking one of the two guest chairs in front of the desk.

Blair resumed his seat stiffly.

Gerard studied the man, trying to place his features. Something about him looked familiar. "So, sergeant of the guard, eh? I take it you served under Sheriff Joyner as well?" he said.

"Sir, it was my privilege to serve under the late sheriff. His death was a terrible loss to the whole town."

Gerard cocked his head. Nothing about Blair's words could be taken amiss, and yet Gerard had the distinct impression that the sergeant was challenging anyone who presumed to fill Joyner's shoes. "Well, I will only be staying as sheriff until after the temple dedication," Gerard said, trying for an amiable tone and seeking to ease the tension in the room.

No sooner were the words spoken than Gerard realized he had made a mistake. Blair's expression turned frosty. "A short-timer, then," he said. It was spoken as an accusation.

"Well, filling in until the mayor can find someone permanent." Gerard scowled. "Wait a minute, now I know where I've seen you before. You were at the inn last night, weren't you? Flirting with that pretty serving maid. What is her name? Kaleen something?"

Blair flushed. "That's not a pretty serving maid. I mean. . . ." He trailed off, flustered and turning even redder. "I mean, that's Kaleen Duhar, and I intend to marry her!"

"Hmm, Kaleen Duhar," Gerard said, watching his glowering subordinate with amusement. "I got on her wrong side, I think. I must be sure to make amends. So, she's your betrothed?"

"Not exactly," Blair muttered. Vercleese coughed. An awkward silence followed.

The air in the guard headquarters had turned decidedly chilly, Gerard noted. He was wondering what a safe topic of conversation was when a member of the guard burst into the room. "Sir, we have a situation brewing over at Stephen's Grocery."

Blair leaped to his feet again. "What is it?" he asked, heading for the door.

"That elf, Kirrit Bitterleaf."

Blair swore under his breath and followed the guardsman out the door, his visitors forgotten.

"Kirrit Bitterleaf?" Gerard asked Vercleese, hastily following.

Vercleese grimaced. "Local leader of the exiled elves," he said, his distaste evident. "They maintain a base in the mountains from which they harass Baron Samuval, but some of them come into town once in a while for supplies."

Gerard and Vercleese hurried down the stairs hard on the heels of Blair and the guardsman. The four hastened across a corner of the Town Square to the base of the vallenwood housing the town's largest grocery. In the street, an elf Gerard recognized as one of those from the inn the previous evening was loading supplies onto a wagon. Nearby, three or four rough-looking, well-armed men looked on. "I hear elf blood is blue," he heard one man say, with a nasty laugh.

"Naw, everyone knows it's yellow," another said.

"Maybe we ought to spill a bunch and see," remarked a third, his hand resting casually on the hilt of his sword.

But the elf continued loading his supplies as if

blithely unaware of the men. The only hint of reaction, Gerard saw, was the muscle in his jaw tensing nervously.

Meanwhile, a number of townspeople had gathered and stood in clusters, watching. From their expressions, they sided with the roughnecks. Gerard turned to Vercleese, his eyebrow cocked in an unspoken question.

"There's a lot of ill will against elves," the one-armed knight whispered. "Some people blame them for all the unrest in the countryside hereabouts. Not that the elves don't deserve some of that, as far as I'm concerned. Officially, they're welcome in town, though few actually come here. Just as well, I say. However, those men"—he indicated the lurking toughs with a jerk of his chin—"are probably some of Samuval's men, the very ones the elves are fighting. They're officially welcome here as well, as long as they don't stir up trouble."

"Looks to me like they're stirring up trouble right now," Gerard said.

Just then, a tomato was launched from amidst the townspeople, striking the elf squarely in the head. He stumbled slightly and dropped the sack of flour he'd been carrying. The townspeople and Samuval's men joined in laughter. The elf whirled to confront his attacker, his hand dropping to the knife at his belt. But it was unclear who had hurled the messy missile.

"Kirrit Bitterleaf," Gerard said, stepping forward.

The elf turned, scowling suspiciously, facing Gerard with his hand hovering over his knife.

"You dropped something, good sir," Gerard continued, keeping his hands well away from his weapons. He spoke loudly enough for all to hear. "Allow me to give you a helping hand."

From the corner of his eye, Gerard noticed Blair had started forward as well, but the sergeant was stopped by Vercleese's hand on his arm. Vercleese gave a slight shake of his head, indicating to Blair that it would be good to let the new sheriff handle the situation.

The crowd had fallen silent. Samuval's men looked on with frowns.

For a moment, Bitterleaf remained tense, ready for action. He stared into Gerard's eyes. At last his hand eased away from his knife hilt, and he nodded. Without any further word, the two of them stooped and lifted the bag of flour, which fortunately hadn't burst, onto the wagon. Gerard gave the elf some assistance with the few remaining items then Bitterleaf climbed onto the wagon and drove away without a word or gesture to acknowledge Gerard's help.

Gerard snorted at the elf's arrogance, then turned to the townspeople, who were staring at him. "I'm sure you all have business to attend to," he said equably.

There was muttering among the crowd, but at last they began to disperse and go their ways. Gerard caught the attention of Samuval's men as they were about to turn away. "As for you folks, I'm the new sheriff around here, and I'll expect more decorum while you're in my town."

"What's decorum?" one of the men whispered to the man next to him.

"I think it's like hanging pictures and stuff on the walls," said his comrade with a bewildered expression.

"And just what is your name, sheriff?" the third man demanded of Gerard.

"I'm Gerard uth Mondar," Gerard said. "And I aim to run a quiet town."

"So did the last sheriff, and look what happened to him," the man muttered to the others, speaking just loud enough to be overheard. They all chuckled nervously.

"What's that?" Gerard asked coolly, his hand edging nearer to his dagger.

"Aw, nothing," said the man as he turned away. "Come on," he called to his fellows. "We'll find better company down at The Trough."

When everyone had gone on their way, Blair turned to Gerard, his expression more deferential than before. "Well done, sir. If you have no objection, the corporal here and I will return to our duties."

"Of course," Gerard said. Then, unable to stop himself, he added with a grin, "And I'll pass along your respects to Mistress Kaleen if I see her at the inn again tonight."

Blair huffed a moment, then stalked away. Vercleese chuckled, joining Gerard. "Betrothed!" he scoffed. "Blair really leaves himself wide open, doesn't he?"

"Who is this Kaleen Duhar he's so intent on marrying?" Gerard asked.

"Oh, Kaleen. She's the daughter of Cardjaf Duhar, one of the wealthiest and most influential men in Solace. He's a landowner from Palanthas, came here about a year ago with his wife and their only child, Kaleen. Since then, he's already risen to be an important figure on the town council." Vercleese watched Blair and the other guardsman as they marched back across the square toward the guard headquarters. Vercleese shook his head. "Blair's a good enough man, even if a bit of stickler for the rules. Everyone in town knows he's sweet on Kaleen. Now you know it, too, though he's got about as much chance with the likes of her as I do catching a kender with its hand in my pocket."

"It seems not everyone was pleased with Graylord Joyner's performance as sheriff," Gerard said as he and Vercleese continued their walk through town. They stayed at ground level now and frequently had to stop to allow wagons and carriages by, or to avoid the swirling throngs of pedestrians who crowded the town. In short order Gerard's boots were caked with the thick mud of the streets, churned up by the many passing wheels and hooves and feet.

"Almost everyone admired Sheriff Joyner," Vercleese replied firmly. "Almost." He gestured in the direction of The Trough. "But of course, that feeling wasn't universal."

"Something to keep in mind," Gerard muttered, peering in the direction of The Trough as he thought about the men who had retreated there. "I suppose it might help if we were to take a look at the place where the sheriff's body was found. Would you take me out there this afternoon?"

"Certainly," Vercleese said. "Although we should steal out there without making any announcements. No sense in letting everyone know what we're up to in the investigation." Louder, he said to an approaching man, "Ah, good morning, Councilman Tos. I don't believe you've had the opportunity yet to meet our new sheriff. . . ."

◆ ◆ ◆ ◆ ◆

By midafternoon the day had grown hot, turning the air muggy as the sun beat down on the puddles and mud left by the rain. Vercleese led Gerard to an untilled field south of town. Gerard slapped at whining mosquitoes as they trudged along. The mud he had accumulated on his boots in town was nothing compared to the heavy layers of it he was picking up here, making each stride difficult. Gerard walked with care lest he lose a boot entirely in the thick, squelching muck.

"Now let's see," the knight was saying to himself. "It's right around here somewhere." He stopped and searched the area for his bearings. "It's been a couple of tendays, and I was out here only the once, before heading out at Palin's request to come get you. We didn't find much." He swung his head ponderously, peering from one corner of the field to another. "Ah, yes, here it is." He led Gerard confidently toward the farthest corner. "I remember now, I think."

He halted before a bit of ground seemingly no different than any other spot in the vicinity. All traces of blood and any impression the sheriff's body might have made on the ground had long since vanished, obliterated by the recent rainfall.

"The Ostermans said they were driving by on the road over there, on their way to town for market," Vercleese said, gesturing back to where they had left their horses. "Tom noticed a flock of crows gathered around something piled on the ground here, and came over to investigate. When he did, he found the sheriff lying facedown here. He was already hours dead."

"Hmm," Gerard said, squatting down and stirring the mud with a finger. The soil gave off a damp smell of rank fertility. There was nothing to see, really, just a few stones, dirt, and some stray flecks of hay. "Hold on." He picked up a couple of the stalks of straw, then stood and looked about the field. "This ground hasn't been planted in hay, at least not recently."

"Hmm, that's right." Vercleese shook his head, studying Gerard closely, apparently still trying to get the measure of his surprising new superior. "Hasn't been tilled in some time, and even then the farmer that planted it was growing potatoes."

Gerard rolled the stalks between his fingers. "Odd place to find hay then, wouldn't you say?"

Vercleese scratched his head. "Now that you mention it, Sheriff Joyner had bits of hay stuck to the bottoms of his boots when we examined his body. But on the other hand, anyone tramping around these parts is likely to pick up a little hay sooner or later."

"Maybe," Gerard said, looking around but seeing little hay scattered elsewhere. "But if he was tramping around, as you say, then the hay would probably come off his boots, wouldn't it?"

"What are you getting at?"

"Maybe nothing," Gerard said, upending his hand and letting the flecks of hay float back to the ground. "Or maybe . . . the sheriff was killed somewhere else . . . then the body was brought here after the murder. Just maybe . . . someone moved him to avoid suspicion falling on them."

"Hmm," Vercleese said, still watching Gerard closely. "Maybe."

"Are there many farms nearby?" Gerard asked, turning to plod back through the mud toward the road and their waiting horses. At each step, the sodden ground sucked at his boots.

Vercleese fell into step alongside Gerard, shaking his head. "Not since the war, anyway. There's mostly elves and Samuval's men in this area these days, lying as it does between their respective bases of operation. It's a troubled area, what with the skirmishes between Samuval's and Bitterleaf's patrols. Too far from town. Most farmers steer clear."

"Might one side or the other, the elves or Samuval, have killed Sheriff Joyner?"

"Not likely, not just for snooping around, if that's even what he was doing. Their quarrel is usually with each other, not the people of Solace. The sheriff was liked even by them, mostly. Heck, he even played a game of Regal now and then with Samuval himself. Used to go over to Samuval's fortress to do it. That was his way of keeping the channels of communication open."

"And the elves didn't find that as being a little too friendly with their sworn enemy?"

"Naw. The sheriff used to go up into the mountains once in a while to talk to Kirrit Bitterleaf, too. Not to play Regal, of course; I doubt that haughty elf even knows there is such a game, let alone plays it with any skill. But Sheriff Joyner took a real accepting view of all the peoples of Krynn, as long as they obeyed the law while they were in Solace."

"But we're pretty far from Solace out here," Gerard said softly.

"True enough." Vercleese turned without another word and continued toward the road.

"I suppose I should have a talk with these Ostermans," Gerard said, falling into step beside his deputy. "Where would I find them?"

"Oh, I doubt you'll learn anything new from them,"

Vercleese said amiably. "But you can try. You'll find them most mornings at the market."

They made the return trek to town in thoughtful silence.

CHAPTER

6

Gerard and Vercleese stood outside the entryway to the new Temple of Mishakal, where
construction had grown feverish. Stonemasons and
carpenters seemed to be competing over which group
could raise the greatest clamor. The taste of stone
dust vied with the smell of wood shavings in the air.
On the ground, blocks of marble were dressed with
hammer and chisel before being raised with block
and tackle to the upper reaches of the structure,
where they were incorporated into the massive walls,
with mortar hoisted from below. Timber was hewn
into appropriate lengths with axe and adz, split into
rough planks with wedges and hammers, then planed
smooth for use in the interior. Overhead, tiles were
being laid in neat rows along the roof, a relatively
noiseless occupation except for the occasional tile
that slid free of a workman's hands and flew in a long,
graceful arc to shatter on the ground.

Gerard, safely out of range, shook his head at the
frenzied activity. It was a wonder no one on the site

had been killed, he thought. "Mayor Palin told me you might find an old friend here," Vercleese said, peering about the grounds. "Lady!" he shouted to the hooded figure of a cleric some distance away. "Oh, Lady! Over this way!"

The cleric, who had been consulting with a man who bore the air of one in charge, looked up at Vercleese's cry and threw back the hood that had obscured her features. To Gerard's astonishment, the individual thus revealed was Lady Odila Windlass. He turned to say something to Vercleese, who grinned back at him as he headed toward Odila. Gerard hurried to catch up.

Just then, the man with Odila blew a piercing whistle, and all noise at the site blessedly stopped for lunch. The man strode away with the plans he and Odila had been discussing.

When Gerard reached the female cleric, he suddenly felt awkward, uncertain whether to embrace her as an old comrade from their days in the knighthood together or to kiss her hand in the more formal greeting that befitted her station nowadays as a titled lady. Evidently, Odila shared his discomfort. Her hand rose partway then hesitated before dropping again to her side. She blushed, her freckles almost disappearing in the rising color of her cheeks.

"Oh, go on, you two," Vercleese boomed, giving Gerard a none-too-gentle shove.

Gerard closed the gap and enfolded her in his arms, pounding her affectionately on the back.

"Hey, Cornbread," Odila cried, "leave one or two ribs intact, will you?" But she sounded as happy to see him as he was overjoyed to be reunited with her.

Gerard held Odila at arm's length and studied her

more closely. She had let her hair grow out from the short, martial cut she had worn during the war. Now it coiled in a pair of braids pinned atop her head. She smiled at him, yet her deep, brown eyes remained sad, and permanent frown lines tugged the corners of her mouth. Furrows etched her brow. She still wore the look of world-weariness she had acquired during the war, when Takhisis impelled her to confront whatever fears and longings inhabited the dark reaches of her heart. That experience had resulted, ultimately, in Odila leaving the Knights of Solamnia and becoming a cleric of Mishakal.

Evidently, Odila still bore the scars from her encounter with the dark goddess.

"How have you been?" Gerard asked. "What have you been doing for the past year?"

Again she smiled the weary smile that was her trademark. "I have spent much of the year studying in Palanthas, becoming proficient in the teachings and rites of Mishakal." She hesitated before continuing. "And healing a little from the effects of the war." She brightened. "But what about you, Gerard? I . . . I have heard that you left the knighthood as well."

"I didn't realize that news spread so fast," he said in a subdued tone.

"Palin told me. He also told me about the situation with your father. I'm sorry, Gerard."

Gerard's mouth tightened. "Yes, well, such a parting was bound to happen eventually, I suppose. If we hadn't quarreled over my leaving the knighthood, we would have disagreed about something else. My father and I just don't see eye to eye."

"Fathers and sons seldom do," she said softly. Then

she laughed, for the first time sounding genuinely amused. "Or so I've heard, anyway."

"So what are you doing here?" Gerard asked, anxious to shift the subject.

"Overseeing the completion of the temple and preparing for the dedication ceremony. Come; let me show you what we're accomplishing here." She pulled his arm, leading him up the six stone steps to the portico and in through the huge double doors, which were propped open for easy access by the workmen. Vercleese followed, but at a discreet distance.

Inside the entrance hall, all was cool and dark. The air bore the sharp tang of newly hewn stone and freshly cut timber. Two worship rooms flanked the hall, one on each side. Ahead stood a second set of double doors, also thrown wide. Odila led Gerard through these doors, their footsteps sounding sharp on the marble floor and echoing in the dim recesses of the building.

Once through the second set of doors, Gerard found himself in the central Chamber of Mishakal. A statue of the goddess dominated the chamber. The benevolence that radiated from the statue's face transcended the mere marble of a sculptor's art, and Gerard caught his breath. If he had been wearing a hat, he would have instantly removed it out of reverence.

The room featured no other ornament, only the clean, graceful lines of the circular chamber. Nothing was allowed to interfere with the effect of encountering the goddess's effigy in the center.

The staccato tap of other footsteps sounded behind them. Gerard turned to see a man approaching, the man Odila had been talking to outside. He was a short, stocky man of middle years who carried himself with an air of authority, although he greeted Odila with a show of obsequiousness. Gerard frowned, instantly taking a dislike to the man.

"Ah, Salamon," Odila said, "let me introduce you to my friends. Gerard, this is Salamon Beach, the architect for the building. A very good and important architect. Salamon is in Solace to take charge of overseeing construction and keeping everything on schedule."

"Under the lady's direction, of course," Salamon said in an oily voice, bowing to Odila.

"Gerard is the town's new sheriff," Odila went on.

Something shifted, becoming furtive in Salamon's manner. "I am honored to make your acquaintance, sir," he said, though he never raised his eyes to meet Gerard's. "Now I know whom to go to should anything untoward come up in our little world here." He laughed mirthlessly as if he had just told a joke. "Although we are quite insular and peaceable, and therefore in scant need of an officer of the law."

"You wished to see me, Salamon?" Odila asked.

"Matters will keep, Lady," the architect said, bowing unctuously again and backing out the way he had come. "I wouldn't want to intrude on the lady's visit." He nodded to Gerard; turned, almost colliding with Vercleese, and scurried away.

Gerard stood staring after the man. Salamon bore close watching, of that Gerard was sure. Although why the man aroused his suspicions, he had no idea.

The tour over, Odila led the way back outside. The bright sunlight struck with merciless intensity after the dimness of the interior. Gerard squinted around at the temple grounds, where workmen reclined, eating lunches taken from wrapped packets. A few workmen, apparently having finished their meals, lay stretched out on the grass, snoring softly. Under a tree, a pair played a game of Regal. The entire atmosphere was one of indolence and relaxation that formed a stark contrast to the tumultuous activity that had characterized the site upon Gerard's arrival.

Odila ushered Gerard toward a large pair of rounded rocks protruding from the ground, and motioned for him to sit. He chose one of the rocks and sat, and she took the other.

"So what do you think of our project?" she asked.

Gerard peered at her. "The temple is most impressive."

Odila beamed, again appearing free of whatever ghosts of the past haunted her. But it was only a fleeting look of pleasure, and soon the serious frown returned. "We still have much to do before the dedication."

"Are you concerned about being ready in time?"

"No, not really. Salamon seems a capable supervisor. He'll get the job done, I'm sure."

But Gerard noticed that her voice lacked conviction.

Just then someone approached and handed a basket to Odila. "Ah, lunch," Odila said, taking out sandwiches and offering one to Gerard. "Will you and Sir Vercleese join me?"

Rather than answering, however, Gerard was staring up at the young woman who had delivered the basket. It was the pretty serving maid from the inn the previous evening.

Odila noticed the direction of his gaze. "Have you met Kaleen?" she asked. "She's been a great boon to me. Not only does she keep everyone fed, but she has turned out to be an invaluable assistant."

Gerard knew he was staring like a fool. He opened

his mouth to say something, but no words came out. Instead he turned his attention to his sandwich, cold roast beef on a bun.

"Oh, I've met Lord Porridge," Kaleen said with a sly wink in Gerard's direction. Gerard felt himself flush all the way to the tips of his ears. "He's staying at the inn, you know," Kaleen went on. "And I can tell you one thing, he simply adores Otik's spiced potatoes!"

Odila turned to look at him with a puzzled expression. But Gerard ignored her and tore off a bite of sandwich, which he chewed diligently, his mouth dry as the Plains of Dust.

That was the first time Gerard ran into Kaleen that day. Later that evening, when he went to the inn for dinner, he saw her again, leaning over a game board across from a thin, dissolute-looking man with shifty eyes. "Gerard," she called to him with easy familiarity, waving the sheriff over. "Mott here is teaching me to play Regal. Ever heard of it?"

Gerard glanced around the large room, unusually quiet this evening, then crossed to Kaleen's table. He nodded to her before concentrating his gaze on the man across from her. The stranger's eyes darted shiftily this way and that, refusing to meet Gerard's.

"Yes, I've heard of Regal," Gerard said, declining to mention that he once had been a regional champion of the game that was quickly replacing khas as the most popular in Southern Ergoth—as well as in Solace, apparently. "You aren't working tonight?"

"Laura gave me the night off. I came by to help out

anyway. So what do you know about Regal?" Kaleen went on, bubbling with excitement. "Mott says I'm a quick learner. He says that at the rate I'm going, I'll quickly win back what I've lost, and then some."

"Does he now?"

Mott awarded Gerard a sickly smile, then glanced away.

"And what, exactly, is it that you have lost?" Gerard continued.

"Nothing much," Kaleen said, suddenly evasive. "Nothing I can't replace."

"So what are the stakes right now?"

Kaleen's voice dropped to a mumble. "Tomorrow's wages." She brightened. "But I'm in no danger of losing again. I'm about to win everything back. Isn't that right, Mott? You said so yourself."

Mott started to stand. "I, uh, have to be going. I just remembered some business elsewhere."

"Sit down," Gerard said softly.

Mott sat.

"Now, if I recall the game properly, there should be a crown somewhere that allows one player or the other to assume control of the board."

Kaleen glanced to the side of the board, where five walnut shells rested. "Yes, it's under one of those," she said. "The player who uses a turn to look under a walnut shell gets a chance at claiming the crown."

"Under a walnut shell?" Gerard responded pleasantly. "Now, what do you think of that, Mott? Any chance that crown is really somewhere else?" Gerard's hand shot out, grabbing Mott's left wrist and forcing his palm up. There, slyly held in place by the base of his thumb, was a game piece shaped like a small diadem.

"Well, what do you know," Gerard said. "Looks like I guessed where the crown was hidden. That makes me the claimant for the throne."

In one swift, liquid move, Mott reached with his other hand for a knife. Gerard twisted the man's wrist until there was a snap. Mott screamed and dropped the knife, grabbing for his wrist with his good hand. Gerard let go, and the man bent over his broken wrist, moaning.

"I think you'd best see to that injury, then be moving along out of town," Gerard said.

"Now, how am I to make a living?" the man gasped.

"Try honest work." Gerard turned away. "But do it in some other town. I don't want to find you still here tomorrow."

"Who are you to order me around?"

"I'm the new sheriff of Solace. And this young woman"—he pointed to Kaleen—"is under my protection. As are all the good citizens of Solace."

Mott swore and stumbled from the inn, hunched over his broken wrist.

Kaleen was staring at Gerard. "My goodness! How did you know that piece was there?"

"Just a lucky guess." Gerard looked around the inn once more, satisfying himself that all else was well, then sat down at Mott's empty place. "He seems to have left his game behind," Gerard said, indicating the Regal board. "Care to play? I can teach you some of the fundamentals." When she hesitated, he added quickly, "Not for coin, though. Just for fun."

She smiled. "Certainly. It sounds as though I could do with some further practice at it before I encounter the likes of Mott again."

For the rest of the evening, they played Regal, with Gerard showing her the finer points of the game. She was a quick learner, and by the last game of the night, she actually managed to beat Gerard, without him making too much of an effort to throw the game her way.

That night, Gerard busied himself in his attic room above the inn, stooping to avoid banging his head yet again on the low-hanging rafters. A candle burned with companionable light on the table beside the bed, casting warm, flickering shadows on the walls and ceiling of the cramped space. Gerard could scarcely pace three strides in any direction before bumping into something. Yet for all that, the room was beginning to feel homey and welcoming. From the open window, a soft breeze caressed the bare skin of Gerard's arms and face. The air smelled of green leaves and full-bodied tree sap. Outside, crickets chirped, turning even the greater expanse of night into a friendly presence. Through the tree branches overhead, stars spangled the heavens. Two of the moons hung low against the horizon.

Gerard lifted a spare shirt from his travel bag and laid it neatly in the little wooden wardrobe in one corner of the room. A tattered, leather-bound book emerged from the bag next and was placed lovingly on the table beside the candle, next to the sheriff's medallion he had set there earlier. He sat wearily on the bed, little more than a cot really, and drew a dagger from the inside of his right boot. Then he pulled off his boots and lay down on the bed. Though he was of medium stature, Gerard's feet hung over the end of the bed, forcing him to draw his knees toward his chin. It was little inconvenience, however, as he was used to the harder accommodations of camp life.

He blew out the candle, but his eyes remained open, searching out the night sky through the window. Somewhere in the distance, a rich tenor voice sang a low, mournful song about lost love, possibly some youth serenading his sweetheart beneath her window. Gerard smiled. Farther away, sounds of revelry swelled up briefly as a door opened, then receded when it shut again.

He couldn't sleep. He singled out one star and studied it, thinking of Kaleen and how she had called him Lord Porridge, and how she had smiled each time she managed a particularly bold move at Regal. In the darkness, he flushed again at the memory of her joking name for him.

He was unaware of when his eyes closed and he drifted off at last. Gradually, however, another scene took shape around him. It was night still, but now he stood outside, before the great doors of the Temple of Mishakal. He felt bidden to enter, and approached the six marble steps with reverent awe. As he came closer, the doors swung, drawn wide by some powerful, unseen hand. He stepped into the antechamber, where he was able to walk confidently despite the dark. In fact, with some part of his mind registering this oddity, torchlight sprang up in his dream as if to guarantee the sureness of his steps. Incense hung heavy in the air, and from somewhere deep inside the temple came the slow, dolorous beat of a gong, summoning the faithful to prayer. Yet the temple appeared empty, and Gerard's steps echoed hollowly.

He proceeded through the entryway and into the central chamber. At first glance, everything seemed as before. But after a moment's reflection, he realized there was a difference.

The statue of Mishakal cradled a bloody body in its arms, covered with a tattered cloak. The statue seemed alert, watching Gerard's approach with stony eyes. When he came close enough, the lips of the statue began to move. Gerard struggled to make words out of the shapes formed by the marble lips, but without sounds to accompany the movement, he was at a loss to understand.

"What?" he breathed into the relative silence of the chamber. "What are you trying to tell me?"

From the agitation on the goddess's face, Gerard gathered the matter involved some urgency, but he was helpless to make sense of what she was saying. He tried to come closer and examine the body she was holding. He wondered if it was Sheriff Joyner. But every time he took one step forward now, the statue receded before him.

So Gerard passed deep into the night, forever taking steps that led nowhere and struggling fruitlessly to comprehend the message the statue was trying to impart to him. His frustration grew as the night lengthened, and his body twitched and jerked unmercifully on his bed.

Across town, Palin lay similarly afflicted in his own bed. Usha, stirred from sleep by her husband's restlessness, debated whether to wake him or let him continue on whatever nighttime journey occupied his soul. In the end, she let him sleep and dream, although she propped herself up and kept watch over him, as if to ward off any dangers he encountered. Palin too spent the night walking toward a statue that stayed out of reach, a statue that held a cloaked and bloody corpse and tried in vain to speak to him. Like Gerard, Palin woke in the morning little refreshed for his sleep, and wondering what the dimly remembered outlines of his dream might portend.

CHAPTER

7

'—hereby call this meeting—"

Gerard caught the speaker in midsentence as he rushed in late to the town council meeting. He hurriedly found an empty seat and slumped in it, trying to avoid the curious stares of the council members and others present. Vercleese was already there, Gerard noticed, seated well back in the room.

The speaker, having paused in his words, glared at Gerard. "—call this meeting of the Solace town council to order," he concluded, scowling around the room as if challenging anyone else to interrupt him.

No one did.

The speaker, a thin, nervous-looking young man, rapped the gavel gravely before turning it over to Palin. Then the thin young man sat and proceeded to take minutes of the meeting, never uttering another word until it was time to adjourn. As secretary to the mayor, he considered calling the meeting to order and adjourning it two of his most important duties.

From the general rolling of eyes, Gerard gathered

this sense of importance wasn't shared by the elected members of the council.

Gerard let out a deep breath and tried to relax. At the last minute, he had decided to shave, and that had made him late for his first council meeting. So much for making a favorable impression, he concluded grimly. He was still groggy from a troubled night's sleep, complete with the strange dream.

Palin, who looked as though he hadn't slept well either, mustered up a smile and seemed to take in each individual personally before he began to speak. "We have a full agenda today, starting with an item concerning a cock Petric Jameson claims is crowing well before dawn—"

"And waking my whole household!" grumbled someone in the room.

"We'll get to that, Petric," Palin said easily. "After that, we have an item regarding the procedure for obtaining a merchant's writ to sell goods in the marketplace, followed by a dispute involving ownership of, and ultimate responsibility for, a dead cow. . . ."

Palin continued through a daunting list of tedious topics, with Gerard's introduction as sheriff appearing as item number twenty-nine.

Gerard groaned. He scanned the council table, noting Kedrick Tos, whom he had met previously on his tour with Vercleese. He didn't recognize three of the other men, merchants he judged from the cut of their clothes, although at the far end of the table sat a fourth man, a gray-haired, sophisticated-looking gentleman whom Gerard decided must be Cardjaf Duhar. The gentleman bore some resemblance to Kaleen. Duhar was listening in deferential silence as Palin spoke, occasionally nodding in response to something the mayor said.

One item on the agenda, a call for a referendum on the matter of accepting "foreigners and others of that ilk" into Solace, caused a considerable stir.

"I'm as tolerant as the next man," announced one councilman who had requested the floor, immediately alerting Gerard to the likelihood the man's remarks would be anything but tolerant. "But I say we're allowing too many questionable types into our town, many of them not even human. Why, just the other day I spied a minotaur walking about in the marketplace as bold as you please." He paused while a gasp of indignation rose from several of the listeners. "I say we have to get back to good, traditional *human* values," the councilman went on, "the kind of values that made Solace such a desirable community in the first place."

There were cries for and against the speaker's remarks among the spectators, and a barrage of comments from a couple of the councilmen. Palin banged the gavel and waited for silence. Duhar gestured discreetly for the floor. When he received Palin's nod, he rose, the only councilman thus far to deliver his remarks while standing, Gerard noted. A near hush fell upon the room as everyone waited to hear what a successful businessman from Palanthas would have to say about the situation.

"You all know that I'm a relative newcomer here in your fair town myself," he said in a measured, resonant tone. He nodded to several of those present. "You have given us a new home, taken us in as members of the community, and even granted me the privilege of lending my meager voice to the governance of your civic affairs.

77

"But I am troubled to hear that not all newcomers to Solace may be so warmly welcomed in the future. True, some individuals may be causing problems, but we have statutes and ordinances for dealing with troublemakers. Most others, and I count these as the great majority of those streaming here, are sincere, law-abiding folk who only wish to share in the many benefits with which Solace is blessed. I say these individuals, human and otherwise, have uncounted skills and qualities to contribute to the common good, and that we should open our doors to as many of them as will come. Why, even a minotaur should find ready acceptance here, provided he obeys the laws governing all. We can only progress to the extent that we continue to grow. Not to grow is to become stagnant. I believe no one in Solace wants that."

He resumed his seat with an air of gravity that held the room gripped in silence. Then a clamor erupted as numerous people strove to air their opinions. Palin banged the gavel furiously. At last he achieved a semblance of order and turned the floor over to a short, chubby councilman who was practically apoplectic with bottled-up emotions. Indeed, the man was red-faced and shaking with urgency, so that he could barely force coherent words from his throat. "Wanton women," he managed to gasp. "Gambling. Fistfights in the street." He stopped, glaring around the room as if to daring anyone to refute him. Abruptly, he sat down, apparently satisfied he had made his point.

Whatever his point might have been, Gerard thought to himself.

And so it went. Eventually, Palin interceded in the debate, quietly urging moderation in the council's decisions and laying out a case for controlled growth. Such was his influence that everyone present listened respectfully, whether they agreed with him or not. In the end, the council voted to defer action on the measure and proceeded to the next item on the agenda.

Two hours later, the council had dealt with only nineteen of the items on the agenda. Gerard jerked awake at one point, having started to doze, and glanced around to see if anyone had noticed. A couple of those around him appeared to be in similar states of semi-consciousness. One man had actually begun to snore. Gerard inhaled deeply and tried to pay attention as the council took up the matter of Goodwife Wilks, who was said to have been selling dark magic charms to both sides in a neighborhood squabble. Not that anyone had a problem with the charms themselves, apparently, but it seemed Goodwife Wilks was also quietly stirring up both sides in the long-running dispute, thereby doubling her business.

At long last, the council reached item number twenty-nine. Choosing his words carefully, Palin introduced Gerard, giving an elaborate account of his service during the war and making much of his having been a Knight of Solamnia. Gerard squirmed self-consciously throughout the glowing address. He had thought that sitting quietly during the council's endless deliberations was excruciating enough, but being the center of their attention was worse. He would gladly have battled a dragon rather than have to endure another moment of this torture.

When Palin finished, the chubby councilman who had spoken so pithily about wanton women, gambling, and fistfights in the streets signaled for the floor. Again, he opened and closed his mouth several times, trying to form his words. His head bobbed vigorously with the effort. "Temporary," he blurted at last. "Serving until . . . qualified candidate chosen . . . duly appointed search committee . . . answering to this council." Then he looked around at all the other council members, scowling fiercely, his somewhat mysterious remarks apparently concluded.

"Yes, well, of course the points made by my esteemed colleague should be taken into due consideration," the next speaker said, as if the first man had made some sense. "In the meantime, Gerard uth Mondar will be serving as temporary sheriff of Solace, and in order to familiarize himself with all the relevant statutes, regulations, and civil codes, should take it upon himself to, uh, familiarize himself with all the relevant. . . ." He stopped, tangled up in his own words. "Here," he began again, after an awkward moment, producing an enormous stack of books, scrolls, and codices, and handing them over to Gerard. "These will tell you everything you need to know. See that you study them." He narrowed his eyes, looking as though he wanted to add that Gerard would be tested on his knowledge of same in due time, but refrained from saying more.

Gerard accepted the stack of documents gingerly, concerned lest it topple and scatter. Across the table, Palin gave Gerard a sympathetic grin.

Before Gerard could leave the room, Cardjaf Duhar rose again and bowed slightly to him. "We are most grateful for your services to our fair town," he declared in his measured voice. "I'm sure Solace will remain the safe, peaceful community we have all loved as a result of your good efforts."

Gerard nodded to Duhar and turned, catching a vaguely hostile look on Blair's face. Evidently the man did not approve of Duhar, or more likely he didn't approve of Duhar and Gerard starting out on such amiable terms. He privately vowed to keep a watchful eye on Blair. Like so many citizens of Solace he had met lately, there was more to the man than met the eye.

A guardsman burst into the council chamber, puffing for breath. He hurried over to Blair and whispered something to the sergeant. Blair scowled, leaped up, and made for the door, then, apparently recollecting himself, turned and rushed over to Gerard instead. "There's some kind of problem down at the jail," he hissed in Gerard's ear, as the others looked on concernedly.

Gerard stood and addressed the council members. "If you will excuse us, gentlemen, it seems duty calls." He bowed as well as he could, considering the stack of documents tucked in his arms, and hastily followed Blair and the other guardsman from the room.

Vercleese trailed Gerard, following Blair and the other guard to the northeast corner of town, where the jail was located. As they hurried along, Gerard pictured every sort of dangerous miscreant and cutthroat confined in the jail, raising havoc and possibly threatening insurrection. So he was surprised when he and Vercleese arrived at the low, solidly built log building, to find the main cell inside filled with a half dozen gnomes. The gnomes were rattling the bars, though not apparently in an effort to get out or attract their jailors' attention, but rather with an eye toward determining the strength and suitability of the bars for some arcane purpose. They were measuring the bars' lengths and diameters, arguing loudly over whether they could serve as rails for some contraption that Gerard gathered was best described as a "rail-directed, self-propelled, steam-powered, multipassenger conveyance," whatever that might be. At least it didn't sound like the device constituted a threat to the town's safety, and the gnomes had served to extricate Gerard from the unendurable town council meeting. For that blessing, he felt grateful.

"Excuse me," shouted one gray-bearded gnome over the general commotion, when he noticed Gerard and the others had arrived. He pointed at Gerard. "Excuse me, are you the new sheriff, the one in charge here?"

Gerard stepped forward, nodding that he was.

"Well, I wish to protest our unfair incarceration. We were peaceably going about our own business when we were unlawfully detained and placed here. Not that it isn't a very pleasant jail, though of course I have no real basis for comparison."

Gerard mentally counted them: right, six gnomes. Well, at least they weren't kender, he thought with relief. Six kender in jail would be a real threat to the general welfare.

He turned and addressed Blair. "What's the charge?" he asked the head of the town guard. "Why are these fellows being held?"

"They've got the road into town from the north completely blocked off," Blair asserted vehemently. Then he appeared to recollect himself, for he added hastily, "Sir."

"Blocked off? How?"

"It's some contraption of theirs, sir—"

"Our rail-directed, self-propelled, steam-powered, multipassenger conveyance," put in the gray-haired gnome, whom Gerard gathered was the leader of the bunch. At any rate, he was the most soot-stained, begrimed member of the group, as well as conspicuously the oldest.

"Their rail-directed . . . whatever," Blair continued, narrowing his eyes. "It's taking up the whole road, and merchants and farmers alike are unable to get in or out of town from that direction."

"How far from here is this?"

"Just a couple of miles or so."

"Hmm," Gerard glanced out the window, where dusk was gathering. It was too late to go out there now. He would have to wait until tomorrow morning to see this gnome contraption for himself.

"I say, we should be permitted to get back to our invention," put in the gray-haired gnome. "We were in the midst of conducting some Very Important Business."

"And what might that be?" asked Gerard.

The gnome took a deep breath, swelling up for what promised to be a long-winded answer, so Gerard quickly added, "The short version. Twenty-five words or less, please."

"Twenty-five or less?"

"That's four already."

"Four?" The gnomes counted on his soot-stained fingers. "Oh, you must be counting hyphenated words separately. They really should only count as one."

"You're up to twenty."

The gnome looked ready to argue, then apparently thought better of squandering his remaining five words. "Testing our steam-powered-self-propelled-rail-directed-relocation-device." Then, seeing Gerard was about to protest, he blurted out, "Hyphenated-words-really-shouldn't-count-as-more-than-one!" He did a quick tabulation on his fingers. "Twenty-five!" he exclaimed with satisfaction.

Gerard pursed his lips but didn't argue. Given the nature of gnomes to extend any technical description into the next millennium, he felt he was getting off lucky to have held it down to this length. "And where are you going in your rail-directed thingamajig?"

"Haven," declared the gnome in a rare one-word reply.

Gerard frowned, puzzled. "Haven? But that's in the heart of Samuval's domain. Why are you going there?"

"Lord Steppenhost, a Very Important Person in Que-Kiri, has contracted with us to develop a mobile transport system for moving people and specified races between Que-Kiri and Haven for the purpose of increased trade and general stimulation between territories." He made vague motions to the east, in the general direction of Que-Kiri. "The rails we've secured to the ground stretch all the way there, allowing us to travel from there to here and back, at will."

"Mm," Gerard said noncommittally. He had his own suspicions about this Lord Steppenhost's motives, which probably included enticing the gnomes to leave Que-Kiri as expeditiously as possible. "Then your business doesn't explicitly involve Solace, I take it."

The gnome shook his head, flinging dust and soot up from his hair and beard in a small cloud around his head. "No, no. In fact, we were engaged in honest debate, trying to decide whether to go through Solace or around it, when we were interrupted by this good man here, and summarily arrested!"

"I say go around it," piped up one of the other gnomes.

"Through it!" hotly declared another. "Right through this jail!"

The lead gnome scowled at this intrusion and went on, "Going through town would entail some decided complications, such as trees and buildings that would be in the way. Of course, we could level these, but that would be unnecessarily destructive. Instead we might raise the entire town hydraulically and set it to one side, providing us with a clear access to Haven."

"And why not just go around Solace?" Gerard asked. "Wouldn't that be, er, challenging?" he added hopefully.

"Oh, going around Solace would involve considerable bother."

"No it wouldn't!" objected the gnome who had spoken up before, precipitating a renewed argument among his fellows.

"More trouble than moving the entire town to one side?" Gerard asked over the ensuing din, forgetting for the moment that it was a gnome he was talking to, and not a rational creature at all.

"Oh, yes, considerably." The head gnome glared at his colleagues to prevent any disagreement, but the other gnomes were now arguing loudly with each other and ignoring their leader.

"I see." Gerard paused, edging away from the argument in the background about flywheels and gears and transfer of momentum, and conspiratorially beckoning the head gnome a few steps closer to him. "And who might you be? The short version."

"Conderammenthlurpbrackennob."

"Well, Nob, you're going to have to trust me. I'm interested in your problem, and would like to inspect your magnificent invention myself. Maybe I might have an idea how to help. But I'm going to have to hold all of you here until I can check this matter out tomorrow."

"Uh. All right."

"All right? That's it, just 'all right?' "

The old gnome shrugged his thin shoulders, and lowered his voice. "We get to sleep indoors and have some free grub, right? Any chance of some of Otik's spiced potatoes?"

"Blair!" Gerard called, turning around and nearly bumping into the guardsman. "We'll hold them here until tomorrow, when I can check this thing out. Meanwhile, Vercleese, I want you to go to where their device is parked and direct anyone trying to get into town from that direction to take one of the more roundabout routes. Blair, you'll stay and watch over our guests."

Blair scowled. "But you know I was planning on seeing Kaleen at the inn—" Abruptly he stopped, grinding his jaw with displeasure.

"Yes?" Gerard said, raising an eyebrow.

"Nothing, sir," Blair said unhappily. Meanwhile, the head gnome had rejoined the others and the debate had resumed noisily. Gerard ground his own teeth at the cacophony. Gnomes were worse than the town council. He headed for the door.

"And where will you be?" Blair asked. Then, when Gerard spun around, the sergeant added petulantly, "In case anyone should come looking for you. Sir."

"I'll be at the inn," Gerard said, softening the blow by adding, "I'll try and send Kaleen over with some, er, grub."

It had turned full dark outside. The hubbub that enveloped Solace during the day had quieted somewhat, although the sounds of music were now added to the mix that fell upon the ear. Gerard picked out the notes of a viol playing somewhere with mournful solemnity, while elsewhere a piper and fiddle wove a spritely tune. Laughter spilled from two or three of the arboreal houses as parties got under way, and small clusters of well-dressed townsfolk strolled along the streets and bridge-walks, enjoying the balmy night air.

Smells of cooking also wafted on the air, reminding Gerard that he hadn't eaten for several hours. The aroma of a roast swan from one house played upon his appetite. He hurried faster toward the inn, his stomach growling in anticipation of some tasty—but mild!—dish for his supper.

"Sheriff!" someone called. "Oh, Sheriff!"

Reluctantly, Gerard paused, allowing a huffing Lady Drebble to catch up with him. Gerard nodded a greeting.

"I wish to register a complaint," Lady Drebble said, panting as she came abreast of him. "A most serious and formal complaint."

"And whom or what do you wish to complain about?" Gerard asked when she had paused at length without continuing.

"Why, my neighbor, Goodwife Gottlief, of course."

"Ah," Gerard said, still waiting to be enlightened. "And what exactly has Goodwife Gottlief done?"

"Nothing. She's done absolutely nothing, and that's the problem."

"Lady Drebble, I'm afraid you're going to have to explain." When she gave him a look of scathing disdain, Gerard hastened to add, "Remember that I'm new to the community. I'm not aware of whatever history of difficulty might exist between you and Goodwife Gottlief."

"Of course," Lady Drebble said, instantly mollified and happy for the excuse to tell her story. "Well, it all began when I first moved to Solace. Right from the start, Goodwife Gottlief was jealous of my status, you know. She likes to take on airs, pretending she is better than she is, while I have never been anything but gracious to those beneath my station. Anyway, as I say, Goodwife Gottlief resented my rightfully displacing her in Solace society. . . ."

Gerard listened with as much patience as he could muster while Lady Drebble recited a lengthy history of wrongs and slights she had endured from the ungrateful Goodwife Gottlief.

"But what exactly is the problem now?" he was finally obliged to interject when Lady Drebble chanced to pause for breath. It was extraordinary how long she seemed able to talk on a single lungful of air, he reflected.

"Why, she didn't even acknowledge me when I went out today, although I purposely passed right in front of her garden where she was busy tending her flowers. It's disgraceful! I bid her good morning, as I always do to my social inferiors, never having been one to hold poor breeding or bad upbringing against one, whereupon she merely sniffed and turned the other way. She should be reprimanded severely!"

"Perhaps even put in jail for the night to teach her a lesson," Gerard added dryly.

"Yes, that's it exactly! I'm so glad you understand the seriousness of her offense."

"Lady Drebble, perhaps you should set the example and adopt a more conciliatory spirit toward your neighbor." When Lady Drebble drew herself up to object to this astonishing remark, Gerard hastened to add, more slyly, "Think how such an approach would bedevil her, as she tried to determine what you were up to." He winked to underscore his point.

"Oh! Why, yes. True, true. It would drive her to distraction, trying to figure that one out."

"Exactly."

Lady Drebble leaned close, placing a conspiratorial hand on his arm. "Sheriff, you are a genius." With a swirl of skirts and petticoats, she swept away to put her revenge into effect.

Gerard let out a deep breath and resumed his own course toward dinner.

The inn was crowded, as always. Gerard slid into a seat as an elegantly dressed couple finished their meal and stood up. He saw Kaleen serving tables across the room and settled back to wait for her but was startled when Laura stormed over to him instead. She plunked a heaping platter of Otik's spiced potatoes down in front of him and glared, challenging him to object.

Gerard forced a thin smile. "Mm," he managed to murmur.

Laura waited.

Gerard picked up a spoon, thrust it into the pile of potatoes, and drew out a dangerously large mouthful. As Laura continued to watch, he shoveled the spoonful into his mouth. He tried to grin, then chewed slowly under her steadfast gaze. His mouth tingled from the peppery flavor. His stomach was already churning in protest.

Seeing him chew, Laura's expression softened. She smiled and turned away, heading back to her kitchen. When she was a safe distance from his table, Gerard discreetly spat the mouthful out into his napkin and pushed the platter of potatoes aside, his appetite ruined. He glanced around the room to see if anyone had noticed his indiscretion. A group of swarthy men in one corner of the room caught his attention. He squinted, trying to see them better, but their cloaks and cowls obscured their faces. One, however, looked familiar; Gerard knew he had seen the cloaked man before, but for the life of him he couldn't remember where.

Then his eyes came to rest on Kaleen and he froze. She was glowering at him from across the room, having apparently witnessed him spitting out the potatoes. Gerard withered under her condemnatory gaze. Reluctantly, he drew the platter of potatoes toward him again and began nibbling on tiny spoonfuls, swallowing with difficulty over the increasingly violent objections of his digestive tract. Presently, the seats in Gerard's immediate vicinity emptied as people sniffed the air and chose to move elsewhere.

Gerard felt himself flush with embarrassment as he shoveled in another mouthful of the spiced potatoes.

CHAPTER

8

The shrill voice wafted into Gerard's room with the cool, predawn breeze. "Three tendays after his death, Sheriff Joyner's murderer has yet to be found."

Gerard bolted upright, cracking his head on the low ceiling that angled sharply across the room. The room was still dark; the sky outside showed the scarcest gray.

"Municipal officials assure this crier that all avenues are being explored and the killer will eventually be brought to justice."

It was a high, piercing voice Gerard almost recognized. He rubbed his head where he had banged it, listening more closely.

"To date, however, no progress has been made and the murderer remains at large."

A kender's voice. That blasted kender who had the job of town crier. What had Palin said his name was? Tangleknot? Tanglefoot? Tangletoe, that was it. Tangletoe Something.

"In other news about town, the two-headed chicken mentioned yesterday turned out to be a pair of chicks standing very close together. Sorry for that. However, I have been assured that one of Mistress Corinne Nestor's laying hens produces only double-yolked eggs."

Now he had it: Tangletoe Snakeweed!

"Those eggs are currently for sale in the town market. Better get there fast, however, as Mistress Nestor says they're bound to go quickly."

Gerard groaned and swung his legs out of bed, working at the stiffness that resulted from sleeping in such a cramped position. The mention of the town market reminded him that he needed to get over there to talk to the Ostermans.

"An invasion of gnomes threatened the town yesterday," Tangletoe continued, his voice receding into the distance. "Thanks to quick action on the part of the town constabulary, the miscreants are now all safely in jail."

Gerard hung his head, remembering he still had to deal with the gnomes. Well, that would come after he had breakfast and talked to the Ostermans.

The kender's voice disappeared altogether, trailing away as the wretched creature turned down another street to shatter the morning peace of other citizens. Well, everyone in Solace should be thoroughly roused by now, Gerard thought grimly. He had no sympathy this morning for layabouts still in their beds. Let the whole town get up in time to watch the sunrise.

He made his way to the inn, where, to his surprise, Laura beamed at him and served him his morning usual—plain porridge without honey or cream—without protest. Evidently, Kaleen had kept his secret, and

Laura didn't know that he had spat out Otik's potatoes the previous evening.

With the porridge soothing his belly, he made his way to the market. The sun had risen while he was at the inn, and the marketplace was awash in early morning light. Despite the early hour, the marketplace buzzed with activity. Well, maybe not buzzed, exactly, Gerard amended. Rather it squealed and mooed and bawled and crowed, as animals of every kind were sold either for the butcher's block or for farmyard stock. The smells, too, included those of animal waste, overlaid with the more fragrant odors of fresh herbs and produce from townsfolk's gardens and farmers' fields. The sounds of haggling from dozens of stalls were part of the symphony.

Animals and produce weren't the only goods for sale. Citizens of Solace were also buying cloth of every kind, from serviceable wools and cottons to more extravagant silks and satins and rich brocades, as well as ribbons, lace, buttons, bows, and other items of apparel. Other stalls sold pins and knives, pots and pans, and every kind of kitchen implement. One enterprising peddler was busy creating dragons from folded pieces of paper—green and red and blue, copper and silver and gold—and selling them to harried mothers whose resistance was being worn away by the clamoring of their children. Merchants were turning up from all across Abanasinia for the upcoming temple dedication and festivities. Gerard even noticed Odila with Kaleen in one section of the market, buying scrolls and ink and quills. He nodded at the two, and they smiled back, their arms intertwined as they moved on. That friendship appeared to be blossoming.

He found the Ostermans' stall readily enough, and asked them about their discovery of Sheriff Joyner's body.

"Oh, it was awful, let me tell you," said Tom Osterman, adopting the manner of one relating a well-worn tale. "There were crows everywhere. That's what first alerted me to the fact that something was wrong. I stopped the wagon immediately to investigate—"

"Now, Tom, don't exaggerate," interrupted Sophie Osterman. "You know you got down out of the wagon to look at that field because you long to buy that land."

"Yes, but I did think something was wrong right from the first. I just didn't say nothing until I was certain."

"Ahem, so you found the body," said Gerard, trying to redirect the conversation. "Did anything look out of place?"

"Well, it was a dead body, for one," said Tom Osterman heatedly. "I mean, imagine how you would feel, discovering a good man like Sheriff Joyner sprawled and murdered like that."

"I see." Gerard nodded thoughtfully, trying to tamp down Tom's flash of irritation. He paused as a boy with a paper dragon careened into the Ostermans' stall, then ran off holding the paper dragon aloft as though it were flying. "Uh, what direction were you coming from?"

"Oh, we'd just been to see Jutlin Wykirk," said Sophie. "I remember distinctly, because he was to be our last stop before coming here to the market. And we were arguing about him, Jutlin Wykirk." Tom looked offended. "I mean, we were *discussing* Jutlin Wykirk. Of course, we forgot all about Mr. Wykirk when we saw Sheriff Joyner's body."

"Hmm," Gerard said. "And why were you discussing this Jutlin Wykirk?"

"A most unpleasant man—" Sophie began.

"But very important hereabouts," interrupted Tom. "He's the town's miller. That's why we had gone there, to get some wheat ground into flour so we could sell it to Brynn Ragulf, the baker."

Gerard remembered the distracted baker with flour smudges all over his face. "Oh, so you do a regular trade with Wykirk?"

"Oh, yes," said Tom. "Everyone around here does, although some folks like having to deal with him less than others."

"What do you mean?"

"Well, old Wykirk doesn't like outsiders," Tom explained.

"Kender, dwarves, minotaurs, any creature of that sort," Sophie added. "But especially elves." She grimaced. "He really carries on about elves. Says they're infesting the countryside. I don't know why he gets so upset. Elves aren't really so bad once you get to know them."

"And when have you ever known an elf?" Tom asked, an eyebrow raised.

"I was speaking in the abstract," Sophie said with a sniff. "Now minotaurs or draconians, they are genuinely unfriendly."

Tom snorted. "You're sounding just like old Wykirk."

"Why, Tom, I'll have you know—"

"So nothing looked out of the ordinary when you found the body?" Gerard said, desperately trying to rein in the discussion. "There wasn't much blood, I gather."

Tom frowned in thought. "You know, now that you

mention it, there wasn't all that much blood I could see on the ground. Oh, there was some, but I've done my share of butchering animals on the farm, and I'd have expected much more blood to have pooled."

"Maybe all the blood soaked into the ground," Sophie offered.

Tom shook his head. "No, I don't think so." But he looked uncertain.

"Well, thank you both," Gerard said. "If you think of anything to add, let me know." He eased away as Tom and Sophie resumed their bickering over the relative merits of the various races of Krynn.

He spotted Laura buying potatoes for the inn. She saw him and waved before returning to her bargaining with a farmer who looked red-faced and ready to fold under her determined assault. Gerard grinned, his sympathies with the harried farmer. He continued on through the market, although he glanced over his shoulder now and then, feeling he was being followed. But he saw no one.

At one booth, Gerard came across a man selling swords, and he stopped to consider the merchandise.

"Finest swords in all of Ansalon," the man boasted, noting Gerard's interest.

Gerard picked up a sword more fanciful than effective, and wasn't surprised to find that the blade was such poor quality steel it couldn't possibly hold an edge, the "jewels" encrusting the hilt were nothing but glass, and instead of balancing close to the hilt, the sword balanced too near the middle of the blade. Nevertheless, he swept the weapon through a couple of practice moves. Suddenly, he was holding nothing but the hilt, as the blade snapped free and went flying.

"Huh!" the merchant grunted, watching the blade narrowly miss a serving wench who was haggling over a pair of chickens. "Now that's never happened before." He sounded almost sincere, then quickly shifted Gerard's attention to another sword. "You've a keen eye for your weapons, good sir. Now take a look at this beauty. You won't find another like it in all—"

"I know, 'in all of Ansalon,' " Gerard finished for him, declining the proffered sword, which was even gaudier than the first.

The merchant nodded so briskly his multiple chins wagged as he continued to hold the weapon out for Gerard's inspection. "That's right—*all* of Ansalon!"

Instead, Gerard picked up a plain, functional leather scabbard, thinking of the much superior sword the smith here in Solace was finishing for him. Gerard would need a scabbard for it.

The merchant winced at Gerard's choice. "Sir, I really couldn't sell you such a miserable specimen as that. Allow me to show you something finer—"

"How much?" Gerard interrupted.

"Oh, a man of your ilk. You really shouldn't buy such a—"

"By the way, you do have a merchant's writ, don't you?" Gerard asked mildly.

"Huh?"

"A merchant's writ. All the out-of-town merchants are required to have them."

The merchant laughed. "Oh, sir, that's a good one. You had me going for a moment."

Gerard studied the man through narrowly slit eyes, letting the silence stretch out.

The merchant began to squirm. "Say, just who do you think you are, anyway?" he demanded.

"I'm sorry, allow me to introduce myself. Gerard uth Mondar. I'm the sheriff hereabouts."

The merchant's belligerent expression sagged. "You're not serious."

"You know, that was my reaction when they first offered me the job."

"You're really the sheriff?"

"I'm afraid so."

"And that business about the merchant's writ?"

"Yes, that is true as well," Gerard said, nodding.

Sweat broke out on the merchant's brow. "Look, I'm sure we could reach some kind of agreement on that scabbard, if you fancy it so."

"How much?" Gerard repeated.

"Tell you what—for you, only twenty steel."

Gerard cocked an eyebrow. "How much?"

"Uh, did I say twenty? Whatever could I have been thinking?" The merchant attempted a chuckle that sounded more like choking. "I meant fifteen."

Gerard stared at him.

The merchant's shoulders drooped. "Twelve," he said miserably. "I can't go lower, even if you are the sheriff."

"I could throw you in the jail, you know," Gerard suggested genially. "We have quite a nice one. The folks here in Solace are very proud of it. It's got a bunch of gnomes in it right now—"

"Yes, well, if I sell you that scabbard for any less, you might as well lock me up, for I'll not being making any profit off this wretched trip," the man said sourly. "Seems no one in town wants a sword these days. Just frippery for this celebration I hear you've got coming up."

Gerard nodded, paid the man, then, taking pity on the merchant, also bought a cheap but serviceable knife. "But if you're going be staying in town, you'd better get a writ," he admonished.

The merchant was already packing his wares. "Stay in this town? Not a chance! I'm heading for Haven, where I hear a man in my line of business stands to make a little steel."

Gerard walked on, idly perusing the goods for sale at the various booths. He still had the uncomfortable sensation of being followed.

The morning was getting on, so Gerard set out for the crossroads outside town where the gnomes' invention was blocking the way. There he met up with Vercleese and Blair, who had brought the whole passel of gnomes with them, along with quite a few townsfolk, who were evidently expecting some kind of excitement. Well, anything involving gnomes often promised excitement.

The contraption in question was the strangest thing Gerard had ever seen, surpassing all other gnome inventions he had had the misfortune to encounter. A huge boiler stood in the midst of six great, flanged wheels that were riding along some kind of track, the rails for which extended behind the device in the direction from which it had come. At the time they were stopped, the gnomes had been busy installing additional rails on the ground ahead of the device, right through the crossroads that formed a major junction into this end of town. Evidently, they had intended to extend these rails through the center of town, bringing the apparatus chugging along with them.

"Does it work?" Gerard asked dubiously.

Nob huffed and snorted. "Does it work! How do you think we got this far?"

That was exactly what Gerard was wondering. The crowd of townspeople was swelling.

Gerard wished he could give Lord Steppenhost of Que-Kiri a piece of his mind.

The gnomes began clambering into and over their machine, firing up the boiler and dragging more rails forward to extend those already on the ground. At first, the vehicle sounded like a herd of incensed bulls, snorting and pawing the earth. Smoke billowed from a stack above the firebox, carrying so many cinders into the air that Gerard was afraid they might start a fire if they got anywhere near the town's vallenwood trees. The racket mounted, sounding like a talon of angry dragons swooping in for an attack. People began looking around nervously.

And the darned machine wasn't even moving yet, Gerard thought, shaking his head. How much worse was the noise likely to be when the thing actually got going?

Gerard motioned to Nob. "How about a demonstration of how well this invention works?"

"Exactly what I had in mind," Nob said. "Of course it's been working fine—better and better after each repair. Still, it has a few kinks, a number of peculiarities, shall we say."

In the crowd, Gerard saw coins changing hands as people began betting on the outcome of the demonstration.

"Show me," he said, jaw out in stubborn challenge.

"Well, uh . . ." Nob hemmed and stammered. "Going

forwards, we have to take time to lay down more of these rails. That's gonna slow us down some."

Gerard shook his head. "I want to see how fast it goes. Crank up the speed."

"We can go backward," said Nob, pointing. "There's already rails in that direction."

"Hurry up," said Gerard, glancing at the sun. "I'm a busy man. I don't have all day."

"Fine then." Nob gestured to his fellows, and several of the gnomes swarmed aboard the machine. Nob himself climbed on last and made a great show of shifting a huge lever.

Steel ground against steel, and the huge wheels began grinding slowly backward. The machine groaned and squealed. The earth trembled. People in the crowd covered their ears.

The thing lumbered in reverse up a small hill, then, as it hurtled down the far side, it could be heard picking up incredible velocity, spinning faster and faster, raising a deafening cacophony.

Then, from the distance, came a loud explosion, and then another, and another. A cloud of smoke and steam burst above the crest of the next hill, followed by more puffs of smoke and steam. The earth was shaking violently. All this commotion was followed by a long silence.

Gerard went to the top of the small hill and shaded his eyes, peering into the distance. The machine and all the gnomes had vanished in the distance. "Halloooo!" Gerard called out.

No one answered.

He returned to the crossroads, where Vercleese and Blair had already begun pulling up the rails. Soon the crossroads was empty of obstruction. A ripple of applause swept through the crowd of onlookers, many of whom were busy paying off their bets.

Gerard smiled, giving an exaggerated bow. He noticed several familiar faces in the crowd, which made him feel more at home than any time since he had left Daltigoth. Among them was the temple architect, Salamon Beach. In fact, he realized now, Salamon had been among the group he'd noticed at the inn the previous night. Also among the crowd, standing apart, was the cowled figure Gerard remembered seeing on the ship on the way over here. Probably some cleric come for the temple dedication, he thought. Some of those clerics were a pretty strange lot.

He waved to a couple of other citizens he recognized from his short time in Solace. Then, with the gnomes' invention gone, traffic began to flow again, with farm wagons and merchant caravans that had been waiting now free to head into Solace. By day's end, Gerard realized, the town would be even more crammed with people, and his duties would become even more demanding.

He sighed and headed back to town, mentally counting the number of days until the temple dedication. Until then, he had a murderer to find and an increasing amount of work to do.

CHAPTER

9

The incident with the gnomes and the problems their invention caused got Gerard to thinking that, to forestall another such brouhaha, he ought to keep track of all the strangers streaming to town for the temple dedication. To this end, he set up registration checkpoints on the three major roads between Solace and the towns of Haven, Gateway, and Que-Kiri.

The checkpoints did not sit well with many travelers. "You mean I have to present my credentials before I can come into town?" a merchant with a wagon-load of wine barrels demanded when he was stopped on the way in from Gateway. "Why, I've been distributing wine in these parts for nigh on fifteen years, and I've never had to suffer such nonsense before."

"It's just a precautionary measure," Gerard explained, while the town guardsman manning the new, brightly painted booth looked on impassively. "Especially with so many new visitors lately. However, you will have to purchase a merchant's writ to do business in Solace."

"I suppose next you'll be wanting to tell me where I

have to stay while I'm in town, and who I can do business with," the merchant groused as he paid for his writ and showed his papers to the guardsman.

The guardsman peered at the merchant's documents closely, unwilling to be hurried, before stamping the papers and handing them back, along with a fresh merchant's seal and an institutional-grade, formal smile. "Have a good stay while in Solace," the guard said. "Be sure to check in with the appropriate authorities at the time of your departure."

The merchant harrumphed and started up his team, the great wagon rolling ponderously with the sound of much sloshing inside the barrels as the merchant made his way toward Solace.

The next man, a tinker with a huge pack on his back, slouched up to the booth and presented his papers with similar grumbling. When it came to paying for his merchant's writ, he refused.

"Look, it's a decision by the town council to require this," Gerard argued.

"I've never had to buy one before, and I'm not buying one now."

"Then I'm afraid you can't conduct business in town."

"Oh?" The tinker's eyebrows rose in mock surprise. "And who's going to stop me?"

"I am," Gerard said wearily and signaled to another guardsman who bundled the tinker, now howling with outrage, off for a night in jail. "Maybe you'll be willing to abide by the municipal ordinances in the morning," Gerard said.

At midmorning he went to see how the other checkpoints were doing, accompanied by Vercleese.

The reaction at each of the other checkpoints was the same: visitors to Solace were taking umbrage at being detained and having their business questioned. No one was eager to pay for a merchant's writ either, when they had never had to purchase one previously.

"Do you think possibly the price of what you are trying to accomplish might be worse than any possible threat to the welfare of Solace?" Vercleese asked Gerard, as they headed toward the final checkpoint, on the road leading to Que-Kiri.

Gerard stuck his jaw out. "It's for the common good. It helps us to know who's coming and going in town. And the writ fees go into the town treasury."

"But Solace has always been a wide open town," the knight said softly.

"Some people might object at first," argued Gerard, "but they'll get used to it."

Solace merchants, meanwhile, were up in arms over another innovation. The enterprising crier Tangletoe Snakeweed had instituted a new practice, taking advantage of the sharp rise in local commerce. He was extolling the virtues of certain merchants' wares for a price while on his rounds. "It's unfair to the rest of us!" a cobbler complained as soon as Gerard and Vercleese returned to town from their round of the checkpoints. "It's an impediment to free trade!"

"That's Evan Grobbel," Vercleese whispered to Gerard. "Although he's better known as Evan the Grouch."

"Why don't you just pay Tangletoe a pittance to tout your goods?" Gerard asked the cobbler, though privately he agreed with the Grouch that the kender had overstepped his duties.

"Why should I have to pay, when the people of Solace already know what fine shoes I make?"

"If everyone already knows you do good work, then you have nothing to worry about," Gerard said.

"But he praises all my competitors!" shouted Evan as Gerard slipped inside the guard headquarters, where he maintained an office. "And besides, it's the principle of the thing!"

" 'The principle of the thing' is the most expensive commodity out there," Gerard remarked dryly to Vercleese. "I wish I could corner the market on that one. I'd retire a wealthy man at a very early age."

Vercleese, absently stroking his mustache, said nothing.

The next couple of hours Gerard had set aside to pore over the volumes of codes, ordinances, and writs he had received from the town council. By lunch time, he was ready to forget them all and pretend he'd never heard of a civic statute, much less been hired to enforce the whole confusing lot of them. His head swam from trying to decipher the endless knots of tangled legalese in order to determine who owed whom what in the matter of one person's well becoming contaminated if another person's chickens jumped in and drowned. Or who was to blame if one man pulled up paving stones from the middle of the road, intending to use them in building a house, while another man stepped into the resulting hole in the dark and broke his leg. But reading about a case involving the statute did make him more wary of where he walked through town at night. Besides, there was another whole section of rules pertaining to pig wastes in city thoroughfares, which posed a threat to pedestrians of an entirely different nature.

Gerard didn't want to encounter any holes in the street, or pig waste, on any of his nocturnal strolls.

He and Vercleese headed to the inn for lunch. Gerard nodded greetings to several individuals they met along the way, pleased to realize that he was getting to know a fair percentage of the town's citizenry. At one point, they encountered a tall, elegant woman whose gray hair was pulled back in a severe bun, giving her a formidable though dignified look. Gerard shot a questioning glance at Vercleese, who introduced him to Goodwife Gottlief.

"Ah, the neighbor of Lady Drebble," Gerard said.

Goodwife Gottlief pursed her lips. "Yes, Lady Drebble. I hesitate to say anything, sheriff, but I fear something may be ailing my neighbor."

"What makes you say that?"

"Every time I have seen her lately, she has been making the most annoying grimaces, as if she is suffering from some severe gastric distress. I thought at first she was trying to smile, but the look is so pained I think now that cannot be the case. I am quite concerned about her health."

"I wouldn't worry about it too much," Gerard said, stifling a chuckle. Then, seeing that Goodwife Gottlief was about to protest, he added, "But I promise I'll look into the matter."

"Thank you, Sheriff." Goodwife Gottlief nodded politely to Vercleese. "Good day, gentlemen." She continued on her way as gracefully as a wraith floating on air, her feet never seeming to make contact with the ground under her long, swishing skirts.

As they continued walking, they heard Tangletoe Snakeweed's voice rising on an adjacent street. "At their meeting yesterday, the town council approved an ordinance requiring all noncitizens of Solace to register with the town guard upon entering the town limits."

Gerard frowned at Vercleese. "Does the town really need a crier? That kender gets on my nerves."

The knight spoke solemnly. "Tangletoe used to be a regular guest in our jail, until he was hired by the town council. It seemed a good solution at the time. He hasn't been arrested now for, let me see, one or two months. That's a record, in all the time he's been in Solace."

"Well, I guess there is a price to pay for the town growing so rapidly," Gerard said in a dubious tone. "Though I often wonder if progress is worth the price, added up."

Vercleese smiled as if Gerard had just made some point echoing the knight's own sentiments. Gerard wondered what the knight might have said of a similar nature, but could think of nothing.

Meanwhile, the kender continued on his rounds, reciting as he went, "Evan the Grou—, er, Evan the Great makes just about the finest shoes in all Solace. Be sure to place your order with Evan the Great today for new shoes to wear to the temple dedication. Best shoes in the whole of Ansalon, probably."

"I guess Evan Grobbel came around to the new way of doing business," Gerard said with a snort. "Didn't take him long, once he realized there might be some profit in it."

"That reminds me," Vercleese said, a pinched look on his face. "I need a new pair of shoes myself."

At lunch, they saw nothing of Laura, much to Gerard's relief. She was off somewhere, enabling

Gerard to have lamb sandwich and a cup of cheese soup without fear of offending her.

After lunch, he and Vercleese strolled around the town, greeting people and checking on complaints. This had become part of his daily routine and was expected of the town sheriff. In truth, though it sounded like lazy, lofty work, Gerard thought, it was wearying in the heat of the day, and the kind of official friendliness and nosiness that he had to force himself to do. It wasn't in his nature to put himself forward thusly, but after his stint in the knighthood, if there was one thing he understood, it was to persevere in any duty required of him.

During the course of their meandering trek, Gerard and Vercleese discussed Sheriff Joyner's murder, debating the possible theories. The investigation was stalled. They had talked to many people in town, without coming up with any viable leads. Now and then Palin asked Gerard for an update, but the upcoming temple dedication was the more important matter, and as there had been no further crimes of note, there seemed no urgency about the murder. Still, it bothered both of them that they didn't yet have a suspect or even a motive.

They came to a ramshackle, ground-level building, where loud sounds of laughter and music and argument already seeped through the cracks in the dirty windows and through the chinks in the poorly made door. A woman's voice inside rose momentarily in a forced, commercial squeal of delight, the sound muffled by the thin walls but still distinct.

Gerard looked quizzically at Vercleese.

"The Trough," said the knight. "If you think it looks disreputable from the outside, you should see the inside. It's even worse. Every couple of years, the place manages to burn down and has to be rebuilt. The owner has taken to never cleaning; he just lets the inevitable fires do the job for him. The only time it ever looks respectable is the day it first opens for business again, after the latest fire."

Gerard chuckled, despite himself. "Well, it's about time we paid the place a visit, don't you think?" He started toward the front door.

Vercleese stopped him with a hand on his arm. "Nighttime is better," the knight said in a low voice.

"Why?"

"It's a den of iniquity, right enough," Vercleese said softly. "But especially at night."

"If you say so," said Gerard, reluctantly turning away.

"One more thing," the knight said, holding Gerard's arm and meeting his gaze. "Every town has at least one den of iniquity, and the council usually leaves this one alone, so long as the mischief and occasional violence remain within limits. If we need to go in looking for something—or someone—then that's what we'll do. Otherwise, it's best not to tip our hand with drop-in visits."

Gerard allowed himself to be led farther along the street, casting a glance over his shoulder from time to time as if The Trough's building itself might commit some foul deed that would compel him to swing into action. But if he secretly hoped he would have to storm inside and round up the establishment's clients and haul them off to jail, he was doomed, for the present at least, to disappointment. The building stolidly refused to engage in any nefarious act.

"Here we have the warehouses of Tyburn Price," Vercleese said, gesturing to the boxlike structures that rose on each side of the narrow road. "Without question, he is one of the town's most prominent citizens, and does an active business in import and export."

Gerard and Vercleese followed a slight curve in the road. "I'm familiar with the name," Gerard said distractedly. "In fact, Tyburn Price contracts for quite a bit of business on my father's ships."

Vercleese nodded. "That would be him. A shrewd businessman—you'll never get the better of him in a deal. But a fine fellow for all that. Now up ahead we have. . . ."

The knight's voice droned on, merging with the piercing buzz of cicadas on the hot, airless afternoon. Gerard longed for the welcome relief of a breeze, but none materialized.

The Trough had set the tone for the neighborhood, and now they found themselves in a rougher quarter of Solace. Gerard and Vercleese kept their hands near their weapons as they strode purposefully through the streets with their ramshackle, temporary buildings, all on ground level. Ragged children played in the gutters, which ran with the wastes of butcher shops, tanneries, and less savory businesses. Gerard breathed through his mouth and marched resolutely on, ignoring the catcalls and hooting of the children as he and Vercleese passed by.

◆ ◆ ◆ ◆ ◆

Later that afternoon, while Vercleese went over to the temple grounds to check on the construction,

Gerard wandered down to the blacksmith's shop to see about the progress on his sword.

"It takes time to fashion a good blade," grumbled Torren Soljack, the smith. "I do good work and don't care to be rushed. Now, if you want to take your business elsewhere, you go right ahead."

Gerard was sitting on an upturned wine cask. If the temperature outside was hot, the temperature inside the smithy was almost intolerable. He wiped his forehead with his sleeve but was unable to stop the flow of sweat from trickling into his eyes. "Where else in town can I get as good a sword?" he asked equably.

"You can't!" Soljack snapped. While the smith talked, he kept up the steady rhythm of hammer blows on the red-hot horseshoe he held over the anvil with a pair of tongs. He seemed oblivious to the rivulets of sweat that glistened on his torso, bare except for the leather apron he wore to protect himself from sparks. He was a mass of burns and scars that shone out white against the bronze coloring of the rest of his skin. "There's nowhere else you can get a decent sword around here. People will tell you, I'm the only one who knows the old arts, which take time and patience." He pursed his lips disapprovingly, but whether of Gerard, lesser smiths, or the world in general, Gerard couldn't tell.

The smith harbored some secret that was eating away at him, Gerard thought. The secret rose up like bile in his mouth, only to be choked back down again. Whatever mystery he was harboring would surely kill him, given time. What secret could be so terrible it was worth such stress and strain?

Gerard didn't budge. The smith said nothing else but glowered at the sheriff from time to time as if with cheerless surprise to find him still sitting there and watching.

Gerard watched in silence for a long time, noting the care with which Soljack shaped even the lowly horseshoes he was forging today. Gerard couldn't help but admire the man, regardless of how unwelcoming he behaved. Off to one side, he eyed his sword, cooling in preparation for its next stage. He wiped his face again. It wasn't likely that the sword would get all that cool today.

"What can you tell me about my predecessor, Sheriff Joyner?" Gerard asked on impulse, thinking here was a man who saw and observed far more than he let on.

Soljack seemed taken aback by the question. "Sheriff Joyner?"

Gerard nodded, struggling for breath in the heat.

Soljack paused, eyeing Gerard suspiciously. "What are you asking me that for?"

Gerard shrugged. Because I was floundering around searching for some topic of conversation, didn't seem to be the right reply, he thought.

Soljack resumed pounding, each blow of the massive hammer showering the air with sparks. For a long time, it seemed he was done talking. Gerard waited patiently.

"Sheriff Joyner was a good man," the smith said at last, his voice a deep rumble in the tiny shop. "He sometimes visited Baron Samuval up at the baron's fortress nearby." He glanced up sharply, catching Gerard's look. "I guess you didn't know about that."

Gerard shook his head, though he did know—or at least he had heard that Sheriff Joyner played a game of Regal with Samuval now and then.

Soljack shrugged. "Strange thing to do, but it was

common knowledge hereabouts. That's the kind of man Sheriff Joyner was. The sheriff had worked out some kind of understanding or agreement with Samuval, allowing Samuval's men to come into town from time to time."

"I think I've seen some of them around," Gerard said, recalling the rough-looking men who had been taunting Kirrit Bitterleaf outside the grocery.

Soljack nodded, as if reading Gerard's thoughts. "Sheriff Joyner permitted Samuval's men to come into town and buy supplies once in a while, and he permitted the elves to do the same. But if they lingered in town, they had to restrict themselves to The Trough and its environs. Otherwise, Sheriff Joyner would lock them up for a day or two. And that wasn't half as bad as the men could expect from Samuval himself once they got back. As a result, they were generally better behaved while in Solace than some of the town's most upstanding citizens."

Gerard thought about what Vercleese had said about The Trough being a necessary evil in the town. Apparently, Joyner had understood the importance of that as well.

"They played a fierce game of Regal, Sheriff Joyner and Samuval, from what I hear," Soljack said.

"It sounds like they spent some very companionable time together," Gerard said dryly, finding it hard to summon any affection for the mercenary who had helped overthrow the elves in Qualinesti.

Soljack shot him a sharp look. "Rumor has it the wily old outlaw chief liked Sheriff Joyner as much as the townspeople did. I don't think he killed him, if that's what you're wondering."

Gerard let out a discouraged breath. That's what everybody said. Sheriff Joyner apparently didn't have a single enemy, which left Gerard with a grand total of exactly no one who seemed to have had a reason to want the sheriff dead.

◆◆◆◆◆

Lady Odila Windlass walked slowly through the grounds of the unfinished temple, relishing the tranquility now that the workday was over. Though the air still smelled of the stonecutters' dust and carpenters' shavings, gone was the din of chisel and saw. For the moment, as dusk settled upon Solace, the site was calm, the grounds fallen strangely quiet except for the chirping of crickets and the soft rustling of the vallenwood leaves. At moments such as this, Odila could imagine how the temple grounds would feel once construction was finished and the unhurried rhythm of clerics going about their sacred duties replaced the chaos of the builders.

As the last red glow of sunset faded behind her, the crest of the mountains to the east, beyond the temple, grew brighter, foretelling the double moonrise soon to follow. Odila paused in her steps to watch, letting her mind sink into meditative prayer. She drank in the night air in slow, measured breaths and felt almost at peace with the world. Or as close to peace as she came these days, since that terrible moment during the war when she had been forced to look deep into Mina's eyes, only to wind up confronting the darkness that reposed in her own soul. All her life since that moment had been dedicated to the struggle against such darkness wherever it dwelt. But she no longer struggled as a warrior did, with knives and swords; rather, she abided by the healing light of Mishakal, which gave her a far more potent weapon.

She hoped in the end it would be enough.

The frightened squeal of an animal erupted nearby, followed by the heavy flapping of an owl carrying off its prey. The attack, though completely natural, nevertheless disrupted Odila's peaceful reverie. She went on into the temple, while Solinari was a mere fingernail of white edging above the mountains and only a reddish glow indicated where Lunitari would soon rise.

Inside, the sharp rap of her steps echoed back at her from the vast emptiness, first of the antechamber, then the main sanctuary. She found herself standing before the statue of Mishakal.

Then other steps intruded on her thoughts, and she recognized the light but confident tread of Kaleen coming from behind her. Kaleen's arrival always prompted a warm smile from Odila, lighting up a face that seldom knew joy these days, and the young woman from the inn usually brought other amenities.

Odila smelled the aroma of freshly brewed tarbean tea. "I thought you might like a mug to ease the tensions of the day," Kaleen said, her voice soft in the reverential silence.

Odila accepted the mug gratefully.

"When was the last time you ate?" Kaleen asked.

"Don't mother me," Odila growled.

Kaleen said nothing, only waited.

Sighing, Odila relented. "I don't know. Breakfast, I guess."

"Perhaps you'd like me to get you something to eat?"

"No need. I'll have dinner presently."

Kaleen didn't move.

"I promise," Odila said.

In the darkness, she could feel rather than see Kaleen considering her answer. "All right," the younger woman said at last, as if she were the one in authority here. "But don't forget. You've promised me."

"I won't forget, you have my word," Odila said warmly.

The sound of Kaleen's footsteps retreated, fading into silence as she left the temple. Once again, Odila was alone in night's embrace. She turned to where she knew the statue stood; she couldn't quite see its details but knew its expression was serene, despite its divine watchfulness. She took a sip from the mug, the steam rising like a faint, steadying breath against her face. "Thank you, Goddess, for Kaleen and others who help support me," she whispered.

Slowly, she sipped the tea, letting her tension ebb away. When she had drained the mug, she felt somewhat restored. She grinned, thinking that tomorrow Kaleen would demand an accounting of exactly what she had eaten for dinner. She had better go make good on her promise.

She walked softly back through the temple, her footsteps quieter now. Just as she was about to step onto the temple porch, however, she froze, overhearing angry voices coming from somewhere outside. Keeping to the shadows of the two great doors of the temple, she peered into the gloomy light the two risen moons now cast upon the yard. She made out Salamon Beach standing between two figures she didn't recognize. The two strange men were pushing Beach back and forth between them, as if he were a ball in some kind of vicious game they were playing. With each shove, they snarled curses or threats, although Odila couldn't quite make out their words. She was just about to hurry to his aid when, with a final push that sent Beach sprawling to the ground, the two men turned away. She got a brief glimpse by moonlight of one man's face, with an enormous, thick mustache that drooped down to conceal his upper lip and a scar that puckered his skin from the corner of his left eye and down his jaw, disappearing beneath his shirt. Then the two men vanished into the dark. Odila rushed over to Beach and helped him stand.

"What was that all about?" she asked concernedly.

He dusted himself off and tried to laugh, although the sound came out forced and hollow. "Oh, it's nothing. Nothing at all. Just a slight disagreement between . . . colleagues, of a sort."

"That looked like more than a simple 'disagreement,' " Odila said.

"It was nothing, truly. You needn't concern yourself," Beach replied, his tone cutting off further inquiry. "Now I really must be off. I have . . . matters to attend to." Then he slipped into the night as well, although not, Odila noticed, heading in the same direction as his two assailants.

Odila was left standing alone in the moonlight, the inner peace she had gathered about her now quite shattered. She shook her head, as if to clear it of disturbing thoughts, and trudged off toward the inn to honor her promise of getting some dinner. But trudging along, she was unable to shake the sense that, despite Beach's assurances, something was very wrong.

CHAPTER
10

You're sure this is absolutely necessary?" Gerard asked, still hoping for a reprieve. Nevertheless, he went ahead and swung up into Thunderbolt's saddle.

"The outlying farms are under your care, too," Vercleese said, handing Gerard a set of papers. "Here, I've taken the liberty of writing down the names of all the families you'll need to visit, along with directions for getting to each farm."

"What about something to eat?" Gerard asked, for he hadn't even had breakfast. "It'll be late in the day before I get back."

"Oh, I wouldn't worry about that too much," Vercleese said mischievously. "I'm sure you'll find something to eat along the way." With that, he slapped Thunderbolt's haunch and sent Gerard on his way.

For his part, Thunderbolt seemed eager for the chance to get out in the countryside, and Gerard felt a pang of guilt at not having seen to it the horse got more regular exercise. But what with the paperwork piling up on his desk and all the petty concerns that he was discovering went with the job of sheriff, there just hadn't been time. "But at least I'll see that you get to stretch those legs a bit today," he promised Thunderbolt, patting the animal's well-muscled neck.

At least it was a beautiful morning for a ride. The rains of a few tendays earlier had dried up completely, and now the weather had settled into the hot, clear days of midsummer. The countryside was awash with verdant growth, from grasses springing up near waist-high along the edge of the road to lush meadows carpeted with dandelions and daisies. Acres of ripening grain—wheat, barley, and rye—waved placidly in the innumerable fields Gerard passed, each set of fields marking another of the various farmsteads of the region.

List in hand, Gerard stopped dutifully at each farm, introducing himself and getting to know the families.

The first family, Brentwood and Dorla Gibbs and their seven children, crowded around Gerard as expectantly as if he were the first contact they'd had with Solace in a fortnight, although Gerard gathered they had just been in town to market a couple of days before. "Yes, sir, we got a pretty good price for the eggs this tenday, didn't we, Dorla?" Brentwood crowed, sounding as if he had been personally responsible for laying every one of those eggs. He blinked his huge, watery eyes and looked around, assuring himself of his audience's amazement. "A fair price this tenday, indeed!"

Gerard nodded and smiled, unsure what reaction was called for. Dorla beamed at their guest, cradling her infant twins one in each arm, while a couple of slightly older children of indeterminate gender peeked shyly around her skirts. The three oldest children, all girls, hung back, pretending indifference to Gerard's arrival, although he noticed they waited ardently enough to hear anything he might have to say.

"But, here, I'm forgetting my manners," Brentwood went on. "I'm just chattering on, and you haven't even met the little ladies."

Gerard smiled at the cluster of children, expecting to be introduced to them. Instead, Brentwood strode out toward the barn with Gerard in tow, to where a chicken coop stood in the shade of a cottonwood tree. "There!" Brentwood announced with a sweep of his arm. "What did I tell you? The finest little laying hens in all of Solace."

"Ah," Gerard said, wondering how long politeness required him to tarry here. The dozens of chickens in the coop looked no different to him than any others he had ever seen.

Then Brentwood said the magic words that changed Gerard's mind about hurrying on his way: "You'll have breakfast with us, of course."

It wasn't really a question, but Gerard nodded eagerly, for the ride through the countryside at this early hour had aroused his appetite.

"Dorla," Brentwood called, leading Gerard back across the farmyard, "put on a mess of them eggs and fry up some of that fine ham for the sheriff, will you? We need to show him some good country neighborliness."

Dorla Gibbs must have anticipated her husband's request, because by the time Brentwood ushered Gerard into the cozy farmhouse kitchen, the air was already redolent of frying eggs and ham. Gerard accepted a seat gratefully at the large table that dominated the room, while a couple of the older Gibbs girls bustled about, setting places and tending to their younger siblings. Soon, the aroma of fresh biscuits in the oven joined the frying smells in the room.

When everything was done, Dorla carried a platter to the table as proudly as if bringing willing tribute to a king. She set the platter down in the middle of the table with a flourish. One of the girls followed hard on her heels with a serving bowl full of scrambled eggs, while another carried a basket of biscuits and a tub of freshly churned butter. But Gerard's attention was riveted on the platter Dorla had carried. On it rested the ham, which loomed as a huge slab of almost solid fat that wobbled obscenely when the platter came to rest on the table.

Gerard's stomach did a little nervous flutter in dread anticipation at the sight of it. He was about to beg off the ham and ask for just a plate of eggs, when Brentwood caught him staring at the white, oleaginous slab. Brentwood broke into a huge grin. "Raised that porker ourselves, we did. Best bacon in, well, miles in any direction, I'll warrant."

As he spoke, he sliced off a generous hunk and heaped it on a plate, around which Dorla mounded scrambled eggs and piled on two or three biscuits. Belatedly, Gerard realized he was to have no say in what he ate or how much he consumed. Good manners dictated he clean his plate.

He belched softly, already feeling that mass of fat sitting in his belly in an indigestible lump.

The Gibbses, meanwhile, were digging into the food with zest. Gerard managed to work his way resolutely through most of what had been dished up for him, although it required every ounce of self-discipline he had learned as a knight not to disgrace himself by promptly disgorging the meal right there at the table. Dorla and Brentwood tried to urge seconds on him, but he shook his head weakly and forced a thin smile. "I really must see to some of the other farms hereabouts," he explained, his lips drawn tight in an effort to keep everything down.

"Of course," Brentwood boomed. "Why, whatever have we been thinking, wife? We mustn't *hog* our guest." He laughed at his little joke with a wave that took in the remaining ham on the serving platter. "I'm sure our neighbors will want to show him hospitality, as well."

So Gerard resumed his trek, holding Thunderbolt to an amble and drinking in deep draughts of air, which suddenly felt close and oppressive in the growing heat. The birds in the trees sang more mournfully than before, and the buzzing of the cicadas had turned shrill. Even Thunderbolt's gentle pace threatened to dislodge the contents of Gerard's stomach. Nevertheless, he managed to make it to the next farm on his list, the one farthest from town, belonging to Biggin Styles.

It was immediately apparent why Styles's place, a pig farm, was located so far from Solace: the stench from the pigs was overwhelming. It burned in the nose and coated the tongue, to the point that Gerard could scarcely remember what fresh air smelled and tasted like. His stomach, already burdened by the Gibbses' ham, rolled over heavily.

Styles was a bachelor, shrewd, bitter, and inordinately proud of his farm. He had come to Solace, he informed Gerard with a haughty air, during the war, along with many of the other recent immigrants who had been displaced from their native lands. But he, unlike the majority of others, had not lacked for industry. In a short time, he had turned this farm, which had fallen into disrepair and which he had purchased for next to nothing, into a going concern. On every side, pigs now squealed and rooted in their pens.

"You can see me in town near any market day, selling the best porkers to be found in all of Solace," he said disdainfully.

Gerard smiled wanly, grateful there was no Goodwife Styles to urge him to sample the bounty of the farm, and hopeful of being able to quickly escape the place and its smell.

"You'll join me for an early lunch," Styles said. Again, it wasn't really a question—more the condescending manner of one bestowing his largess on an undeserving social inferior.

Gerard gulped hastily. "Oh, no, I really couldn't—"

"Nonsense!" Styles waved the objection aside. "I can't have you leaving here, saying that Biggin Styles lacked social graces."

"No, really, I wouldn't think of saying—"

"Sit down. I'll soon find us something worthy to eat."

"Please, just no ham," Gerard begged, as Styles ushered him firmly to a chair.

Styles froze, anger flashing in his eyes. "Why, I'll bet you've been over to the Gibbs place." He shook his head and scowled. "Them and their paltry fare. I'll wager they carried on the whole time about their *wonderful* ham, didn't they?" He turned back to his kitchen. "As if anyone in this county had pork to compare with Biggin Styles. Well, you won't get any of that kind of ordinary food here." He fished around in a cupboard and came out with a huge pottery jar, which he placed on the table. "There!" he announced grandly. "A Styles farm specialty." He dug into the jar with a long-handled fork and plopped a couple of sodden, vinegary smelling forelegs, complete with split hooves, onto a plate, which he then pushed in front of Gerard. "Now here's real food! Pickled pig's feet. You won't find the likes if 'em anywhere."

Gerard stared at the plate and swallowed hard, pretty certain it was true: he wouldn't find the likes of this particular treat *anywhere*.

"It really gets your mouth watering, don't it?" Styles continued, evidently mistaking Gerard's reaction. He served up a couple more feet on a plate for himself. "Well, don't stand on ceremony. Dig in!"

Gerard hesitated. He gingerly bit into one of the delicacies, chewing, swallowing, then stifling his gagging as he nearly choked on it. As Styles watched him, he gave a thin smile and finished off the rest. Then, pleading the urgency of his mission as an excuse to leave without eating the second, he said he really must go. Styles stared at the remaining pig's foot balefully. "I guess I'll just have to send that one along with you," he said. "You can have it for your dinner."

While he wrapped up the hoof in an evil-smelling, soggy paper, Gerard asked whether Styles had ever seen Sheriff Joyner wandering this far from town on his excursions through the countryside.

Styles froze then turned on Gerard, his expression glowering. "Joyner! Why are you asking me about him?

Did one of my pesky neighbors say I had something to do with his murder?"

"No, no," said Gerard hastily, palms out to deflect the man's anger. "I'm just trying to get a sense of where the man might have visited before his death, that's all."

Styles cast his squinting glare on Gerard for long moments before finally relenting. "Take advantage of a man's hospitality and then ask him something like that," he grumbled, just loud enough for Gerard to hear, as he finished wrapping the pig's foot. "I must be daft to be so generous with folk."

When he had finished, he thrust the package at Gerard. "Here, something to help you remember the name of Biggin Styles!" he cried. "Now that you know what good pork is, you'll never be satisfied with anything less."

On the road again, Gerard turned the contents of the package over to the first cur he found roaming the countryside. The dog peered at the pig's foot for long moments, studying the item from every side, before finally dragging it off into the weeds, whether to devour it or bury it, Gerard little cared. At least the awful thing was gone.

The next place on his list was the mill belonging to Jutlin and Agnes Wykirk. Gerard was already feeling logy. It seemed everywhere he went people were determined to feed him.

Here, at least, no pork products of any sort were forced upon Gerard, just a hunk of heavy, sour-tasting bread and a mug of bitter beer. The Wykirks sat at the table as he ate, Jutlin watching him with an occasional cackle like a bantam rooster strutting in the chicken yard, while Agnes simply glared at him without saying a word, as if Gerard's mere presence somehow called the propriety of her kitchen into question. A large kettle bubbled on the hearth, but whether it was dinner cooking or whether Agnes Wykirk had been in the midst of making soap, Gerard couldn't tell. He was just glad he wasn't expected to partake of any of its dubious bounty.

It was no wonder Jutlin Wykirk was so skinny, if this bread was an example of his wife's cooking.

Out in the mill yard again, Gerard leaned for a moment against Thunderbolt and tried to steady himself. His stomach was roiling. "When was the last time you saw Sheriff Joyner?" he ventured, trying to make conversation in order to forestall the effort required to mount the horse.

Jutlin grinned at him. "What do you mean?"

"Well, I gather he used to go visit Samuval from time to time," Gerard said. "And sometimes he went to see the elves. That would put him in the neighborhood of your mill, now and then."

"Elves!" Jutlin spat. "All those wretched creatures—elves and dwarves and every other vile sort—hanging about Solace these days, crowding the place. Even draconians, from what I hear!"

"So you didn't see Sheriff Joyner before he was murdered."

"Depends on what you mean by 'before,' don't it?" Jutlin kept on grinning, reminding Gerard of a young child who has just learned to bandy words with his parents. "I might have seen him a day or two before, or it might have been longer." He shrugged. "I can't rightly say."

"Tell me, did Sheriff Joyner welcome the various races to Solace?"

Jutlin's expression clouded. "No more than anyone else in town. They all like to go on about how growth is good for the community. As far as I'm concerned, what would be good for the community would be to run all them out of town. Keep Solace for human folk."

"So you didn't like Sheriff Joyner?"

"Oh, the sheriff was all right, so long as you didn't get him onto the subject of what he called 'tolerance.' There was never any bad blood between us, if that's what you mean. Yes, I can truly say I liked him well enough."

Gerard nodded and, having put off the inevitable as long as he could, swung heavily into the saddle. He sat for a moment and forced himself to take deep, steady breaths, studying the tumbledown mill and huge, decrepit barn. Then with a wave, he eased Thunderbolt onto the road.

At Corly Ames's place, he was induced to try the sourberry pie, one of the tartest dishes he'd ever tasted, while Trent Linden's wife (Gerard never did catch her name) served him up a generous bowl of cabbage soup. By the time he reached the Ostermans' place, he could barely stay alert in the saddle, and he wondered how he could politely decline any further country fare.

Tom and Sophie were delighted to see him again. They took him around the farm, showing off their chickens (Gerard was beginning to wonder if farmers detected a level of personality in the creatures that was indistinguishable to mere townsfolk, they carried on about their chickens so) and their fields of wheat. "I'm still hoping to acquire that extra field," Tom said with a hint of shy pride. "That would allow me to considerably enlarge the farm."

"You mean the field where you found Sheriff Joyner's body?"

Tom's cheerful expression fell. "Yes. Though it'll bring sad memories, of course, working that field now. I expect it'll take quite a bit of time before it's just another field again."

"Well, thank you for showing me about the place," Gerard said as they arrived back in the farmyard around the house. "I'd best be on my way."

"What! Before you join us at table? Sophie and I wouldn't hear of it! It's a tradition when the sheriff comes calling to sup together. We always looked forward to Sheriff Joyner's visits."

Gerard protested weakly, knowing from the start that his words were falling on deaf ears. All too soon he was seated at the table in a huge farmhouse kitchen that would have sufficed to serve everyone at the Inn of the Last Home on a busy night. Sophie slaved furiously at the stove while Tom droned on about acreage under cultivation and crop yields and market prices. As he spoke, a pungent, peppery odor began to permeate the air, and Gerard felt like weeping.

"Here you go!" Sophie said at last, plunking a large serving dish down on the table. "I know Laura Majere sets great store by her spiced potatoes, and that recipe's a treasured family secret. But I'll wager my spiced potatoes will stand up against anyone's!"

Gerard groaned inwardly. If anything, Sophie's potatoes smelled even more robustly flavored than Laura's. At the risk of committing a grave breach of etiquette, he grabbed the nearest serving spoon and began dishing himself up a modest helping, figuring he was likely to get off with smaller portions if he served himself than if he left the job up to his hosts. Indeed, Sophie frowned at the small amount on his plate and looked ready to object.

"I can't wait to try them!" Gerard exclaimed, shoveling in a mouthful before Sophie could interrupt . . . and almost dropped his spoon on the table. The potatoes were hot! Not stove hot, but spicy hot, peppery hot, peel-the-skin-off-the-roof-of-your-mouth hot. Gerard gasped and gulped at the mug of ale Tom had set before him. The burning sensation diminished only as long as he kept drinking, for soon as he stopped for breath, the searing pain returned full force. "More!" he choked, finishing his ale and pushing the mug toward Tom. "Please, some more."

Tom laughed good-naturedly and refilled the mug while Sophie beamed as though Gerard had just paid her the highest form of compliment. "I'm glad you like them," she said, blushing.

Gerard didn't try to correct her misapprehension. He continued drinking ale, though at a slower rate. Finally, he was able to tolerate the twinges that continued to plague his trembling mouth. He set the mug down, wiped his lips with his sleeve, and looked at his plate.

One mouthful down, and who knew how many more yet to go. He let out a deep breath and resolutely picked up his spoon. As Tom and Sophie looked at him, beaming, and eagerly beginning to devour their own hefty servings, Gerard began toiling through the rest of the portion on his plate.

By the time he was through, his stomach was

heaving and his head was spinning with the effects of the ale. He had to have Tom's help clambering back into the saddle. He headed back into town at the gentlest pace he could coax from Thunderbolt, who was still impatient for a good run. His shadow stretched far into the field on his right. Even at a plodding walk, the potatoes and ale were not long with him. Indeed, all the day's victuals were soon left behind at the side of the road.

He had made an entire sea voyage at the height of a storm, he thought miserably, and never once was seasick. Yet here he was now, unable to keep simple farm fare down on a neighborly visit through the countryside.

From now on, he resolved, he would stick in town where he belonged.

CHAPTER

II

One morning a few days later, Gerard hummed as he strolled along the bridge-walks, nodding and greeting people. He got a wan smile from the bemused baker, Brynn Ragulf, whose mind was undoubtedly far from Solace, sailing the high seas and living a life of adventure. "Rising," Ragulf said distractedly in answer to the stock question citizens always asked about how the bread business was doing, despite the fact that Gerard hadn't asked. "Always rising." He wandered off, already back in his reverie, oblivious to the flour that dusted his face and clothes.

Gerard's reception from Kedrick Tos, the gangly goldsmith and councilman who fancied himself a ladies' man, was more effusive. "Sheriff, just the man I wanted to see! I have an idea for helping to ensure the safety of Solace from attack. A ditch and palisade constructed around the entire town." He waved his hands expansively to indicate the scale of the project.

Gerard smiled. "And who do you think is going to attack?"

"Oh, I don't know. Brigands, I suppose. Outlaws. Villains of every stripe. We should be prepared in any event, don't you think?"

Gerard tried to envision digging a trench around the whole of Solace and erecting a palisade alongside it. Such a structure wouldn't even protect the town against imaginative kender, supposing the project could ever be completed in the first place—a proposition Gerard highly doubted. Even the checkpoints on the major roads into town were drawing criticism from a number of merchants and private citizens alike. Anything more ambitious than that would never find sufficient support from the rest of the council. "I'll take the matter under consideration, Councilman," he said thoughtfully, knowing Tos would forget all about the idea now that he had passed it along to Gerard. Tos was enthusiastic that way, and absentminded afterward.

Tangletoe Snakeweed passed beneath the bridge-walk, crying out the news of the day—or what passed for news in his spiel. "For all those who were wondering, it turns out Lady Drebble will be all right," Tangletoe announced grandly. "Healer Argyle Hulsey says Lady Drebble's features merely froze for a while from the unaccustomed effort of arranging them into a smile. Argyle Hulsey says it was the worst case of rictus she's ever seen outside of a three-day-old corpse, but Lady Drebble's face should be back to its habitual expression within a few days."

Early though it was, the town was already bustling. Horses, carts, and wagons passed along the streets below, raising clouds of dust, now that the days were hot and dry, that rose even to Gerard's perch among the trees. By day the cicadas droned; by night the crickets chirped. And always there was the turmoil of a town undergoing unprecedented growth, with all the opportunities and problems that afforded, which meant that the town sheriff played a vital role.

Gerard drank in the morning air. There was real satisfaction in his job, a kind of contentment that had eluded him all those years he had served as a knight. Who would have thought, he mused, that he would find a source of such pride here in Solace, where he had been forced to endure such humiliation during the war?

He reached the home of Palin and Usha and knocked. The door opened almost immediately, revealing Palin in his usual early-morning garb of embroidered robe and slippers. Gerard tried to stop in every day to talk with the mayor. After Palin heard of Gerard's misadventures on his farm rounds, he made a point of inviting the sheriff to daily breakfast, assuring him that his eating habits were his own. So Gerard had began showing up as a regular guest at their morning table.

The Majeres were willing to serve Gerard plain, unsweetened porridge without cinnamon or cream, if that was his desire. But he was gradually tempted by the blueberry muffins and jam or honey, with stacks of buttermilk pancakes swimming in syrup, which Palin and Usha often enjoyed.

"Come on in," Palin said, showing Gerard to his customary chair. "What's the word out in the world this fine morning?"

Gerard sprawled in the chair Palin had offered him, feeling right at home. "The word is that Lady Drebble's face froze when she attempted to smile at Goodwife Gottlief. At least, that's what Tangletoe Snakeweed is claiming this morning on his rounds."

Palin laughed as he took his own chair. "For once, I can believe the kender got his facts right. Lady Drebble's face *would* freeze if she tried to smile, especially if the recipient was to be Goodwife Gottlief. But you know, I really think you're the one who is to blame."

"Me?" Gerard sat up straight. "What did I do?"

"You encouraged Lady Drebble to take a more conciliatory approach to Goodwife Gottlief, don't you remember? You suggested to Lady Drebble that it would drive her neighbor crazy trying to figure out what was up."

"How'd you hear about that?" Gerard mumbled.

"Oh, a good mayor has ears."

"Vercleese told you!"

"Whatever my source of information, I think you should own up to some level of responsibility in the matter."

"All right, what of it? What do you want me to do? Should I apologize to Lady Drebble?"

"Apologize? Why, I should say not! I rather think your actions should come before the town council for a commendation."

"Hmph!" Gerard snorted, realizing Palin had been making light fun of him. "If appearing before the council means having to attend another one of the council's interminable meetings, I'd rather face Lady Drebble's frozen face any time, thank you very much."

"Suit yourself," Palin said with a grin. Then he glanced up as his wife entered. "Usha, I'm sorry. I got busy talking business with Gerard and forgot to help you finish fixing breakfast."

"I heard what kind of business you two were discussing," Usha said dryly as she carried a tray laden with food and dishes in from the kitchen. "But that's all right; I saved the cleanup for you."

"Ah." Palin tried unsuccessfully to keep his face from falling. "Well, that's only fair, I expect." He helped her transfer items from the tray to the table.

For a while, there was no further discussion—business or otherwise—as the three set upon the omelets and biscuits with honey Usha had prepared. At last, Gerard sighed contentedly and pushed back from the table. He shook his head when Usha offered him the basket with what remained of the biscuits. "What can you tell me about Cardjaf Duhar?" he asked, keeping his tone light.

Palin looked at him and raised an eyebrow.

"I only ask because I see Kaleen practically every day at the temple grounds, or every night at the inn," Gerard explained hastily. Then, feeling he had said more than he intended, he felt his face flush. "That is . . . look, I just can't imagine a free spirit like her born to a man as seemingly worldly and business-oriented as her father, that's all. I'm curious."

Usha smiled and stood. "I'll leave you two to discuss *business,*" she said. She patted Palin affectionately on the arm. "And I'll leave the dishes to you."

"Kaleen follows her own path," Palin said after Usha had gone. "And it's to her father's credit that he stays out of her way."

He went on to explain how Duhar had recently retired to Solace from Palanthas, where he had extensive business interests, because he felt Solace was a more suitable environment in which to raise his only child, Kaleen. Duhar remained more familiar with life in the large city, however, and retained a cosmopolitan view of the world.

"Although Duhar is never anything less than respectful toward Solace's traditional leaders, he seems to regard the opinions of some of us as quaint and out of step with Solace's future," Palin explained. "He favors virtually unlimited growth and development, wanting to welcome as many new arrivals to the town as possible. He argues that it is selfish of Solace's long-term inhabitants to resist making the town as welcoming as possible to new people in a troubled world."

It was primarily through Duhar's efforts, Palin added, that Solace had become the home to the new Temple of Mishakal, for Duhar was one of the principal financial backers of the building project. "Yet he doesn't strike me as an especially religious man," Palin continued. "Rather, I think he sees the temple as one more civic establishment, helping to forge the ties of a stronger community."

"And what about Kaleen's mother?" Gerard asked.

"Ah, Gatrice Duhar. She's an elegant, self-possessed woman from Palanthas high society who has never really felt at home in Solace. I suspect that she resents Cardjaf's decision to move to so backward a place, a decision in which she had little part—as she has on occasion publicly reminded him. Nevertheless, she attempts to make the most of her situation by educating the women of Solace in the cultural refinements she feels appropriate for one of her station."

"I see."

"Yes," Palin concluded tartly.

Gerard, sensing that Palin was going to say no more on that topic, tactfully switched gears. "I gather you and Cardjaf Duhar don't always see eye to eye."

"Oh, we don't, but who does? We're always extremely

respectful of one another. It never degenerates into anything personal." Palin sighed. "No, we don't always see eye to eye. As I say, Duhar favors unlimited growth, a view he has convinced certain others on the council and in the town to adopt. I fear that Solace is in danger of losing the very quality that makes it special."

Gerard saw Palin's eyes blaze with real pride as he spoke of Solace, and he knew the man had found his true calling as mayor. It was clear Palin loved the town and relished being responsible for helping to build and oversee its future.

Caramon would have been proud, Gerard reflected sadly, wishing the elder Majere had lived long enough to see his son in this surprising role.

"How is the murder investigation going?" Palin asked when the conversation seemed in danger of stalling.

"Progress is slow, I have to admit," said Gerard, feeling guilty. "But I've been mulling things over, and I think it might be a good idea to pay a visit to this bandit Samuval. You know, get the measure of the man, look him in the eye, and ask him just what he knows about the sheriff's death. I understand Sheriff Joyner actually used to visit Samuval occasionally."

Palin nodded, then pursed his lips. "I suppose it might be a good idea to talk to Samuval personally. But be careful," he warned. "Joyner had a kind of personal truce with the ruffian. Vercleese can guide you part of the way to that fortress of his, but after that you'll be on your own. Samuval would take two men coming as a threat, but one man, carrying a white flag . . . well, you'll probably be safe enough. Samuval is a villain, but he's not a totally unprincipled scoundrel, and he probably wouldn't attack you without some sort of reason. And he'll know all about you already because he has plenty of spies and confederates who pass through town and will have already passed along information about Solace's new sheriff. I'm sure he'll be anxious to meet you, if only to gauge how much of a threat you might pose to him in the future. Maybe you can put a scare into him. It's best that he keeps his distance from Solace."

Gerard found this explanation less than reassuring, especially since he and Samuval had met briefly during the war and he regarded him as a scoundrel without honor. Fortunately, Samuval wouldn't remember him. The sheriff stood. "Well, I'd best get going. But first, let me help you clean those up." Gerard indicated the dirty dishes with a sweep of his hand.

Palin winced. "I don't think Usha would forgive me if I made you help with dishes. You're our guest, and besides, it's my job. But here, before you leave, there's something I want you to see." Palin led the way to the back of the house and ushered Gerard into a room that turned out to be Usha's studio. She was busy working on a painting, a portrait of Odila, dressed in priestly raiment and standing in front of the temple as it would look when finished.

"Why, that's beautiful!" Gerard said. Then, stepping closer, he took a better look. Within the architectural details and the shadows cast by the building lurked vague, distorted images suggestive of grinning skulls and bloody shrouds, dripping daggers and gallows' ropes. "Oh!"

Usha jabbed her finger vexedly at the painting. "Don't worry. I don't know what all of this means yet," she explained. "I don't know what it has to do with Odila or a temple devoted to healing. I'm afraid maybe it foretells some unhappy event or disruption that is to befall during the dedication ceremony, but I won't be sure until the painting settles and is done."

Gerard was puzzled, knowing little of magic and less of magical painting of the sort Usha specialized in. The Knights of Solamnia had an almost hidebound objection to magic and even though Gerard was no longer a knight, he still shared this attitude. Magic made him uncomfortable, suspicious. "I don't understand," he said warily, intending no discourtesy. "How did those strange images get there if you yourself didn't paint them?"

"This is one of my gifts from the gods that I can't really explain myself," Usha said, gazing unhappily at her work. "Sometimes, when I'm painting a scene or portrait, my mind just goes kind of blank. When I come to my senses again, it's almost as if the painting has painted itself. Sometimes, I won't even notice until the next morning. Then I don't know whether the auguries appeared from my own hand or whether they were etched there magically overnight, in my absence. Often, it takes a while to see what is being revealed, although this example is less subtle, more legible than most. And sometimes the auguries vanish by the time the work is finished. Are they warnings to be heeded, or are they sent to cause the very things they show?"

"What do you mean?" Gerard said. He gestured vaguely at the painting. Palin, his hands clasped behind his back, stood there listening, without saying anything.

Usha was quiet for a while. At last, she began to

speak. "Once, I was asked to paint a portrait of a wealthy businessman in Solanthus," she said softly. "He was an influential man, very powerful, and like other men of power, he boasted many enemies.

"All went well with the portrait at first, and the businessman was very pleased with my work. Then a strange thing began to happen. First, the eyes in my painting became glazed, as in death. I would restore their look of vitality each day, putting in the points of reflected light that characterize vital eyes, only to have them turn cloudy again each night. After that, I began to find the mouth open each morning as if in a silent scream. Finally, a bloody line started etching itself across his throat, opening further each day until the bloody line became a gaping wound.

"With great unease, I showed my client these omens and told him they might be warnings of what is to come, unless he took steps to prevent things. He concluded that his enemies were out to kill him, and immediately set out for Palanthas until such time as it seemed safe to return." Usha paused, as if unwilling to continue. "On the way, he was set upon by robbers," she added at last, speaking so softly Gerard had to strain to hear. "He was killed. His throat was cut." She looked Gerard full in the face. "So you see, I must have inadvertently caused his death by showing him what the picture revealed. In a way, I contributed to his death. And now I don't know whether to warn Odila of these portents, or whether it would be better for her if I keep silent."

"But she has to be alerted!" Gerard said vehemently. "We can't just sit by and let whatever it is befall—not if there's a chance we could stop it."

"Gerard, weren't you listening to what I told you? I helped cause that businessman's death!"

But Gerard wasn't listening. He stumbled back from the painting, his eyes wide with horror. "I had a dream a few nights ago," he said in a whisper. "I was standing in the new temple. The statue of Mishakal was holding a body, a corpse, and trying to tell me something, but I couldn't understand what Mishakal was saying. Nor could I tell whose body it was, for it was covered in a bloody sheet."

Usha gasped and clapped a hand over her mouth.

"What?" Gerard said. "What is it?"

But it was Palin who answered. "I had the same dream. And I, too, couldn't tell whose the body was."

"It might have been Odila's!" Gerard declared, turning toward the door.

"Wait," Usha called. "Don't do anything that might cause this fate to happen."

"He must do what he thinks is right, dear," said Palin.

"I must go to Odila," Gerard said, hurrying from the room, "and at least tell her."

Without further ado, he made for the stairway that would take him to ground level, the bridge-walk trembling beneath his frantic steps, and there he met up with a panting guardsman rushing in his direction. "At the temple!" the guardsman gasped, bent forward with his hands on his knees as he tried to catch his breath. "A terrible accident. . . . Must tell the mayor."

"Was anyone injured?" Gerard asked, already feeling a tight foreboding.

"At least one dead." The guardsman straightened.

"Who?" Gerard demanded to know. "Who is dead?"

But the guardsman merely shook his head and resumed his sprint in the direction of Palin's house. Gerard raced toward the temple, fearing the worst.

CHAPTER

12

Gerard burst onto a scene of chaos and panic. On one side of the temple grounds, the scaffolding that had supported workmen had partially collapsed and swung away from the building at a crazy angle. There, people were swarming about aimlessly, trying to help and mostly getting in the way. The few individuals who appeared to possess some sense of purpose were digging among the rubble of fallen beams and stone, evidently looking for victims.

Several injured workmen and clerics had been taken aside and were grouped in a cluster at one edge of the site. Some of them sat dazedly, favoring hurt arms and legs. Others lay stretched out on the ground, moaning occasionally. Odila moved among the injured, offering what comfort she could.

Gerard hurried over to her.

"Are you all right?" he asked, noting with concern a bad scrape above her left eye where oozing blood was congealing to form a dark crust.

She nodded, her face still blank with shock.

"What happened?"

"Some sort of accident. The scaffolding just gave way at one corner."

Gerard scanned the ranks of injured. "An accident! Is anyone badly hurt?"

Odila shook her head, her braids coming loose and spilling hair down one side of her face. "Just one person, and unfortunately that is Salamon Beach," she said, nodding to a figure completely covered with a tattered cloak. "He was right underneath the structure when it collapsed."

Gerard strode over to the figure and peeled back a corner of the cloak. Salamon Beach gazed up at him with milky, sightless eyes. His features sagged with the weight of death. Blood pooled on the ground beneath his head, the back of which had been crushed by falling debris. Gerard covered the dead man again, then started in sudden recognition.

Salamon Beach, cloaked like this and cradled in the arms of Mishakal's statue, plainly evoked the bloodied figure in his dream.

So was this what the dream, and for that matter Usha's painting, had been trying to tell him? That there would be some sort of accident here? If it actually was an accident.

More people arrived on the scène as word of the tragedy spread throughout Solace. Kaleen led Argyle Hulsey, the local healer, over to attend to the injured. The healer moved swiftly and professionally among them, assessing the extent of the various injuries.

"How is Stonegate?" Odila asked Kaleen. "Was he badly hurt?"

Kaleen shook her head. "Shaken up, and his arm

badly bruised, but he's all right."

"Who is Stonegate?" Gerard asked, coming up behind them.

"The chief foreman on the project," Odila explained. "He works—worked—directly under Salamon."

"So he would stand to benefit from this misfortune."

Odila stared at him. "No! What do you mean?"

"Just that this Stonegate might not have liked being the architect's underling. Maybe he wanted to be in charge and saw this as his only opportunity for advancement."

Odila shook her head. "Gerard, you are too wrapped up in the pressures of being sheriff. You don't know Stonegate. That's not like him at all."

"Maybe," Gerard said, chastened. But he made a mental note to question this Stonegate as soon as the possibility presented itself.

Kaleen watched Argyle Hulsey proceed through the ranks of the injured. "Maybe I should see if I can help, even if it's only to offer those who are hurt some tarbean tea." She moved off to consult with the healer.

"I don't know what I'd do without her," Odila said with a sigh, watching Kaleen stride purposefully away. "She's become my right hand in the preparations for the dedication, and she's not even one of my clerics."

"She's certainly a competent young woman," Gerard said, staring after Kaleen as well. She had a saucy step, even in the midst of this unhappy scene, that was a pleasure to behold.

"As for doing without someone, now I don't know what I'm going to do without my architect," Odila said ruefully, turning back to Gerard. "It's a sad loss. And I fear it'll put us days behind."

Across the way, someone had apparently organized the workmen into tackling the job of dismantling the damaged scaffolding. The scaffolding swayed precariously, but held together as men began removing the pieces plank by plank and strut by strut.

"Salamon Beach certainly seemed like a, uh, valuable person," Gerard said, searching for tact. "But difficult."

"Yes, he could be difficult," Odila agreed. "Although he and I were able to get along all right. And he was worth all the extra bother of dealing with him."

"Did he have any enemies that you're aware of?"

"Salamon? No, not enemies exactly." She paused, then hurried on. "There was something strange that happened a few nights ago. I had almost forgotten, until now."

"Go on," Gerard urged when she fell silent again.

"Well, I was coming out of the temple after dark. Everyone else had gone for the night, and I don't think Salamon knew I was still here. I spotted him arguing with a couple of men. They were really pushing him around and abusing him. Then they finished their business and took off into the night. When I asked Salamon about it, he tried to laugh the matter away, but something was wrong. I just couldn't tell what." She shook her head. "For that matter, I still don't know."

Gerard frowned, thinking about the curious incident. On the side of the temple, the attempt to dismantle the scaffolding had hit a snag. Gerard stared in that direction but couldn't make out what the difficulty might be. "These men," he said, "did you recognize them?"

Odila shook her head again. "Never seen them before. But I did get a good look at one of them. It was only by moonlight, but I wouldn't soon forget a face like that." She described the thick, brushlike mustache that obscured the man's upper lip, and the vicious scar that ran from the corner of his left eye down to somewhere under his shirt.

Gerard scratched at his beard, self-conscious about disfiguring scars that left their bearers immediately recognizable. "Could they have rigged an accident of this sort?"

"Oh gosh, I don't know." Odila shrugged. "It is probably nothing more than an inopportune accident. A construction site like this is certainly a dangerous place. This just serves to remind us all of that fact. We all of us need to be more careful, I suppose."

"I suppose." Gerard let the matter drop. Judging by the worried expression on her face, Odila had enough to fret about right now. He decided not to pester her anymore that day about Salamon Beach. And now was not the time to tell her about Usha's painting either. A dwarf with his right arm in a makeshift sling hurried over just then, a sheaf of pages rolled under his left arm. "Lady," he said, bowing to Odila.

She acknowledged the greeting with a nod and turned to Gerard. "This is Stonegate." Then, addressing the dwarf, she asked, "Do you have any idea how long it'll be before we can get started again? And will we be able to complete the project without Salamon to oversee the design?"

"We're clearing away the debris, Lady. It's difficult to be certain at this point, but I believe we'll soon be able to resume work and be back on schedule in a day or two. Of course I would not presume to fill the architect's shoes," he added seriously. "But fortunately, he had brought us to within sight of completing the project. I believe I can get us the rest of the way."

Odila dipped her head in a grave nod, then absently tucked the loose end of her braid behind her ear. "Thank you."

The dwarf's barrel chest swelled with pride. "Lady," the dwarf said simply. Gerard had to admit he seemed an upstanding fellow, not the suspicious type. Stonegate started to turn back to the construction site, then paused and added to Gerard, "I almost forgot. Someone who says he works for you wanted you to come see something before we proceed with any further repairs."

"Oh? Was it Vercleese uth Rothgaard, my deputy?" Gerard asked, falling into step with the dwarf.

Stonegate shrugged, wincing at the discomfort that caused to his injured arm. "Humans are hard to tell apart, forgive me for saying so. Except for Lady Windlass, I cannot distinguish one of you from another."

His words were meant kindly, but his manner remained indifferent. Privately, Gerard thought all dwarves looked alike, too. But clearly, this Stonegate viewed all humans with scorn. Gerard resolved, later, to learn all he could about the dwarf, and whether he might have had anything to do with causing the accident and the death of Salamon Beach.

Stonegate led Gerard to the base of the scaffolding, where the workmen now stood milling about, waiting to resume their tasks. Gerard was surprised to see Blair standing by the scaffolding rather than Vercleese. The sergeant nodded to Gerard in greeting and indicated one of the main struts, where the rope lashing that had secured part of the structure now hung in pieces. "I wanted you to see this, sir," he said in a low voice, indicating the segments of rope.

Gerard stepped closer. He expected to see the rope frayed from whatever wear and tear had caused it to break. Instead, he saw the clean edges of a careful cut, each strand neatly severed.

"Looks like it wasn't an accident," he said.

"My thoughts exactly," said Blair. "Someone did this deliberately. The question is who and why did it collapse just when it did—when Salamon Beach was standing underneath the structure?"

"You think he might have been targeted?"

Blair gave him a faintly contemptuous look. "Don't you?"

Gerard refrained from telling the sergeant just what he thought, although he intended to upbraid him on a more private occasion, letting him know that his impertinent tone was not appreciated and would not be tolerated. "Did anyone witness the accident?"

"A couple of the workmen noticed two rough-looking men they hadn't seen before hanging around shortly before the collapse occurred. One of the men he described as having a thick, coppery mustache and a prominent scar down the left side of his face. No one saw where the pair went or even when they left. They seem to have vanished in the commotion."

Gerard raised an eyebrow. The descriptions matched those of Odila's strangers who had assaulted Salamon Beach a few nights before. Their confrontation must have been more serious than the architect let on—serious enough, perhaps, to get him killed. Gerard nodded. He'd have to see whether anyone else in town could identify these two men. "Well done, Sergeant," he said, clapping Blair on the shoulder. The sergeant shrugged, as though to say it was all in a day's work.

Vercleese arrived just then, and Gerard showed him the rope and filled him in on the "accident," including what Odila had told him about the incident a few nights earlier. Right after that, Palin hurried up to the group, and Gerard explained everything all over again.

Meanwhile, Stonegate stood impatiently to one side, huffing and snorting, clearly anxious to get work started up again and resentful of the humans' wasting of time. The death of his former boss seemed to matter less to him than putting the whole project back on schedule. Finally, Gerard turned to the dwarf. "All right, we're through here for now. But I expect you to inform me if you come across anything else suspicious or see anyone loitering about whom you don't recognize. Is that understood?"

Stonegate hesitated.

"Lady Odila would want you to cooperate in this," Gerard added.

"Oh, well, in that case, of course I'll let you know immediately," the dwarf said, bowing his head before the mere thought of the lady who evidently held him in thrall. Then Gerard and the others walked slowly back to the area where the injured had been grouped.

"So we have another possible murder," Palin said quietly to Gerard. "Do you think it could be related to the death of Sheriff Joyner?"

Gerard scratched his chin. That thought had occurred to him as well. "It does seem unlikely there would be two such unusual murders so close together in time, unless there was some connection," he said cautiously, "although the methods used in the two cases were very dissimilar. Until we get more information on this latest killing, however, we can't know for sure."

Kaleen and Odila were waiting for them where the injured were being treated. Odila looked more her usual self, the color having returned to her face, but Kaleen was beginning to show the strain of having been exposed to injury and death. Gerard thought that she herself could do with one of the mugs of tarbean tea that she had been distributing to the victims.

Only a couple of the injured workmen remained, most having returned to their jobs with minor cuts and scrapes, Odila explained. A few had been taken by Argyle Hulsey to her shop in town for additional treatment. "And she wants to see Salamon's body as soon as we can bring it to her," she continued. "She wants to examine it more closely than she was able to do here."

A crashing noise caused Gerard to spin around nervously, but evidently it was only the controlled demolition of the damaged scaffolding, which now lay in a heap beside the temple wall. Dust from the crash swirled about the men who stood there, to one side. When the dust cleared sufficiently, they swarmed about the ruined woodwork, dismantling it and salvaging any useable timber. Stonegate was back in his element, now that the petty disruption of death and injury was over with. He was barking orders and consulting the rolled pages with drawings of the project.

When Gerard turned back to the conversation, Odila and Kaleen were engaged in some kind of mild argument. "What's the matter?" he asked, trying to play peacemaker.

"She wants to take Salamon's body to Mistress Hulsey," Odila explained. "But I want her to go home and get some rest."

Gerard looked at Kaleen, who swayed a little where she stood, she was so obviously exhausted. "Let her accompany the body back into town," he said. "But only on condition that she go home and get some rest afterward."

Odila frowned but nodded.

"I'll go with her," Blair said quickly. "Just to make sure she gets home all right."

"No, I'll go with her," Gerard said firmly, earning a hostile look from Blair. "I want to hear what the healer says, and I want you and Vercleese to see what you can find out about these two men who assaulted Salamon the other night. Circulate their description, find out if they're still in town, and bring them in for questioning."

"But—" Blair began.

Gerard cocked an eyebrow at him, squinting fiercely.

"Yes, sir," Blair said, his voice sulky and his face in a scowl.

"I'll join you at Argyle Hulsey's shop," Palin said as Gerard turned to leave. "There are a few things I need to do here first in order to reassure everyone that we are in control of the situation."

"Are we in control of the situation?" Gerard asked only half jokingly.

Palin shrugged. "People will want to think we are, at any rate. It's my job to calm their fears."

Gerard nodded, offered Kaleen his arm for support, and ushered her to the wagon where the body of Salamon Beach was laid out. The whole time, he was uncomfortably aware of Blair's furious stare following the two of them as they walked away. Only when the wagon was bumping and swaying on its way to town, with the two of them safely aboard, did he begin to relax.

Eventually, he and the surly sergeant were going to have to have a confrontation.

◆ ◆ ◆ ◆ ◆

Meanwhile Usha had taken a break from working on Odila's portrait.

The house needed cleaning, and that took an hour or so. Then she cut some flowers and placed them in a vase on the table. Afterward, she felt she really must get some bread dough mixed. When the dough had been kneaded and placed in cloth-covered pans to rise, Usha washed the flour from her hands and looked about for some further distraction. There was nothing else to do. Everything was now in its place. The house was spotless. All was as it should be.

Usha frowned.

At last, she walked resolutely into her studio, where she mixed her paints and gathered her brushes. Only when all was ready did she remove the protective cloth that always hung in front of one of her paintings in progress.

And froze.

The half-seen images that had been there previously were gone at last. But in their place was a far worse portent, for one wall of the temple was now unaccountably dripping with blood.

Usha dropped her implements, letting the cloth fall

back across the face of the painting, and ran for the temple, knowing for certain that a death had already occurred.

CHAPTER

13

Palin was talking with Odila, when Usha came hurrying toward them, her skirts hiked up and her face flushed. "Are either of you hurt?" she gasped, out of breath.

"No," Palin said, taking her gently by the arm. "We're all right."

Usha glanced quickly around the temple grounds, her eyes coming to rest on the sight of workmen dismantling the collapsed scaffolding. For all the activity, the work site was eerily hushed, affected by the mood of the disaster. The workmen were going about their tasks without any of their usual banter or singing. "And the others? Was anyone hurt?"

"Most everyone escaped with little or no injury," Palin answered.

She looked at him sharply. "Most?"

"The architect for the project, Salamon Beach, is dead."

Usha's shoulders sagged. "I expected as much. Not him, precisely, but I feared someone had died." She looked up into Palin's face. "When I went to work on the painting today, blood was dripping down the temple wall." She pointed to where the scaffolding had been. "That wall there."

"Your auguries were true, unfortunately," Palin said equably. "Would that they could tell us who did it as well."

"Who did it? You mean this was intentional, not an accident?"

Palin nodded.

"Someone, or more than one person if you like, severed a rope that bound the scaffolding," Odila said, joining the conversation. "We don't know yet, however, whether they intended to kill Salamon or whether they were just trying to delay construction of the temple. Salamon may simply have been standing in an unfortunate spot when the scaffolding gave way."

Usha stared at the temple a moment. "It's hard to imagine someone wanting to disrupt construction of a place devoted to healing," she said at last.

"There may be dark forces at work here," Odila said. "Certainly Mishakal has her enemies among the gods."

"We can only hope your fears prove ungrounded," said Usha, laying a gentle hand on Odila's arm.

"Now that you're here," Palin said to his wife, "perhaps you can help Odila comfort the survivors."

"Where are you going to be?" Usha asked, puzzled.

"I've arranged to meet Gerard at Mistress Hulsey's shop," Palin said grimly. "We need to learn all we can from Salamon Beach's corpse."

◆ ◆ ◆ ◆ ◆

Kaleen had fallen asleep in the wagon, her head resting on Gerard's shoulder. He tried to move as little as possible, not wanting to disrupt her rest, but his muscles burned with a cramp beneath his shoulder blade. Unfortunately, he had been sitting in an awkward position when she fell asleep. He grimaced and forced himself to hold still. Kaleen had been spending long hours working at the inn, as well as assisting Odila, and she was clearly spent. Before dozing off, she had tried gamely to hold up her end of a conversation, but constant yawns had betrayed her exhaustion.

He studied her while she slept. Her pretty face looked almost haggard, and there were dark circles under her eyes. Poor girl, Gerard thought. She needed this brief rest.

As the wagon bumped and jostled along the pitted road into town, he fell to thinking about whether there could be a link between the murder of Sheriff Joyner and the death of Salamon Beach. Gerard could conceive of no motive that would connect the two deaths, but it was odd they had happened so close together in time. Perhaps there was a conspiracy afoot to undermine the dedication of the temple, and Sheriff Joyner had stumbled upon the plot in its early stages. If so, what kind of conspiracy was it, and why did the sheriff and the architect have to die?

The wagon rumbled to a stop before the imposing house of Cardjaf and Gatrice Duhar, one of the newer, ground-level buildings that had become popular in Solace since the war. Gerard gently shook Kaleen awake, secretly enjoying the opportunity, if truth be told, to brush her shoulder. "We're here," he said.

"What? Where?" Kaleen asked blearily, peering

about her. She frowned. "What are we doing here? We're supposed to be going to Mistress Hulsey's shop."

"I told the wagon driver to stop here first," Gerard answered.

"You did? Why?"

"Because you need to be at home getting some rest." When she looked as if she wanted to object, he quickly added, "Consider it an order from the sheriff."

He was rewarded with a thin smile.

"Well, if it's an official command, then I guess I had better obey." She yawned deeply. "I suppose I could do with a little nap before going to work at the inn tonight."

"You need more than a nap," Gerard said. "You need a good night's sleep. I want you to consider staying home tonight; let someone else take your shift at the inn. I'm sure Laura can cope." Again, she looked ready to argue. "Please, Kaleen," he added gently. "You're so exhausted you can hardly stay on your feet. The temple dedication is coming up in just a few days now, and you don't want to be so worn out you can't enjoy yourself."

"I suppose not," she said dubiously.

"Good. Then that's settled." He helped her down from the wagon.

Just then, the front door was flung open and Cardjaf and Gatrice rushed out, their faces wracked with concern. At least, Gerard assumed the tall woman with the imperious eyes was Kaleen's mother; Cardjaf he recognized from the town council meetings.

"We were so worried," Gatrice said, wringing her long, slender hands. "We heard about the accident and were just about to hurry over there to make sure you were all right." Her gaze fixed on Gerard, her eyes growing bigger as she took in the sheriff's presence. "You are all right, aren't you?"

"I'm fine, Mother," Kaleen said, allowing herself to be held in the older woman's awkward embrace.

"All those long hours you've been putting in over at that new temple, and now it turns out to be an unsafe place," Gatrice went on, abruptly dropping her arms and leading her daughter toward the house. "I told your father we never should have left Palanthas to come here. I have a good mind to forbid you from going back to that dreadful temple." When Kaleen opened her mouth to speak, Gatrice hurried on. "But we'll talk about that later. Right now, let's get you inside. You're near collapse, poor thing." She threw a perfunctory smile of gratitude in Gerard's direction then resumed fussing over Kaleen as they entered the house.

Cardjaf looked awkward, a manner strikingly at odds with his usual self-possession. He couldn't find the right pose; one moment his hands hung uselessly at his sides, the next moment they were clasped with false bravura behind his back, then finally he raised them up and executed a half-gesture of apologetic explanation. "My wife," he explained as Gatrice led Kaleen inside. "She's never quite forgiven me for uprooting her from Palanthas. But we are grateful to you for bringing our daughter safely home."

Gerard, made uneasy by Gatrice's disapproval and Cardjaf's awkwardness, responded with a formality that came out sounding more brusque than he'd intended. "The situation isn't really as bad as you may have heard. There was some damage, but the foreman, a dwarf by the name of Stonegate, assures us they'll have construction back on schedule within a few days."

"But someone was killed, we heard."

Gerard hesitated. "Yes, Salamon Beach, the architect. Actually, we think the accident may have been concocted to cause his deliberate murder."

Cardjaf shook his head solemnly. "I hate to sound callous, but I hope you will get at the facts of the matter. What happened at the temple will affect the town's reputation, especially if does turn out that this death was intentional. We can't afford any negative repercussions."

"A man is dead, Councilman. For Salamon Beach, the repercussions are already negative."

Duhar treated Gerard to a penetrating stare. "Two men are dead, Sheriff. Surely you haven't forgotten about your predecessor? It doesn't help matters that this disaster occurs on the heels of another mysterious incident. I trust that sooner or later you will get to the facts of that incident also."

Gerard felt his face flush.

"But there, I'm forgetting my manners," Cardjaf said, turning abruptly cordial. "You brought our daughter safely home to us, and for that, as I say, we are truly thankful." He hesitated. "She's been putting in long hours with this temple nonsen—" He broke off, looking embarrassed. "With this temple business," he amended, "becoming a kind of unofficial liaison for that visiting cleric, what is her name? Cordelia? Something like that."

"Lady Odila," Gerard said stiffly.

"Odila, yes, thank you. This new preoccupation worries her mother. And, I may as well admit it, the situation worries me, too. We have plans for Kaleen's future, and they don't include her becoming infatuated by empty religious rhetoric. Kaleen has been having many long, soul-searching conversations with this Odila person, and I fear the cleric may be taking advantage of our daughter's emotional vulnerability to plant silly notions in her head."

Gerard bristled, knowing Odila was far from being the type to take advantage of another person's emotional vulnerability, or to plant silly notions in anyone's head—especially Kaleen's.

"Well," Cardjaf concluded, "I for one will be glad when this temple is finally dedicated. It's been good for business here in Solace, but enough is enough. So I hope this unfortunate incident at the temple today won't delay the dedication. The sooner that the necessary observances are over and done with, and all these visiting clerics return to their proper homes, the better. And now, if you will excuse me, I had best be seeing to the welfare of my wife and child. They've had quite enough time for a little mother-daughter heart-to-heart talk, don't you think?" He awarded Gerard a knowing, indulgent smile and strode up to the door of his house.

Gerard climbed back into the wagon, silently fuming.

A few minutes later, the wagon driver pulled up in front of Argyle Hulsey's shop, where a small crowd had already gathered in anticipation of watching as the dead man's body was brought inside. Gerard, still annoyed over his exchange with Cardjaf Duhar, put a couple of the men in the crowd to work carrying Salamon Beach into the shop. The pair had come to the scene wanting a close-up look at the dead man, Gerard reflected sourly; now they were getting a closer view than they bargained for. Of course, they'd probably be bragging about their involvement and making the most of it in the town's taverns and inns before nightfall.

Now the two jockeyed for who would grab the man's legs and who would grab the arms, so close to the bloodied head. They squeamishly took up their burden at last and lugged it inside, depositing the former architect with undignified haste on his back atop the worktable made ready by Mistress Hulsey. Then the two hovered nearby, as if expecting a reward for their meager contribution to the day's drama. One of the pair, who was unusually tall, kept brushing against the clusters of dried herbs that hung from the rafters. In his confusion, he backed up against a counter along the side of the room, where he almost upset the potions Mistress Hulsey had been in the process of making. Indeed, the air in the shop hung heavy with the potent aromas of herbs and minerals, not all of them pleasant. It made the room feel uncomfortably cloistered.

"Thank you," Gerard said dryly, as he directed the two men toward the door. "That'll be all."

"Maybe we should stay a while," the shorter of the pair said. "You might need our help with . . . with something else before you're finished."

"We'll let you know if we do," Gerard said, flashing an insincere smile. He closed the door on them as they were still protesting and turned his attention back to the table, feeling a little dizzy from the multitude of thick odors in the room. At least they covered the smell of death, Gerard thought.

"We'll need to undress him," Mistress Hulsey said, apparently unfazed by the stuffy air and the manner of the two men. Her voice was matter-of-fact. They set about peeling off the architect's clothes, cutting them from his body where necessary to avoid shifting his head any more than they had to. Soon the body lay undressed, and Mistress Hulsey walked slowly around the table, surveying the corpse from every possible angle, occasionally moving in closer to study some feature in more detail, then stepping back and resuming her unhurried examination. When she had completed her slow circuit, coming again to her starting point, she stopped.

"Well, a couple of fingers are broken," she declared, indicating the left hand of the dead man. "There's no swelling, so they were probably broken by falling debris at the time he was killed." She pointed to a large scrape on his right shin. "That abrasion, too, probably happened at the time of death as there appears to have been little bleeding from the wound afterward. His heart had already stopped beating." She frowned, pulling the eyelids well back from each eye and peering at them, then closing the eyes and exploring the dead man's mouth. With practiced equanimity, she pulled the tongue this way and that, examining the oral cavity from all vantages.

"What is it exactly that are you looking for now? I mean, in his mouth," Gerard asked, curious.

"Evidence of poisoning," she said.

"Poisoning? But surely he was killed by scaffolding when it collapsed."

She looked at him with a cool, detached gaze. "We don't know that for certain. We only know it *looks* that way." Abruptly, she shrugged. "However, I don't detect any evidence of poisoning, so you're probably right. Let's turn him over and get a look at the back of his head."

Argyle Hulsey was a small, birdlike woman, so it

took some straining for the two of them to flop Beach over without rolling him right off the table. When they finally had Beach facedown, she made another careful circuit around the table, coming to a stop at the shattered head. Blood and tissue matted the man's hair, and shards of bone protruded from the gaping wound. A portion of the gray, lumpy brain lay exposed, looking crushed and pulpy. Though Gerard had seen his share of dead men in his knightly days, he forced down the bile that rose in his throat.

Mistress Hulsey poked dispassionately at the edges of the wound then lifted the hair to expose the nape of Beach's neck. "That's odd," she said, pausing in her inspection.

"What's odd?"

"That." She pointed with her free hand to a small tattoo that had been hidden by Beach's hair. High up on the neck, just below the hairline, were a pair of stylized bones with a four and a three showing on their uppermost faces.

The shop door opened, then closed again, and over his shoulder Gerard saw that it was Palin who had entered quietly.

"What does it mean?" Gerard asked.

"It's the sign of a secret society," Palin said, coming to stand beside Gerard and leaning forward for a better look. "I've seen it before."

"An evil brotherhood?" Gerard asked.

Palin shook his head. "Not really. It's an elite gambling society. They have no religion except bones and cards and other games of chance. They're willing to risk everything on their nightly gambling rituals. Generally the members are criminals, but some from all levels of society are addicted to games of chance, and if they can afford to play and lose . . . well, then they're welcome."

Mistress Hulsey nodded. "I've heard of this organization, too. Generally criminals, as you say. That's why it's a bit odd to find this tattoo on a man like Salamon Beach, architect of a temple devoted to Mishakal, the goddess of healing."

"The tattoo identifies members to each other," Palin explained.

"It sounds as though I should learn as much as I can about this society and then ferret out its members here in Solace," Gerard said.

"Yes," said Palin, frowning. "Though I can't easily guess what a secret gambling society might have to do with the temple accident, or the architect's death."

Gerard couldn't guess, either. Nor did he have a clue as to how to go about gaining access to so secretive a fraternity. Maybe if he took up gambling in the evenings, frequenting the various taverns and inns. Then if he spread enough coin around, word would spread about his "addiction." Members of the society might then be encouraged to approach him.

Vercleese was busy seeking anyone with knowledge of the two ruffians who had been seen assaulting Salamon Beach. But he had to keep one eye on the individuals he questioned and another on his partner, Blair Windholm. The sergeant of the town guard was acting sullen; he wasn't doing his share of the job. Maybe Blair was simply put out because he hadn't been allowed to accompany Beach's body—and the lovely young Kaleen

Duhar—back into town. However, if he had an ulterior motive for his desultory assistance, Vercleese wanted to know.

"I don't think it's likely that the two people we're looking for are the same ones who trampled your garden and helped themselves to some of your carrots," he said gently to Mora Skein, the plump, angry seamstress they had met coming out of Stephen's Grocery.

"But you said you're looking for a couple of men who might have been up to no good, and that certainly fits the description of whoever stole my carrots. My *prize* carrots!" she added, leaning closer for emphasis. "You know, they always take the ribbon at the local fair."

"But we're looking for men with distinct faces. You said you didn't get a good look at your carrot thieves. It might have been just some of the neighborhood boys out doing a little mischief."

"Mischief!" Mora's eyes widened with outrage, and her face darkened. "My best carrots, and you call that mischief?"

"Come on," Blair growled. "We're getting nowhere here."

Mora turned on him. "And you! The town guard can't even protect my vegetable garden, and you pretend to defend all of Solace?"

Blair backed up a few steps, his hands up as if to ward off Mora's words. "I'm sure we'll catch whoever's done this to your garden, ma'am. But first we have to find these two men, who might have committed a real crime—"

"Real crime!" Mora shrieked, gathering attention from passersby. "Desecrating my garden and robbing me of my priceless carrots doesn't qualify as a real crime? I'll have you know that Mistress Dinmore has had her eye on the annual gardening prize for years and will gloat for the rest of her life if she can win it, now that my best carrots have been stolen. She was already out in her yard this morning, smiling in her false way as I discovered the damage to my garden."

"You're right, Mistress Mora," Vercleese said hurriedly, taking her arm and drawing her quietly away from Blair and the collecting crowd. Deftly, considering he had only one arm, the knight took out a small notebook and scribbled some words on it. "I've officially noted your loss, and we will of course investigate the theft of your carrots with all due dispatch. Indeed," he said over his shoulder to Blair, "we might start by talking to some of the folks down at The Trough."

They bade Mora as polite a farewell as they could and rushed away. Blair was muttering imprecations, and Vercleese clapped him on the shoulder. "Buck up. Soon we'll be among ordinary ruffians down at The Trough. They'll seem positively cooperative by comparison, I'm sure."

But the clients of The Trough answered Vercleese's and Blair's questions with surly monosyllables, and none who were present fit the descriptions of the two men Vercleese and Blair sought. Try as he might, Vercleese couldn't find anything suspicious or cagey in the customers' replies. It was as if the two ruffians, striking though their appearances might have been, had drifted into Solace as unnoticed as the evening mist and vanished without leaving a trace.

Vercleese's jaw was clenched in frustration as they marched back to the guard headquarters to meet Gerard and tell him they had learned nothing new.

CHAPTER

14

Gerard and Vercleese heard Tangletoe Snakeweed coming long before they saw him. They had just picked up their horses from the stable and were riding toward the southern edge of town.

"It was the greatest calamity of modern day Ansalon," the kender sang out from a nearby street. "Stones and bricks and chunks of mortar flew everywhere, falling with a mighty roar all around the temple grounds. Timbers shivered with deafening cracks. The dust thrown into the air blocked the sun for most of an hour, threatening to bury alive those who didn't choke to death first. One whole wall of the new temple collapsed in a heap of rubble. I alone among the few survivors managed to maintain my presence of mind, hurrying here and there heroically to tend to the fallen. . . ."

Gerard turned to Vercleese. "Did you see the kender on the scene at the new temple yesterday?"

Vercleese shook his head.

"Me neither," Gerard said. "He must have been hurrying heroically."

"Perhaps we were too dazed by the magnitude of the disaster," Vercleese added with a wry grin.

Gerard made an elaborate show of checking his pockets and purse. "Huh, that's peculiar. I have all my belongings. Another indication that I didn't have any brush with a kender."

"Or maybe Tangletoe wasn't in the 'borrowing' mood. That would be an occasion worthy of recording in the histories kept at the great Library of Palanthas." Vercleese laughed. "People would flock from all across Krynn just to read the account and marvel at it."

"Meanwhile," Tangletoe went on, "Stephen, renowned throughout Solace for his grocery store where the prices are much more reasonable than anywhere else in town and where all the races of Krynn are welcome to do business, had this to say about the accumulating, confusing number of municipal codes enacted by the town council: 'I don't know why we have to have this accumulating, confusing number of municipal codes enacted by the town council. Why do we vote these guys into office if they're just going to tax and regulate us out of business afterward?' That's an exact quote from Stephen himself, folks, or near enough anyway, minus the curse words.

"In other items of the day. . . ."

The kender's voice receded down an adjacent street, swallowed up by the clamor and bustle of another business day in Solace. Gerard and Vercleese wove through the numerous wagons and carts that made their lumbering way through town. Horses snorted and whiffled, donkeys brayed, workmen shouted oaths and directions, barrels thundered as they were rolled up and down gangplanks and across cobblestones, children laughed and called out singsong rhymes, often mocking the workmen, and men and women passing by carried on lively conversations.

For a town that had witnessed "the greatest calamity of modern day Ansalon" just yesterday, Gerard thought, Solace seemed to have dragged itself out of the apocalypse and resumed its normal pursuits with admirable alacrity.

Soon he and Vercleese left the turmoil of town life behind them, riding swiftly down a hard-packed dirt road. The horses leaned into the effort, eager to stretch their legs. Dust swirled up behind them, then dropped without a breeze to carry it. They pounded across the bridge of Solace Stream, passing near Jutlin Wykirk's mill with its creaking, slowly turning wheel.

They continued south. When the horses began breathing harder, the men reined them in, letting them resume a steady canter. Although not yet midmorning, the day was already clear and hot. Gerard wiped the sweat from his face with a sleeve. After a time, trees closed in around them, just a few here and there at first, but soon growing thicker until the road narrowed to a mere track and the horses had to proceed in tandem instead of abreast. The day, formerly so bright and clear, now seemed gloomy. Gerard hadn't realized how many birdsongs had enlivened the air around him earlier, until now when they abruptly fell silent. He shivered in the unexpected chill and drew his doublet tighter about him for its scant warmth. At last, Vercleese, in the lead, signaled a halt and slid from the saddle, watching the woods around them warily.

"Just for the record, let me say it again: I don't think this is a good idea," the knight muttered. "I used to try to talk Sheriff Joyner out of it as well. But he always claimed he was lucky."

"He wasn't lucky to be murdered," Gerard said. Though he was striving to lighten the mood, he regretted his bad joke instantly. Darken Wood pressed close around them, dragging at their spirits. Gerard too dismounted. Something akin to magic prickled along his arms and neck, raising the hairs as if he were standing in the midst of an electrical storm.

"No, in the end he wasn't lucky," Vercleese said grimly, staring hard at Gerard.

Gerard shrugged and wrapped Thunderbolt's reins around a branch protruding from a deadfall. Vercleese had been arguing with him about this all morning, without making any headway.

"That Samuval is a snake," Vercleese went on, unwilling to let the matter drop. "I'm telling you, I wouldn't—"

"Which way?" Gerard interrupted.

Vercleese stared at him.

"Which way?" Gerard repeated, more gently this time.

Mutely, Vercleese pointed into the forest.

Gerard nodded and clapped his deputy on the shoulder. "You have your instructions," he said, still speaking in a firm but gentle tone. "I'll meet you here this afternoon."

Vercleese put a foot back into his horse's stirrup, then hesitated, looking imploringly at Gerard.

"Don't worry. I'll be all right," Gerard said.

Vercleese hoisted himself into the saddle again and rode off slowly, muttering to himself and not looking back. With a grim smile, Gerard watched his loyal deputy go. Then he shuddered at finding himself alone in Darken Wood, feeling much less brave than he had tried to act a moment before. With a resolute breath, he started off on foot in the direction Vercleese had indicated.

The land climbed, becoming rocky and hilly. Underbrush snagged at his clothes and tore at his skin. Gnats and mosquitoes whined around him, sometimes half blinding him in thick clouds. He bled from a dozen tiny marks, a combination of mosquito bites and thornbush scratches. Sweat poured off him. And still the hair-raising presence of magic caused shivers to run up and down his flesh.

He came at last to the top of a bluff, where he stood on a rock outcrop looking out over a clearing some distance beyond. In the midst of the clearing stood the fortress Baron Samuval was erecting in the clearing. The nearly completed wooden stockade was made of thick poles set into the earth, their sharpened ends pointing to the sky. In the open field surrounding the wooden fortress, soldiers and dark knights drilled, churning to dust a ground long dried from the rains. Gerard counted half a dozen dark knights and maybe three times that number of men at arms. The latter made for a motley army, consisting mostly of rough-looking humans, but also a sprinkling of draconians, goblins, ogres, dwarves, and even one or two renegade elves. But what the force lacked in the niceties of appearance, they more than made up for in martial skills, for Gerard noted with professional approval (and personal distaste) the precision and confidence with which they handled themselves. This would be a formidable force for any enemy to face.

That meant that Kirrit Bitterleaf's elves must amount to an equally impressive force if they were resisting Samuval's occupation of their realm; otherwise Samuval wouldn't be wasting the resources to erect this fortress and station so many of his soldiers here on the Qualinesti border.

Gerard took a white scarf from where he had looped it over his belt and proceeded down the bluff, waving the scarf overhead. Within moments, the gate of the fortress had boomed open and a squad of soldiers hurried out, marching straight toward Gerard. He stopped and waited, doing his best to look unconcerned as the half dozen heavily armed, burly soldiers clustered around him. He nodded to them as if there were nothing unusual about their meeting, striving to conceal the loathing he had for these men who occupied the elven realm.

The leader of the squad gave him a fierce once-over, looking as though all he really preferred to do was to kick Gerard halfway to Qualinost. Instead, he cleared his throat, looked to his companions for support, then formally addressed Gerard. "My lord Baron Samuval sends his greetings and requests your presence with him in the compound," he said in a gravelly voice that nevertheless managed to sound almost sissified delivering so composed a message.

A couple of the soldiers snickered, but the leader shot them a glare that quickly brought silence.

"That means you're to come with us," the leader added in a more menacing tone, drawing closer, in case Gerard had failed to comprehend that he was now a de facto prisoner.

"As you wish." Before Gerard could start toward

the fortress again, however, the leader of the soldiers grabbed the belt that held Gerard's dagger and unbuckled it.

"You won't be needing this," the leader snarled, tucking dagger and belt under his arm.

Gerard shrugged indifferently and made his way quickly down the bluff, leaving the soldiers falling all over themselves in an effort to catch up and flank him as a proper military escort. Gerard whistled unconcernedly, all the while studying the fortress as he drew nearer. Kirrit Bitterleaf had his work cut out for him if he intended to go up against this kind of defense. But of course the wily elf wouldn't make a direct attack; he would harass Samuval's supply lines and whittle away at patrols that dared to venture beyond the fortress's protection.

At the gate, Gerard had to wait a few minutes to be admitted, giving his captors time to catch up. They huffed and sweated, being burdened with armor, and before the gate opened, the leader approached Gerard with a dirty, folded scarf. Gerard cocked an eyebrow. "What's this for?"

"Baron's orders," the leader snapped. Gerard allowed the scarf to be wrapped around his eyes and tied securely behind his head, all the while wondering why Samuval felt the need for it. Was Samuval concerned Gerard would learn the exact number of soldiers quartered at the fortress and communicate that intelligence to Kirrit Bitterleaf? Had Sheriff Joyner been received on his visits here with similar distrust?

Once the blindfold was in place, Gerard heard the gate creak open, admitting the noise of construction, for inside carpenters were hammering, sawing, hewing, and planing, trying to complete the fortress. The cacophony was reminiscent of the temple construction, Gerard reflected wryly. And, just as at the temple grounds, the air here was redolent with the tang of freshly cut wood. But here too was the noise of soldiers marching in cadence with heavy, booted feet, of officers barking out orders, and of smiths pounding metal in their forges.

One of the soldiers prodded Gerard sharply in the back, propelling him into the midst of the din. He stumbled along, shoved periodically to indicate where he should go. He tried to sort out the sources of sounds, but it was an impossible task. There was too much to take in. Besides, his purpose here, he reminded himself, wasn't to learn the number and disposition of Samuval's forces; it was to learn all he could that might help him solve Sheriff Joyner's murder. Much as Gerard would have liked to lead a troop of knights in here and clear out the riffraff, that wasn't the sheriff's obligation. His job now was to parley with the man he detested.

Abruptly, a rough hand on Gerard's chest brought him to a halt, and he heard a door open. One of the guards announced him and pushed him inside. The door closed and the blindfold was whipped away from his eyes. A quick glance around revealed a crude but efficient wooden room that apparently served as Samuval's headquarters. There were windows on two of the walls, with closed curtains leaving the room gloomy despite the hour of the day. The noise from outside could still be dimly heard through the thick wooden walls. A couple of candles flickered on a large worktable, on which a rolled map had been spread. A middle-aged man of medium height with the powerful arms of an archer was bent over the map. He paused, ran his hand through his short salt-and-pepper hair, then rolled up the map and turned at last to Gerard. A ripple of recognition washed over his initial expression of cool composure. "So it *is* you!"

Gerard gave a mock half-bow. "At your service, *Baron*." He gave the final word an emphasis that undercut its authority.

"They told me it was you. But what is a Knight of Neraka doing as sheriff of Solace?"

"I am a former knight, but of Solamnia, I hasten to emphasize, not Neraka," Gerard explained.

"But when I saw you once before, in the siege outside Solanthus, you wore the armor of Neraka. And you had a prisoner, a young woman who was a Knight of Solamnia."

"So I did, and that armor enabled me and my 'prisoner' to escape."

"So you were a spy," Samuval said, his lip curling in a sneer.

"Yes."

"Well, now I have you again. But this time, no disguises."

Gerard nodded. "No disguises."

Samuval laughed. "Well, that war is over. Now we must come to terms with the present." He accepted Gerard's dagger from the leader of the squad that had brought him in, then made a gesture to an aide who had been standing at mute attention at the back of the room. The aide approached Gerard and patted him down thoroughly, finding and confiscating a couple of other knives he had strapped to his arm and shin. The aide tossed the weapons onto the table.

"Fools!" Samuval hissed to the soldiers who had brought Gerard in. "Didn't you check him for hidden weapons first?" The leader of the squad cringed. "I'll deal with you later," Samuval said angrily and dismissed the soldiers with a sharp gesture. The soldiers spilled from the room in rapid disorder, so anxious were they to escape their leader's wrath.

Samuval sighed, waving to one of the crude wooden camp stools around the table. "Sit," he told Gerard. "Let's have tea together and discuss whatever you came here for like the two gentlemen we are."

Gerard refrained from saying what he thought of the outlaw leader's claim to gentility.

"And while we are enjoying our tea," Samuval went on, "perhaps like your predecessor you will join me in a game of Regal. We are, after all, two civilized people." He shot Gerard a glance as if struck by sudden doubt. "You do play Regal, don't you? I mean, you are civilized?"

"I play a fair game," Gerard acknowledged, sitting. "I was the Southern Ergoth champion in my age category for a time," he added, noting Samuval's amused reaction.

"Good." Samuval smiled and motioned again to the aide, who placed a small camp table between them and proceeded to set up a game board. Then the aide brought two steaming mugs of tarbean tea from a stove in one corner of the room. Watching the aide, Gerard recollected all the times he had served similar duty while a Knight of Solamnia, preparing tea for his superiors though he longed for an opportunity to fulfill a more significant role. Now here he was being served in turn, pretending to civility with this ruthless captain of a brigand army. What was Samuval up to? The outlaw acted as though he were starved for a friendly game of Regal.

Gerard sipped his tea gingerly, for in truth he detested the stuff. He gathered his thoughts. Now that he was here, he wasn't sure just how to bring up the subject of Sheriff Joyner's murder. Besides, Samuval seemed to have some sly purpose of his own in mind.

Samuval looked at him with a sudden cold hatred in his eyes. "You must think you made quite a fool of me during the war, claiming to be a Knight of Neraka. Worse, you made a fool of Mina. But I think it's time we evened the score." He turned toward the aide. "Brok! Bring in any men who are presently off duty. They will be privileged to watch while I teach our . . . *guest* here the finer points of competition."

Brok gave Gerard a sneering grin before going outside. When he returned a few minutes later, he was accompanied by a dozen or more of Samuval's brutish-looking men. They clustered around the small table. Gerard didn't like the odds but realized he couldn't do anything about it.

"Look, the baron's gonna play him at Regal," one man laughed, and the others joined in. They pressed in close, inspecting Gerard like a side of beef. Gerard returned their stares as levelly as he could. For all their motley appearance, he noted their swords and knives as shiny and new, made with distinctive curved blades. Samuval himself wore a sword befitting the title he had conferred upon himself, a richly ornamented, curved weapon with a jeweled hilt and decorative scabbard.

Samuval rotated the game board so the green, or Life, pieces faced toward Gerard, and the red, or Death, pieces were toward his side. Looking up, Samuval caught Gerard's questioning gaze. "For the sake of argument," he explained with a malicious wink. This brought another laugh from his men, some of whom stood so close, Gerard could feel their hot, fetid breath on his neck.

Samuval was playing some psychological game, Gerard understood, and he had already made his first move. This game of Regal might endanger Gerard's very life.

One after the other, they switched around the five cups to the side of the board, under one of which lay the Crown. During play, a person could give up turns in order to look under the cups, in hopes of crowning a Courtier and raising it to the level of a King. As the board was prepared, Samuval's men began taking bets on the outcome of the contest, although they were hard pressed to find anyone willing to wager against their leader.

"Your move," Samuval said when everything was ready. "Green goes first."

Life before Death, of course. Gerard was being granted the first move. The sheriff opened cautiously, advancing a Thrall two spaces.

"Ah, Kargaard's Gambit," Samuval said with a grin, moving one of his Thralls forward in turn. "A classic opening and here is my response."

Gerard had never heard of Kargaard's Gambit, and wasn't sure it even existed. No, the wily freebooter was probably just trying to shake Gerard's confidence.

"Pleased as I am to have your company," Samuval said almost idly, as he studied the board, "you didn't come all this way just to play a friendly game of Regal with me, did you?"

Gerard sipped his tea with elaborate disregard for the men whispering and sniggering around him. He suppressed a grimace at the taste. "I came to see what light you could shed on Sheriff Joyner's murder. I understand you and he were friendly, and that he sometimes came here to play you at Regal as well." He advanced his Thrall another space.

Samuval responded in kind, then sat back and nodded. "I tolerated Sheriff Joyner, but that was only because he, at the behest of the Solace officials, made the town a neutral place for me and my men. Nor did he harass me outside the town limits. Of course, his actions were constrained by ordinances from the town council. To go against the council would have been stupid, and one thing Joyner wasn't was stupid." He grinned. "Besides, he played a pretty mean game. I can trounce every man at this outpost, so it was refreshing to face such a competent opponent from time to time."

Gerard started to take another sip of tarbean tea, then put his mug down instead. He didn't think he could bear to swallow another mouthful. He tried bringing one of his Soldiers into play, but Samuval deftly countered his move. "So what do you know about the sheriff's murder?" he asked, launching an offensive against Samuval's Courtiers, the highest-ranking pieces on the board.

Samuval casually made a move to beat him back. "Ask the elves about that one," he said, causing his men to laugh again.

"Yeah," muttered a man in Gerard's ear, "ask the elves."

Gerard finally succeeded in bringing one of his Soldiers into play. "What would the elves know?"

"I hear they left you a special message," Samuval said, laughing at some private joke. "You know, *morgoth?*" He captured Gerard's Soldier and removed it from the board.

The man was surprisingly well informed, Gerard thought. "What's the meaning behind *morgoth?*"

Samuval shrugged, moving one of his own Soldiers forward. "All this fuss over one dead sheriff!"

Gerard started to rise. "Well, you're right. That's what I came to talk about. If that's all you can tell me, we might as well cut this game short."

A rough hand on his shoulder forced him down again. "Sit. Finish the game." The men behind and those hovering to his sides laughed uproariously at this.

The game dragged on with mounting tension. Gerard had to admit, Samuval made a formidable opponent. The men around him spat laughter in his face at every advance their captain made, occasionally poking him or clapping him hard on the shoulder. Twice Gerard sacrificed a turn in order to look under a cup, but in neither case was he successful. At one point, one of Samuval's Thralls was in a position to be captured and removed from play. So Gerard took the Thrall from the board, even though he puzzled at his opponent's willingness to sacrifice even so minor a piece.

Samuval swiftly answered Gerard's move by switching two of his pieces, putting him in a much stronger position. With a start, Gerard realized that Samuval's maneuver had left Gerard's Courtiers open to attack from at least two quarters. He stared at the outlaw chieftain.

"Yarus's version," the older man explained.

"But you never said. . . ." Gerard's protest trailed off, unfinished.

"No," Samuval said, treating Gerard to another wink. "I never did."

From then on, Samuval had Gerard hard on the run. Piece by piece, he ate away at Gerard's forces, constantly threatening the Courtiers. Gerard found himself sweating. He had the feeling Samuval was toying with him, that he could have ended the game long before now if he had so desired. But instead he wanted to drag out Gerard's defeat, humiliating him in front of the men.

Samuval, meanwhile, seemed to play only half-attentively. He moved a Priest into position to threaten Gerard's remaining Soldier. Gerard blocked Samuval's Priest with a Courtier, and looked his opponent in the eye unflinchingly.

Samuval chuckled and took one of Gerard's Priests with a Thrall, a daring move that he made look effortless. Gerard clenched his jaw and pulled his forces tighter around his Courtiers.

Samuval affected a thoughtful frown. Then he casually took another of Gerard's Courtiers with a Merchant, leaving Gerard's last Courtier vulnerable on Samuval's next move, regardless of what Gerard did during his turn. "Game," Samuval said amid the hooting and catcalls of his men. The outlaw leaned back. Abruptly, his expression turned scowling and serious.

"You play a good game," Gerard admitted. "So are we done talking about Sheriff Joyner? Am I free to go now?"

Samuval shrugged, a gesture of uncertain meaning.

Gerard slowly rose and began to make his way through the press of Samuval's men, who gave way reluctantly before him. He reached for his belt and dagger from the table. Brok stopped him.

"I'll keep those, if you don't mind," Samuval said tersely.

"I'm not exactly in a position to object, am I?" Gerard said.

"No, you're not. And I'm not ready for you to go back, not just yet." Samuval jabbed a finger at Gerard. "You have lost, and now you must pay the penalty for losing."

This brought howls of laughter from his men as they closed in tighter around Gerard.

A few minutes later, Gerard found himself standing with his arms bound behind him and an evil-smelling canvas bag pulled snugly over his head. At Samuval's insistence, and with the eager help of his men, Gerard had been forced to remove his doublet, his tunic, and his boots. He shivered in the sudden chill of being dressed in only his knee-length singlet.

"*Now* you may go," Samuval hissed in his ear. "And don't think to presume upon my hospitality again."

The butt of a pike thrust into Gerard's back started him walking, guiding his steps roughly whenever he chanced to stray from the proper path. At the fortress gate, he was abruptly halted by another jab in his stomach. His breath flew out of him in a sharp gasp. The gate to the fortress creaked open, and Gerard was shoved outside. Someone whisked off the bag, although Gerard's head was still bound tightly in a dirty cloth. He could only see by squinting out of one eye.

"Now don't dawdle," chirped the leader of the soldiers who had first taken Gerard captive. "If I were you, I'd hightail it back to Solace." His voice turned into a snarl. "Before night falls and it gets plenty cold around here. And before the baron changes his mind."

The man laughed and shut the fortress gate behind him.

Forcing himself to walk erect even while he felt his back offered a perfect target for any arrow or crossbow bolt, Gerard headed toward the bluff from which he had first observed Samuval's lair. He felt uncomfortably exposed, wearing only his singlet. Besides, the cloth wrapped around his head made it difficult for him to see much. Behind him, he could hear Samuval's soldiers laughing and taunting from the fortress's walls. The rough ground cut and jabbed his feet. Awkwardly, he climbed the bluff, heading toward where he had tethered Thunderbolt.

The trek took a long time, with Gerard stumbling and falling several times. The afternoon shadows lengthened and gave way to the gloom of dusk. Vercleese was pacing nervously when Gerard limped through the underbrush. The knight looked up in horror at Gerard's condition. "What happened? Are you hurt?"

"Just my dignity," Gerard growled as Vercleese unwrapped the cloth from his head and cut his bonds. Gerard stood a moment, working the blood back into his hands. By the time Gerard was ready to mount up, Vercleese was grinning, although he at least had the good grace to turn aside from Gerard's angry gaze.

"Oh, shut up," Gerard snapped as if he had overheard Vercleese's thoughts. "Let's just get back to

Solace, all right? And don't ever mention this incident to me again."

"Anything you say." Vercleese snickered.

Gerard resolved to treat his deputy to silence during the entire seemingly endless ride back to town. They took side streets to get to the inn, although still there were people about who stared wide-eyed at the sight of their sheriff riding stiffly erect in his undergarments. At the base of the great vallenwood tree that housed the inn, Gerard realized the only way to his quarters was through the inn's common room, which would be thronged at this time of day. He let out an exasperated breath and turned to Vercleese, who struggled to keep his expression impassive.

"Can you find me a ladder?" Gerard asked.

A short while later, he slithered through the window of his room and landed unceremoniously in a heap on the floor. He got up slowly, nursing his injured feet, scratching at the innumerable bug bites that covered every inch of his skin, and flopped into bed. Through the open window, he heard Vercleese whistling a cheerful tune as he carried the ladder away and led the horses to the stable. Gerard scowled. Thankfully, within moments he had fallen into an exhausted sleep.

CHAPTER

15

Gerard woke late the next morning, stiff, sore, and itching all over. The bug bites didn't account for all of the itching, he discovered, for apparently he had brushed against some poison ivy on his trek back from Samuval's fortress; he had a red, irritated rash all down the side of one leg. With effort, he kept from clawing at it, although it appeared he had scratched it plenty during the night, making it worse. It itched and burned something fierce.

The sunlight poured through his window. Somewhere, a meadowlark sang. On the streets and the bridge-walks beneath Gerard's attic quarters, Solace already bustled with purpose and energy.

Gerard scowled, dressed in fresh clothes, then went to put on his boots, only to realize they were still in Samuval's possession. The first order of the day would be a trip to the cobbler, through the crowded streets, in his bare feet.

He tiptoed downstairs, hoping to avoid running into Laura or any of the others who worked at the inn.

In that regard he was successful. But if he hoped to make the entire trek to the cobbler's unnoticed, he was doomed to failure. A woman in the silk skirts and lace collar of Solace's new high society saw him emerge furtively from the stairs at the base of the vallenwood tree, and she pointed and giggled. Her companion, a man in similarly elegant attire, turned at the sound and also caught sight of the sheriff. His laughter caused a ripple along the street as more and more people turned to stare and join in the laughter at Gerard's expense.

To aggravate matters (just when Gerard thought matters couldn't possibly worsen), Tangletoe Snakeweed chose that moment to turn onto the street, in the midst of his rounds. The kender was dressed grandly, in a manner he reckoned suitable for a town crier; he wore a long, formal, brocade coat with split tails and wide lapels, which was adorned with an abundance of gold braid and two heavily fringed epaulets. Even the ever-present topknot that was such a distinguishing characteristic of his race was done up with multicolored strands of yarn.

"The sheriff was witnessed last night sneaking back into Solace in his underclothes," the kender was in the midst of shouting, "—oh, hello, Sheriff. I was just talking about you."

For this last part, the kender's voice, which had been pitched to carry, dropped in volume to a normal level, as he came nearly face-to-face with Gerard.

"So I noticed," Gerard said miserably.

"Would you care to comment on what happened last night?" Tangletoe said, his voice taking on an eager, confidential tone. "It would make a great counterpoint to what some of the townsfolk are saying about you.

Lots of nasty gossip, you understand. I have statements from citizens and could use one from your point of view. You know, trying to explain the situation."

Gerard attempted to limp away, but the kender kept pace with him. "I have nothing to say," Gerard growled.

Tangletoe, noticing Gerard's hobbled gate, stared at his feet. "Say, where are your boots? Why aren't you wearing them?"

"I sent them out for repair," Gerard said, still attempting to brush past the annoying creature. "I'm on my way to pick them up now, so if you'll just excuse me."

An increasing number of townspeople had been attracted by the commotion and were stopping to stare and chuckle at his expense. But the kender remained glued to his side.

"I know what," Tangletoe said with breathless enthusiasm. "I'll go ahead of you and announce your coming. That way people will make way for you and be able to express their, uh, sympathy at your plight." He glanced again at Gerard's bare feet. "You know, you really shouldn't be walking out here like that. You might step on a rock or sharp stick and injure yourself."

Over Gerard's vehement objections, Tangletoe proceeded down the street ahead of him, calling out in a loud voice, "Make way for the sheriff, who was glimpsed last night sneaking back into Solace in his underclothes, apparently returning from a secret tryst or assignation. Watch out for that pile of horse manure, Sheriff. You don't want to step in that with your bare feet. Make way for the sheriff, who must have had his boots stolen or something. The sheriff has refused to deny any of the rumors, which have raised considerable concern among the town's leading citizens. . . ."

The four blocks to the cobbler's shop felt interminable. All the most important and influential people in Solace seemed to be on the streets this day, attending to business or out for a stroll. In rapid succession, Gerard spotted Councilman Kedrick Tos, the goldsmith; Bartholomew Tucker, the wine merchant; Tyburn Price, the import-export dealer; even Lady Drebble and—worst of all—Gatrice Duhar. The last-named stared at Gerard's unshod state in openmouthed amazement. Even the relentless sun beating down on Gerard as he limped along seemed to mock him. He felt his dignity wilting like a head of day-old lettuce.

At last he and his unwanted herald reached the cobbler's shop. Gerard ducked gratefully inside, leaving the kender to shrug his shoulders and continue on his rounds undaunted.

"One explanation for the sheriff's odd behavior is the rumor that he enjoys dwarf spirits on occasion and has been known to burst into bawdy tavern songs in public. I would like to sing you a snatch of one of these songs, but, uh . . . but they are inappropriate for children's ears."

The inside of the shop was claustrophobic with the odor of freshly tanned leather, and dimly lit from closed shutters. Gerard was relieved to have finally escaped public scrutiny.

The cobbler, a wizened little man with a frizz of gray hair encircling a bald crown, paused where he had been tapping nails into the heel of a shoe and looked up. He squinted at a point on the wall which was slightly to one side of Gerard. "Yes, uh, sir, may I help you?"

Gerard shifted into the man's line of sight, although the man seemed to take no notice of the change. "I need a pair of boots."

The corners of the man's mouth crinkled into a smile. "Ah, boots. Yes, I make boots. I could make you some."

"No, you don't understand, I need them today. Right now."

The man's smile slipped. "Right now? But it takes time to make good boots. Besides, there are other orders ahead of yours. I'll need to measure your feet, and then maybe I can have them by next tenday. Yes, that's right, I can have a fine pair of boots ready for you by then."

"But I need something to wear in the meantime."

The man peered about the floor in a fruitless effort to locate Gerard's feet. "But what are you wearing now?"

Gerard rolled his eyes in exasperation. "I obviously have nothing on my feet right now."

"Huh? You don't? Be careful. You might pick up a splinter or stub a toe."

"I don't have any boots," Gerard said with slow, deliberate emphasis. "I'm not wearing anything on my feet. That's why I'm here. It's a kind of . . . *emergency.*"

"Ah," the old man said. "An emergency. Don't get many of those."

"Look, do you have something I can wear temporarily? I'll take anything!"

"Well," the old man said slowly, "I might have *something* that would do the job, as long as you aren't too picky."

"Believe me, I'm not in a position to be picky," Gerard said under his breath as the old man turned to rummage in a worn, ancient sea chest behind him.

A few minutes later, Gerard hobbled awkwardly from the shop, trying to convince himself that any shoes were better than no shoes. The ones he had been loaned were brown and dusty and the worst of it was they were several sizes too big for his feet, so he had to curl his toes and lift his feet awkwardly merely in order to shuffle along, making a clopping noise.

The cobbler, after much pleading, had agreed to move Gerard's order to the top of his list and have a new pair of boots ready for him the following day.

The barefoot uproar was nothing compared to the public reaction he stirred now, with much laughter and pointing fingers. Many people appeared to recognize the shoes and sympathized with him for wearing them. "So old Jason finally found someone desperate enough to buy those monstrosities, did he?" said one man, clapping Gerard jovially on the shoulder. "He always said they would sell. He just didn't realize twenty years would have to pass first."

"Interesting idea you've got there, Sheriff," said another. "Boots you can grow into, huh?"

Oddly, Gerard found his duties kept him behind his desk all that day, and he didn't hazard leaving the office until well after dark.

That night the inn was more crowded than ever. As the date for the temple dedication neared, more and more people were flocking into town, crowding the streets and leading to arguments and even occasional fights over the town's dwindling lack of accommodations.

At first Gerard and the town guard had been locking

disgruntled visitors in the town jail overnight, until Gerard realized that some of those needing a place to stay had staged fights just to find a bed for the night. Down at The Trough, it was said, there was an ongoing wager over how many nights in a row someone could wangle a stay in jail—bed and board at the town's expense.

Gerard had been forced to issue new directives to the guardsmen: short of violent crime, no one was to be held overnight. It was amazing how dramatically instances of civil disturbance had fallen off once participants realized they weren't going to get arrested for it.

Gerard found himself feeling abject and defeated when he finally crawled downstairs from his attic quarters. He slid onto a seat next to Vercleese, who was meeting him for a late-night dinner.

"I told you that Samuval is a snake," Vercleese said, evidently misinterpreting Gerard's malaise. "You shouldn't have gone in there alone. Something like this was to be expected from him."

"You also told me my only chance of getting inside the fortress and talking to him was to go there alone," Gerard objected. "You said if two of us showed up, he'd have cut us down as spies, white flag or no white flag."

"Well, yes, I did say that," said Vercleese, hastily adding, "and it was perfectly sound advice."

Gerard stared glumly at the tabletop.

"So, at least you got in and out alive. What did you learn?" Vercleese asked with forced brightness. "Anything useful?"

Gerard sighed and shook his head.

"Nothing? Nothing at all?" Vercleese insisted. "I

mean, all that effort and all the grief you went through afterward, coming back without your clothes and all, and he didn't tell you anything you didn't already know?"

Gerard considered a moment, then shook his head again.

"Well, maybe he really didn't have anything to do with Sheriff Joyner's murder."

"I don't think he did," said Gerard.

"I mean, if he had had something to do with it, he would have bragged about it long before now," Vercleese continued. "He's far too smug to keep quiet about something like that. Besides, as I keep telling you, he never seemed to have any particular animosity toward the sheriff."

Gerard peered gloomily around the room while Vercleese kept talking. In one corner of the room, a string trio was setting up. As Gerard watched the performers go about tuning their instruments (a viol, rebec, and lute), Kaleen swung past Gerard's table on her way to serving a large family spread over two tables nearby. She shot him a pitying glance. He felt himself flush and looked away. He didn't need pity. All he really wanted right now was a pair of boots that fit.

"So what about Jutlin Wykirk?" Gerard asked Vercleese. "I asked you to pay him a visit. You agreed there's something suspicious about that man."

"Well, it's nothing I can put my finger on," Vercleese answered. "I just never have liked the man, and it's not just because of the way he rants about elves and kender. You hear enough of that right here in town. For that matter, I'm no fan of the elves either. Slippery creatures, they are."

He paused, in case Gerard wanted to say something about elves or kender, but the sheriff remained silent.

"But there is something about Jutlin that gets under my skin," Vercleese agreed inconclusively.

The string trio had finished tuning up and now began playing a fast-paced reel. Gerard would have tapped his toes to the infectious rhythm if his boots didn't feel so heavy and cumbersome—and if he felt like toe tapping. "So you went out there like I asked," he continued, "to Jutlin's. Did you get a look around?"

Vercleese nodded. "He's always very neighborly in that regard. He gave me a tour of the whole place. Everything was neat and tidy. I walked around the barn, poked around inside the shed, even had a cup of tarbean tea with Jutlin and his missus." Vercleese grimaced. "Now there's a sour one. I don't think that woman had one good word to say the whole time I was in her kitchen.

"Anyway, I didn't find anything out of the ordinary, and he insists he never saw Sheriff Joyner that day. He remembers the Ostermans stopping by, though. He has a fondness for their potatoes—and a crush on Sophie, if you ask me."

Silence again descended on the table, in spite of the sprightly music of the trio.

"You must have your suspicions of old Jutlin, too," Vercleese said at last. "Why would you send me over there to visit him otherwise?"

Gerard grinned weakly. "Oh, I was tired of your fussing over my visit to Samuval. I just wanted to keep you busy while I was away."

"Well I'll be!" Vercleese fumed wordlessly a moment. Finally, he stood. "I think it's time for me to turn in," he said stiffly. "I'll see you in the morning."

Gerard let him go. He felt he'd done the right thing, and there was something about Jutlin Wykirk that bothered him. But if Vercleese was still upset in the morning, he'd apologize then.

Across the room, Laura stormed out of the kitchen, a huge, steaming platter in her hands.

To his surprise, she plunked it down in front of him. It held the largest single portion of Otik's spiced potatoes Gerard had ever seen. Then she stood back, tapping her toes and glaring at him.

"Um . . ." Gerard began, uncertain what to say.

Kaleen hurried up to the table. "Maybe Sir Gerard would like a little bread and stew instead tonight." She reached to take the platter, but Laura clamped a hand on her arm and shook her head. With a jerk of her head, Laura gestured for the girl to go about her business. Behind Laura's back, Kaleen shrugged sympathetically at Gerard then scurried away.

Gerard scarcely noticed. He kept staring at the huge platter of potatoes. And Laura kept glaring down at him. Gerard picked up a spoon. Summoning his courage, he shoveled up a spoonful. Laura waited. He put it in his mouth . . . and tried to smile . . . and chewed.

The string trio launched into a mournful air that seemed particularly appropriate for the moment.

Laura took a seat across from him, still watching. "None of your tricks now," she said sweetly.

Gerard felt himself flush, partly through embarrassment and partly from the spiciness of the dish. When he felt he had chewed as long as he could, he swallowed. The potatoes were a long time going down.

Kaleen appeared at his elbow again, a large mug of

ale in her hand. She set it down in front of him and caught his eye. "Otik's fine ale makes the potatoes slide down real smooth," she said.

He took the first of several big swigs and found it was true.

Twenty minutes later, Laura stood, looking smug as Gerard scooped up the last of the potatoes. She set the three empty ale mugs on the now-empty platter and hurried back to the kitchen with a look that told Gerard she had temporarily forgotten her other customers and was just now remembering them. He grinned, feeling unaccountably all right and swaying happily to the infectious music of the trio. Someone belched loudly and Gerard looked around for the culprit before realizing it had been him. He grinned all the harder.

A few tables away, he noticed Blair sitting alone, his eyes hungrily watching Kaleen as she swept here and there through the room, serving customers. Gerard reached for the remaining mug of ale, almost knocked it over, and righted it before it could spill. But when he brought the mug to his lips, he discovered it was already empty.

Darn! Now who had gone and done that to him! He glared suspiciously around the room, his eyes alighting on Kaleen. For a moment, he watched her, giddy with gratitude. She was the one who had kept him from having to eat all those potatoes without the saving grace of Otik's ale. Gerard would never have managed had it not been for her.

He became aware of Blair scowling at him, watching

him watch Kaleen. Gerard swung his attention to the sergeant, trying for a flinty glare, then brought his eyes back when they careened right past Blair and off to the side. He hiccupped, feeling a little dizzy from the unaccustomed shimmering of the room. He wished Blair would hold still.

The trio was playing another lively tune. Gerard tapped toes that now felt delightfully numb. Even the itch from the bug bites and the poison ivy had receded into the fog of his mind. He tried to concentrate on what he knew about Sheriff Joyner's murder, but everything was spinning in his brain. Sheriff Joyner, the Ostermans, Usha and her magic painting, the dead architect, the gambling society, the elf-hating Jutlin Wykirk, the elves. The elves. The. . . .

He couldn't keep them all straight anymore. For some reason, he found his whirling thoughts vastly amusing. He laughed at his own foolishness and reflexively reached for his mug, hesitated when he remembered it was empty, then discovered Kaleen had apparently brought him a refill while he wasn't looking.

Good girl, that Kaleen. Steady, dependable. He could see why Blair liked her so.

People had shoved the tables back, crowding them together even more to create a clear space in the center of the room for dancing. Gerard watched the couples whirl and twirl. He swayed zestfully to the music, caught himself from toppling, and applauded the dancers.

Someone tapped him on the shoulder. He looked up to find it was Kaleen—good old Kaleen!—taking off her apron. She curtseyed charmingly. "May I have this dance?"

"But you're working," he managed to say, despite a mouth that felt strangely full of cotton.

"I just finished for the night." She held out her hand. "Come on!"

"Oh, no, no, I rarely . . . that is, I *never* dance! Won't! Can't!"

She pulled him to his feet. "Come on, Lord Porridge, dance with me."

Gerard looked around anxiously, seeking some escape. From his table, Blair was glaring daggers at him. For some reason, that decided Gerard. "All right," he mumbled. "I'll try."

He stood up, kicking off his oversized shoes.

"It's easy. Just follow my lead." She drew him past Blair and into the center of the room.

Kaleen began twirling when she reached the cleared area. Gerard lifted one foot tentatively, then the other, almost forgetting to put the first foot down. He giggled. A few people in the crowd pointed to his bare feet and laughed. Gerard laughed with them. Feeling more confident, he began flinging himself around in time to the music. Some people laughed, some scowled (mostly the ones he bumped into), but everyone pushed back to give him more room. Soon the whole roomful of people had started clapping to the beat. Kaleen spun and swirled gracefully. Gerard showed her some particularly daring moves of his own. The musicians played as though they would never stop.

Laura heard the crowd shouting and clapping and stepped from the kitchen to see what was going on.

There were Gerard and Kaleen in the center of the room, dancing like mad (if what Gerard was doing could be called dancing) while the rest of the room looked on merrily. She frowned a moment in puzzlement, then broke into a huge smile. Who would have thought, she mused. Those two together. And yet now that she considered it, it seemed a likely match.

Humming to the music, she went back into the kitchen, twirling and doing a little sidestep of her own just before the door closed behind her.

CHAPTER

16

Gerard woke the next morning feeling as though his head were being slammed repeatedly by a door. He groaned and started to roll over, wondering who would want to bludgeon him to death, only to discover that moving about wasn't such a good idea. He clenched his jaw to keep from retching.

After a while, the nausea passed, leaving only the repeatedly slamming door. He risked opening his eyes, winced, then held them open by dint of willpower. He swallowed with great difficulty, for someone seemed to have heaped a great deal of dust in his mouth.

It was probably the same person trying to beat him to death with the door. He rolled his eyes around to find the source of his suffering. His eyeballs hurt, but at least moving them wasn't as bad as moving his whole head. At last his gaze fixed on something that moved with the same rhythm as the pounding in his skull. He blinked, the only gesture of disbelief he could manage. A bird had gotten into his room during the night and was fluttering against the windowpane, trying to get out.

Every time those soft, feathered wings collided with the glass, another explosion went off in his head.

He considered his options: rescue the bird and stop the pounding or give up gracefully right here and die. Then he remembered Kaleen and decided to make the ultimate effort to go on. He gritted his teeth, mouthed a quick prayer to any god who happened to be nearby, and swung his legs out of bed.

They crashed to the floor, sending excruciating pain coursing through his legs. Eyes wide open now in surprise, he eased his head over the side of the bed for a look at the latest sensation. His feet were blotchy with purple bruises, lumpy with blisters, and swollen to twice their normal size.

He had a murky memory of someone—possibly him—dancing wildly with Kaleen at the inn last night. If it really had been him (and he hoped it wasn't, recalling what an atrocious dancer he had always been), then he had undoubtedly danced for hours. No wonder his feet hurt so bad!

But what about the thundering in his head? What about the queasy stomach, the Plains-of-Dust feel of his mouth and throat?

Dimly, he saw one giant mug of ale after another pass through his hands, each one starting out full and mysteriously ending up empty.

No wonder he felt so rotten. With infinite slowness, he pushed himself upright until he was sitting on the edge of the bed. All right so far. He massaged his feet until the stabbing pains diminished, then forced himself to stand. It was like teetering on shattered glass but gradually felt better.

Sitting up straighter, he opened the window the

rest of the way and let the bird out. Without its wings beating against the windowpane, the thundering in his head subsided to the level of breakers crashing a little way out at sea. Here on the shore, there was an illusory sense of calm. Now, with the bird gone, even the breakers gradually stopped crashing. The storm had passed. He was beached like so much flotsam, but everything would be all right.

Sailors are familiar with hurricanes at sea and with the eyes of such storms, where all is gripped in strange and fleeting tranquility. Gerard experienced just such a moment of serene indifference, before the hangover returned full force. He took an experimental step toward the door. Agony radiated from his feet, jerking him upright and slamming his head against the low rafters.

When the room steadied again, he was lying on the floor, uncertain whether to grasp his head, his stomach, or his feet. Everything hurt.

The next time, he was much more cautious.

In due time, he was hobbling down the stairs and making his way to the cobbler's shop. He didn't even attempt to put on his temporary shoes. Instead, he walked gingerly on his swollen, bare feet. He realized he was running late for the service at the temple.

The streets were quieter today, as if everyone were busy somewhere else, attending some important function, which was exactly what he should have been doing, Gerard reminded himself. But at least fewer people meant fewer eyes to stare at his miserable plight, fewer mouths to whisper about "that strange man we heard about with the bare feet," as one woman phrased it to her husband within Gerard's hearing. The husband eyed the footgear Gerard carried under his arm and snickered.

At least that wretched kender wasn't about, Gerard thought. He hated to imagine what fantastic escapade Tangletoe would have made of a peculiar incident like this. It might even top Gerard coming back from Samuval's fortress in his undergarments.

Something flickered out of the corner his eye. Gerard kept walking—or lurching, rather—as if nothing had happened, but he scanned the buildings and alleys around him as he went. Nothing. Yet for a moment there, he could have sworn he had seen something, and that he was being followed.

He kept his guard up after that. He might only have imagined it, he told himself. The incident did, however, serve to take his mind off his misery. Soon he reached the cobbler's shop. "Yes?" said the withered old cobbler, again looking at a spot where Gerard was not. "May I help you?"

Gerard frowned, again stepping into the man's line of sight. It was unnerving to think of having a pair of boots made by a man so nearly blind. How could he see to do his work properly? Yet when Gerard explained who he was and the cobbler brought out the boots for his inspection, Gerard had to admit the cobbler knew his craft. The boots were handsomely made, a rich brown with soft, supple leather that came up to mid calf. He returned the shoes he had borrowed, and eagerly, Gerard pulled on the first boot.

It was a tight fit, what with the swelling in his feet. In the end, the cobbler had to help him. Together, they pushed and pulled as Gerard gritted his teeth against the needles shooting through his foot and up his leg.

At last the boot slipped into place. To his surprise it fit comfortably. Cautiously, Gerard put some weight on that leg. It was tender, but certainly bearable. He and the cobbler wrestled the other boot into place, and Gerard let out a small sigh of contentment. For the first time since waking up, he wasn't enduring pain at both ends of his body. In fact, now that he had a moment to think about it, he realized the throbbing in his head had diminished and his stomach had settled somewhat. He smiled for the first time that morning.

The day was looking up.

This time, however, he resisted the urge to get cocky. He paid for the boots, gladly including a hefty surcharge for the speed of the work. With the cobbler nodding gratefully and bidding farewell to an uninhabited space along the shop wall, Gerard headed back. He was going to be very late. He paused at the doorway and checked the street, but no one seemed to be lurking about.

By the time he reached the temple grounds, people dressed in their finest clothes were beginning to appear, coming the other way. Gerard swore under his breath. He had missed the service entirely. He passed Kedrick Tos, Bartholomew Tucker and his wife (Gerard realized he still hadn't learned her name), Lady Drebble (whose son accompanied her with much put-upon sighing and rolling of the eyes), Brynn Ragulf and his whip-thin wife whose steely gaze missed nothing, Cardjaf and Gatrice Duhar, Argyle Hulsey, and even the glowering Torren Soljack. Each person he encountered stole a glance—some casual, some more pointed—in the direction of Gerard's feet as he nodded and passed. Some even looked disappointed at seeing the new boots on his feet. Gerard felt his mouth pull into a thin, tight line. It seemed the town sheriff had quickly become an object of considerable amusement among its citizens.

He hurried on.

On the temple grounds, construction had been temporarily suspended in order to accommodate the morning's open-air service. Now carpenters and masons milled about in the background, waiting to resume work. The scaffolding had been rebuilt along the wall where the "accident" had occurred, no doubt to the disappointment of some curious individuals who had come that morning hoping to witness a scene of carnage and mayhem. In the temple yard stood the clerics who had just finished conducting the service, including Odila in a brilliant white robe that gave her an ethereal look. Gerard was taken aback. He still tended to think of her as a soldier, a Knight of Solamnia, he realized, and hadn't yet adjusted to seeing her as a cleric. Her hair was done up in the tight, braided coils she favored these days, further emphasizing her new calling.

Next to Odila stood Kaleen, who also looked much different than Gerard was used to seeing, for she was dressed in the simple, severe robe of an acolyte. Unlike Gerard, who still felt like something that had been mauled by a saber-toothed tiger (albeit, that was an improvement over how he had felt earlier in the morning), Kaleen looked composed and rested, none the worse for wear for having spent the previous night dancing. She noticed Gerard as he picked his way through the thinning crowd and flicked him a generous smile that further improved his mood.

Talking to Odila was Vercleese uth Rothgaard, which surprised Gerard. He hadn't pegged Vercleese as a religious man. The knight was dressed very soberly, with his mustache waxed, his beard trimmed, and his empty sleeve pinned up so it wouldn't flap around.

Gerard hung back, letting Vercleese and Odila finish talking, for it occurred to him they might be discussing matters of the soul. If so, they deserved a little privacy. After a while, Vercleese, who had been listening as Odila spoke, nodded and stepped back. She put a hand on his remaining arm, smiled at him, and turned to Gerard, indicating the private audience was over. He drew closer, feeling awkward when confronted with her in full cleric outfit.

"Um, I'm sorry I missed the service."

She smiled, lighting a face that looked drawn. Her face was pale, and the circles under her eyes emphasized the pressures she was under. But the smile was as charming as Gerard remembered, all the prettier for the scattering of freckles that spilled over her nose and cheeks. "That's all right," she said. "I'm sure your official responsibilities required your presence elsewhere."

He flushed, thinking that his "official responsibilities" that morning had been to overcome a hangover and pick up a pair of new boots. "Yes, well, hmm. . . ."

"I haven't had a chance to talk with Palin or Argyle Hulsey yet," she continued. "Did the healer's examination of Salamon Beach's body turn up anything interesting?"

"Ah, yes, that proved rather intriguing," Gerard said, warming to the new topic. "It seems your architect was a member of a secret gambling society." He described the tattoo on the nape of Beach's neck, lifting the hair on his own neck as he spoke, to show her where it was affixed.

Odila nodded, her mouth tight in a disapproving scowl. "That explains a lot," she said. "He was always disappearing at nights, off doing something mysterious. He must have been gambling somewhere. I'm sorry. It never occurred to me, though it's so obvious in retrospect."

"The Trough would be my guess," Gerard said with grim conviction.

"Well, he was a good architect, even if a somewhat unpleasant, cold man in many ways," said Odila. "May his soul find rest, wherever it has gone. I'm grateful he left us with such a thorough set of plans. Work on the temple will continue and succeed."

As if waiting for that signal, the dwarf Stonegate, who had walked over to them during their conversation, coughed politely into his fist. Odila turned to him, and he gave a clipped, professional nod.

"Ah, I see the workmen are ready to get busy today," she said. "We've held them up long enough. Now it's time for us to get out of their way." She moved to one side of the temple grounds, drawing the other clerics with her. Again, Gerard was reminded of her official status and felt strangely awed. Lady Odila Windlass had made something of her life since leaving the knighthood, whereas he . . . all he had accomplished so far was to fill a temporary position as sheriff, prove inadequate at solving or preventing murders, and make himself a laughingstock.

Stonegate barked orders to the workmen, who began swarming over the nearly completed structure, picking up their tools and filling the air with the noise of purposeful activity.

"Have you found out anything more about the two mysterious men who assaulted Salamon that night?"

Odila asked quietly, screening her words from any prying ears.

Gerard shook his head. "But I'm on the lookout for the one with the thick, copper mustache and the scarred face. He shouldn't be that difficult for anyone to remember or recognize."

"So do you believe it was an accident or murder?" Odila asked.

Gerard hesitated. "I'm keeping an open mind," he said at last, although he was pretty certain it was the latter.

Across the temple yard stood a cluster of clerics, discussing the service and organizing their duties for the day. The sight of all their various robes, each signifying some religious order or level of office, reminded Gerard of the strange cleric he had noticed aboard the ship coming over and then again when the gnomes had demonstrated their invention. Gerard had not seen that particular cleric around the temple and thought to ask Odila about him.

"Do you know all the clerics here?" he asked.

"Well, I either know them, or they inevitably introduce themselves when they arrive and join the activities. So yes, I guess you could say that one way or another I've gotten to know them all. Why?"

"There's one I've noticed, I wonder if you can tell me something about him, or the order he belongs to." He went on to describe the strange cleric to her, or at least the dun-colored robes the man had worn, for Gerard never had clearly glimpsed the cleric's features.

Odila frowned. "He doesn't sound like anyone I've seen or met, lately. I don't recall ever having seen anyone wear that particular type of robe. He may not be a cleric at all. It sounds like the kind of robe sometimes worn by outlanders from the area around Khur. I hear sometimes they get mistaken for clerics. Apparently it's a common manner of dressing in that land."

"Ahem," said Stonegate, who had again come to stand by Odila's elbow. The dwarf looked about him with apparent unconcern, but it was obvious he desired Odila's attention.

Odila gave Gerard a wan smile. "I'm sorry, but I really must go. My duties beckon." She hurried toward the site, plunging deep into discussion with the dwarf.

Gerard looked around for Kaleen, but she too had disappeared. He was sorry to have missed her, for he was hoping for a word with her before she left—all very casual and above board, of course!

He headed for Palin and Usha's house, eager to find sanctuary there. As he walked, savoring the increasing comfort of his new boots, his hair began to prickle on the back of his neck, and again he had the feeling of being followed. Perhaps it was that the birds along the side of the road were falling just a little too quiet as he approached, as though his wasn't the only presence that disturbed them. But though he listened hard, he heard no rustling of the underbrush or other indication that anyone was on his heels. Then, just as he had about lulled himself into a feeling of complacency, of having been needlessly apprehensive, something whizzed past his head and stuck with a bone-chilling *thunk* in the trunk of a tree, just inches from his face. Gerard had just time enough to register the fact that it was a knife with a piece of paper impaled on the blade.

He dropped to a crouch and scanned the surrounding woods. He eased his dagger from its sheath, feeling very exposed. If the person had been just a little more accurate with his throw, the knife might have been protruding from Gerard's ribs even now.

The forest was silent, as if holding its communal breath against the death struggle that surely must ensue.

Except that nothing happened. Gerard saw nothing, heard nothing else, despite the fact his senses were keyed to full alert. He seemed all alone in the woods. Only the knife protruding from a tree, still trembling with force, attested to things being otherwise.

After a while, he realized the finches and sparrows were again chirping and flitting amid the underbrush. Slowly, Gerard stood and resheathed his dagger. He made a mental note to check with Torren Soljack on the progress of his sword, feeling ridiculously underarmed should real conflict erupt. And apparently that time was fast approaching. He wrenched the knife from the tree and read the appended note. The message was clear enough. *Morgoth.* Beware! But was the word intended for his eyes to see, or were the townspeople expected to have found the message pinned to his corpse?

He tucked the note away, slid the knife into his belt, then continued on into town, warily now. Nothing further interrupted his progress, and soon he stood at Palin and Usha's door. Palin's eyebrows lifted questioningly as he ushered Gerard inside. When they were seated, Gerard handed Palin the knife and note. Palin's eyebrows rose even higher. Gerard related the incident in the woods.

"I don't like this at all," Palin said, when Gerard had finished. He turned knife and note over and over, as if willing some further facts to be gleaned from them. "First Sheriff Joyner, then Salamon Beach, and now a warning you were apparently meant to deliver, dead or alive. It's beginning to look like there's a concerted effort afoot to undermine authority in Solace, inviting anarchy and chaos. I can't help thinking the temple dedication is somehow involved."

"Perhaps," Gerard said.

"And I understand you ran into a stone wall with Baron Samuval, too."

Gerard rubbed absently at the bug bites that still itched all along his arms. "News travels fast in this town."

"I'm afraid you can blame Tangletoe Snakeweed for all the local gossip," Palin said.

"Samuval's a dangerous fellow, to be sure," Gerard went on. "But I can't say I feel certain he killed either the sheriff or the architect. In fact, if pressed, I'd have to say my hunch is that he didn't. He didn't have any real reason. Besides, it's hard to figure why he'd let me go free from his fortress, only to sneak into town a couple of days later and try to aim a knife at my ribs."

"There is something in that," Palin said, looking thoughtful.

Silence stretched for a moment between them.

"I was hoping to speak with Usha," Gerard said at last. "I wanted to talk to her about Beach's death and see whether there's been any unusual changes in her painting lately."

"Ah yes, Usha." Palin rolled his eyes with a dramatic flair and pointed to a poorly made sandwich nearby. "She's acting very secretive and preoccupied. After learning about Salamon Beach's death, she locked herself inside her studio, vowing not to come out until she's done with the painting."

"How long will that be?"

Palin raised his hands, palms up. "Who knows?"

"Can't we . . . ?" Gerard made furtive gestures in the direction of the studio.

"Interrupt her?" exclaimed Palin. "Only at the risk of certain death, I'd say. You were better off in the woods paired off against an invisible assailant. Usha doesn't take kindly to interruptions when she's preoccupied with one of her paintings. And you know, Gerard, artists have deadlines, too, just like architects. When Usha gives herself over to a deadline . . . well, Takhisis herself couldn't get her to budge. No, I'll give her your message when she emerges—*if* she emerges— and shows any desire to communicate." He shuddered. "If the painting doesn't go well, that's not always the case. Meanwhile, carry on as best you can, my friend. Carry on."

CHAPTER

17

First thing the next morning, Gerard donned his doublet and hose and pulled on his new boots, sighing with satisfaction at the smooth fit of the leather enveloping his feet. Then he went to see Torren Soljack.

"It's not ready yet," the smith growled when Gerard asked about the new sword.

"All right," Gerard said, looking around the shop until he located an upended barrel. He sat down on it, putting on a considerable show of making himself at ease.

"What are you doing?" Soljack demanded.

Gerard looked up as if startled at the question. "Waiting."

"You can't do that. Not there."

"Oh, don't worry, I'm comfortable enough," Gerard said. "This will do just fine."

The smith scowled at Gerard for a long moment before finally turning his back on the sheriff and resuming his work. He heated an axe blade to a red-hot glow at

214

the forge and hammered on it with his massive hammer atop the anvil, striking off showers of sparks. His blows seemed to Gerard a trifle more forceful than customary. All at once, the axe blade cracked. Soljack flung down the hammer and swore. Then he turned on Gerard.

"How long do you plan on sitting there, spying on me?"

"Why, until it's ready," Gerard said, with as much innocence as he could muster, neglecting to mention that he had somewhere else to be soon and wouldn't be able to wait at the smithy much longer. He had given Vercleese the slip that morning without the wily old deputy becoming suspicious. "I assume it's just a matter of applying a few finishing touches at this point," he said to Soljack, then frowned at the damaged axe head where it lay cooling on the anvil. "Although I gather that wasn't supposed to happen."

Soljack drew in a deep breath, swelling up like a bladder full of air, or like the bellows he used to heat his forge. "What in the name of all that's holy would you know about it?"

Gerard shrugged. "Nothing. That was merely a casual observation from a disinterested observer."

"Well, you're right. It's ruined! I'll have to start all over."

"In the meantime, then, I suppose you'll have time to finish my sword."

Soljack glared at him. Gerard met his gaze without flinching. All at once, the smith threw back his head and laughed, a huge, bellowing rush of sound that pushed at the ceiling and walls of the shop and spilled out onto the street, causing people to stop and stare in surprise.

It was the first time Gerard had seen the man so much as smile, let alone laugh. He suspected it was an expression as foreign to the other townspeople as it was to him.

"By the gods, but you're a stout one," Soljack said at last, wiping an eye. "Not many men would stand up to me." He grinned a moment, before subsiding into his usual dour expression. "Very well, Sheriff, you shall have your sword, and that right quick."

It was as though a window had been briefly blown wide, only to be slammed shut again as soon as the owner of the house found it standing open. Yet as the smith began working on the sword, attaching the hilt and grip, then touching up the blade and sharpening it to a fine edge, Gerard felt himself no longer the focus of the man's ire. Whatever Soljack's gripe with the world, Gerard suspected the smith himself stood at the center of it, and not anyone around him who intruded upon that internal, personal storm.

Less than an hour later, Soljack barely acknowledged Gerard's gratitude as the latter accepted the finished sword and belted it in place. By the time Gerard left the smithy, Soljack was back to studying the cracked axe head morosely, his face again fixed in its usual scowl, seeking a way to salvage the time he had invested in the offending implement.

But Gerard wasted little thought this time on the source of the smith's antisocial manner, for a question had formed in his mind as he sat and out-waited the man. He strode purposefully through town, receiving the salutations of the people he encountered with brief nods. If he hurried, he had just enough time to get to where he was going before he had to be somewhere else. He found the shop he was looking for, ducked in beneath the clusters of drying herbs suspended from the ceiling—he recognized fastbind and haleboar and sweet lady's bonnet among dozens of other specimens—and hailed the proprietor.

"Mistress Hulsey, I wonder if I might have a moment of your time."

Argyle Hulsey straightened from the mixture of herbs and spices she was reducing to a powder with a mortar and pestle. The aroma of mint rose in a heady cloud from the crushed mixture, overwhelming the more delicate odors in the room. She shrugged the tension from her narrow, birdlike shoulders and peered at Gerard. "Sheriff?"

"You examined the body of the late Sheriff Joyner, did you not?"

She looked at him with a combination of curiosity and irritation. "You know that I did."

"Tell me, did you discover anything of an, um"—he thought how he might phrase the question without giving away the answer he anticipated—"of an *unusual* nature on the body?"

"Unusual?"

"You know, such as strange markings?"

"Well, I would certainly call the word cut into the flesh of his chest unusual in that regard. What was it now? An Elvish word, I believe. *Morgoth?* Yes, that was it."

"I mean other than that etched word, of which we all know. Was there anything else?"

She shook her head; then her gaze became more piercing. "Sheriff, exactly what is it you are wanting me to say?"

He spread his hands helplessly. "Did you look under the hair on his neck, as you did with the architect, Salamon Beach?"

"Of course." Understanding lit her face. "Oh, you mean the tattoo."

"Precisely."

"Well, why didn't you simply say so, instead of sounding like Lady Drebble's fool of a son, Nyland?" She brushed away his attempted explanation with an impatient gesture. "No, Sheriff, Graylord Joyner's body possessed no such tattoo as did the body of Salamon Beach."

Gerard felt a hoped-for connection between the two deaths slip away. "You're sure?"

"Of course I'm sure," she snapped. "Do you presume to question my professional competence?"

"No, no," he said hastily. "I merely . . . well, I had hoped perhaps there would be such a tattoo, which would suggest a common between the two men."

She shook her head. "I knew Sheriff Joyner for a good number of years," she said with a tightness in her voice that made Gerard think there might have been more to their relationship than simply professional association. "I can assure you, he had no such tattoo, nor was he a gambler."

Gerard nodded, although the thought occurred to him that if Sheriff Joyner didn't gamble himself, that didn't mean he wasn't somehow connected with those who did, especially if there was anything about this gambling society that might cause it to run afoul of municipal authorities. In such a case, it would be extremely useful to the members of the society to have the sheriff in their purse.

He thanked the healer and left her shop, no further enlightened than he'd been before coming there. But Gerard made a mental note to discuss with Vercleese the possibility that Sheriff Joyner might have been somehow involved with the gambling society. The deputy was aware of much that went on in this town, and had worked closely with the former sheriff.

Right now, Gerard had an appointment of a very private nature to keep.

Vercleese stood within the shadowed doorway of a tailor's shop and watched Mistress Hulsey's doorway until Gerard reappeared. Vercleese ducked back out of sight and told himself this wasn't really as bad as it looked, spying on his superior. Gerard wasn't behaving like himself this morning, wandering around town and evading him. Something was making the sheriff very anxious.

Given all that had been happening in town lately—the two deaths and the attempt on Gerard's life the day before—Vercleese was determined to keep an eye on the younger man, for his own safety.

Gerard was hurrying down the street now, paying little attention to his surroundings. If he was walking into a trap, he was certainly going into it with his guard down, Vercleese reflected.

The knight frowned and wondered what could possibly be so important that Gerard, normally so cautious, would pay such little heed to his own safety. Vercleese darted from doorway to doorway in Gerard's wake, raising eyebrows from the many passersby

who noticed him. But he was obviously justified in
his efforts to remain hidden from Gerard's sight, for
Gerard began to pause and glance behind him, as if
fearful. Whatever the young man was up to, he was
acting very furtive, which to Vercleese's mind only
called that more attention to him.

He hoped Gerard wasn't attempting to do something foolish, such as confronting a murder suspect
by himself. This seemed all the more likely, after
Gerard picked up his new sword from Torren
Soljack. Was the sheriff headed for some kind of dramatic showdown?

Vercleese was surprised when Gerard turned down
a street with shops and businesses catering to the more
prominent citizens of Solace. The knight's eyebrows
shot up, unconsciously mimicking the looks he was
receiving from all who spotted his peculiar behavior.
He slipped into the shadows of yet another doorway,
startling the proprietor inside, who looked up sharply
then waved in friendly greeting. Vercleese smiled
wanly and returned Kedrick Tos's wave, hurrying on
before the councilman could ask what in the world he
was doing.

With a last wary glance around, Gerard ducked
into an unmarked doorway. Vercleese waited several
minutes then, when Gerard didn't reappear, followed
cautiously. When he peered around the doorway,
risking a look inside, he saw that the door opened not
directly onto another shop, as he had expected, but onto
a short hallway with a couple of closed doors at the end.
Vercleese tiptoed down the short corridor, his hand
on the hilt of his sword. A strange, rhythmic tapping
came from the other side of one door, along with what

sounded like someone humming. Very slowly, Vercleese opened the latch and pushed the door open just enough to peek inside.

In the middle of an empty room, Gerard stood facing a tall, imperious woman who was rapping the floor sharply with a long staff she carried in one hand. At the same time she was humming a lively air. For a horrified instant, Vercleese thought she must have placed Gerard under some kind of terrible spell, for he jerked and twitched spasmodically in time to her beat. Abruptly, however, the woman stopped tapping the staff, and clapped her hands in annoyance, bringing Gerard to a halt. "No, no, not like that at all! Are you utterly bereft of rhythm?"

Gerard glowered shamefacedly at the floor.

"Once more, and this time try to feel the music!" She began humming again and resumed the rhythmic rapping with her staff.

With a smile, Vercleese quietly closed the door and moved with a stealthy tread back down the hall, determined to preserve Gerard's secret, regardless how tempting it might be to let on that he knew. Some secrets deserved a modicum of privacy, and to Vercleese's thinking this was one, for Gerard was engaged in as heroic and momentous a struggle as any he'd ever faced.

The new sheriff was learning to dance.

Early that evening, resting in his attic room, Gerard sat at a small table by the open window and worked industriously as the daylight waned. His quill scratched again and again across a page that soon filled with the lines of his fine, precise hand. He paused periodically to dip the nib in a small pot of ink nearby, careful not to overturn the ink it with a careless elbow or a sudden flourish with the quill. Then he blotted the excess ink from the nib and resumed writing. At one point, he stopped long enough to light a small lamp, the daylight having faded.

On one corner of the table, a small stack of completed pages grew under his relentless efforts.

Meanwhile, the day of the temple dedication quickly approaches, Gerard wrote. *It's only three days away at this point, which means that one way or another it will be all over by the time you read this letter. The town is full to bursting, sometimes leading to angry confrontations between longtime residents and newer arrivals, although for the most part, the atmosphere is festive. But the commotion makes the town somewhat raucous at all times of the day and night, and I've become rather grateful for my tiny attic space high in a tree.*

He stopped to reconsider that last line then crossed out *tiny attic space high in a tree,* substituting instead *accommodations comfortably removed from the general activity.*

This job is challenging, but also extremely rewarding, he continued, *and I find myself relying heavily on my training as a knight.* This last part he added with specific thought toward justifying his leaving the knighthood, wishing to affirm that his earlier schooling had not been wasted. *I almost regret that the term of my position here will be coming to an end with the dedication as I have become quite fond of the town and its citizens.* He paused, struck by the unexpected truth of that last sentence, then went on. *Palin has been an immense help through all of this, as has my deputy, another former knight*. He chose not to mention that Vercleese had left the knighthood after serving a full span of duty, quite a different case than his.

In fact, I have made any number of new friends here—Gerard was thinking of Kaleen, but refrained from mentioning her, knowing that to do so would immediately raise unreasonable expectations—*and have been learning all kinds of new*—he hesitated in his scrawl, thinking of the dancing lessons, then finished instead—*skills. The former sheriff's murder and various other unexplained incidents have yet to be solved, but I've been pondering them and feel I'm getting closer to learning the truth behind these unhappy events.*

And now I need to prepare for the next stage in our investigation, a task that will require some delicacy in handling. I will, of course, be careful, and remain as always your faithful son,

Gerard.

He glanced over the final page then, satisfied, sprinkled it with sand to dry any remaining ink. This done, he blew the sand away, ordered the sheaf of pages he had accumulated, and folded and sealed them into a neat packet. He addressed the finished letter and added it to the others he had written, all of which he stored in a drawer under his spare clothes. Feeling he had discharged his filial obligations for the moment, despite never having actually sent any of the letters he wrote, he stood, being careful for once not to bang his head on the rafters; buckled on his new sword; and hurried out into the twilight for his appointed rendezvous.

Up on the bridge-walks, where he traveled at first, the last glow of sunset still lit the way. He frequently had to slow his steps as he worked his way through the throngs of revelers headed for one occasion or another. The celebratory mood of the town was definitely reaching a fever pitch as the dedication approached. Down below, the streets were more clogged than ever, despite the growing darkness, and Gerard refrained from descending to ground-level as long as possible. Eventually, however, he left the bridge-walk and made his way quietly to stand in the darkest shadows across from the front door of The Trough. Even at this early hour, the evening rituals were well under way inside, with music and the practiced squeals of laughter from the establishment's female clientele emerging through the closed doors and windows.

Vercleese materialized out of the darkness at Gerard's side. "Is everything ready?" Gerard asked quietly.

"We're just waiting for word from Blair," Vercleese whispered.

Scarcely had he spoken when Blair emerged from around the back of the tavern. "He's here," Blair said, his voice equally hushed. "I've been watching the back door. Just had to be patient. He went in with another man about an hour ago."

"All right, keep your eye on the back door," Gerard told the sergeant of the guard. "If either of those two men comes out, you know what to do." As Blair melted away again, Gerard turned to Vercleese. "I'll go in alone. I need you to watch the back door with Blair."

"What? You mean I'm not going in with you?" Vercleese sounded as disappointed as he was disapproving.

"I need you to remain out here," Gerard said, putting a hand on his deputy's shoulder. "Don't worry, I'll be all right. I've been in some pretty tight situations in my time."

Vercleese, well versed in the proprieties of command, lowered his eyes. "Just be careful," he grumbled, heading after the sergeant.

Gerard smiled into the darkness. Then, with a display of more confidence than he felt, he strode across the street to The Trough's front door. The slap of his new sword against his leg felt welcome. At the threshold, he took a deep breath then flung the door wide. It flew back against the wall, making a loud noise that announced his entrance. Gerard stepped inside.

The large common room, smoky from a flue that hadn't been cleaned recently and wasn't drawing adequately, was already full of carousing ne'er-do-wells. A quick glance around told Gerard that not all the patrons were die-hard criminals, most were simply on the shady side of the law. To a man—and a few women, he noted—they looked astonished to see the sheriff poaching on their territory. At the counter, Gerard saw Samuval's aide, Brok, set down his mug and blink. Gerard gave the man a neutral nod.

A sudden scurrying at the rear of the room caught his attention, and Gerard turned just in time to see Bartholomew Tucker, Solace's leading wine merchant, scurry through the back door. Gerard grinned, wondering how many other prominent citizens would be sneaking out tonight.

Gerard stepped boldly into the dragon's lair, making an effort not to wrinkle his nose against the stink of moldy rushes on the floor or the scorched meat that seemed to be the principle food item on the tavern's menu. In the farthest corner of the room, he spotted a gaming table, where a group of swarthy men were busy playing cards, affecting disinterest in his arrival. He looked steadily from one to another, five faces in all, moving through the room in such a way as to be able to stare at each, studying each in turn. He marked the five carefully in his mind and made his way to the counter near Brok.

With a gesture, he indicated the ale barrel to the surly, scowling innkeeper, who filled a mug and plunked it down in front of Gerard, withdrawing his hand from the mug only after Gerard had paid. Gerard took a sip, grimaced at the bitter taste, and set the mug down again. He was almost developing a taste for the stuff. Shifting his sword more comfortably on his hip in case he needed to draw it, he went to stand next to the gaming table.

One of the men at the table had a thick copper mustache and a ragged scar down the left side of his face.

A dun-colored cowled robe hung from a peg in the wall near the gaming table. Gerard made a mental note of the interesting fact. An unexpected bonus, he thought. But time enough for the cowled man later. He glanced at each of the five faces again, coming to a stop on the fifth, the man with the copper mustache and the ragged scar. The five men interrupted their card playing, waiting for Gerard to say or do something, with thinly veiled impatience.

"You!" Gerard said, pointing to Copper Mustache. "Come with me!"

"What am I supposed to have done?" Copper Mustache demanded scornfully, making no effort to obey. However, his right hand crept off the table and out of sight.

"I don't know yet, but I'm sure I'll think of something," Gerard said. "Maybe you have some ideas of your own in that regard. But right now, I want you to come with me. I have some questions that need answering."

The man stood abruptly, pushing away from the table and revealing a cudgel in his hand. The other four men shoved back. One darted away, heading toward the door at the rear of the tavern. Gerard noted his flight, but kept his attention riveted on Copper Mustache.

"Don't seem fair," drawled Copper Mustache, as he stood there, ominously fingering his cudgel. "You with a sword and all."

Gerard made a point of unbuckling his sword and laying it on the table. With his eyes, he warned the other three remaining men to move farther away, and they promptly backed off.

"The polite thing for you to do now would be to put your weapon down as well, sir," he said to Copper Mustache. "What is your name anyway?"

"I'll tell you one thing my name isn't—it's not STUPID!" cried the man. He lunged at Gerard. Gerard deftly sidestepped the man's cudgel, grabbed up a stool, and brought it down on Copper Mustache's head as he hurtled past. The man dropped to the slimy rushes, his cudgel flying from his hand. Gerard leaped to place a knee on the man's back and quickly lashed his hands together behind him. He dragged Copper Mustache to his feet, retrieved his sword, and, with the sword drawn now and held out before him to ward off any attempted rescue of his prisoner, he backed from the room, pulling the still-stunned Copper Mustache after him.

Out front, Blair and Vercleese were already waiting with another struggling prisoner, the man who had attempted to flee the gaming table out through the back door of The Trough.

"Everything went all right?" Vercleese asked, sounding as anxious as a mother hen.

Gerard nodded. "Just fine."

"Shall we take them off to jail?" Vercleese asked when Gerard made no movement in that direction.

"Let's wait a minute," Gerard said. He guided the group away from the door of the tavern and seated them beneath a tree, where he gagged the two prisoners so they couldn't speak.

"Why—?" Blair asked.

"Shh," Gerard warned.

They waited in silence a few moments then Gerard spoke. "Wait here," he whispered and made his way back to The Trough. He repeated his previous grand entrance, letting the door crack loudly against the front wall. The room had emptied some, the back exit evidently having become quite busy after he left. Those who remained looked to be the hard cases.

With everyone watching him, Gerard strode up to the counter, where his mug still sat waiting. Casually, he let his eyes drift around the room, until they came to rest on the empty peg on the back wall where the dun-colored cowled robe had hung. Only two men remained at the gaming table. Gerard matched their faces against those memorized from his previous visit.

That allowed him to recall the face of the missing man, the one who had left wearing the cowled robe.

Oh, yes, he'd know that face well enough next time he saw it.

"Forgot something," he announced loudly to the room. With everyone watching, he downed his ale, belched magnificently, and departed, letting the door stand open.

CHAPTER

18

Gerard sent Blair off for the wagon and horses that, earlier, Gerard had arranged to have tethered nearby. "Is everything ready?" Gerard asked Vercleese when Blair was gone.

"Yeah," said Vercleese, sounding none too happy about it. He started to say something else but was interrupted by the rattle of the wagon and the clop of approaching hooves. Blair drew up in front of the little group and hopped down from the driver's bench. The three pulled their prisoners to their feet and hustled them into the back of the wagon, where they bound their feet.

"Now where?" Blair asked.

"To the jail, of course," Gerard replied.

"And who's going to stand guard all night?" Blair asked sullenly. "Me?"

"Not necessarily," Gerard said, tugging on his beard as he mulled the matter over. "You've worked hard tonight and could probably do with a good night's sleep. No, I think we could probably find a citizen willing to volunteer his services, guarding these prisoners tonight."

"A volunteer?" Blair said. "Isn't that a little, er, unusual?"

"That's right," Gerard said, as he and Vercleese untethered their horses from behind the wagon and mounted. "However, this is an unusual case, calling for unusual measures."

When he gave directions to Blair, however, it was Vercleese who exploded. "Are you out of your mind? Why don't you just stick your hand into a hornets' nest and get it over with!"

"Nevertheless," Gerard said, "that's where we're going. Get him up, Blair."

Blair flicked the reins and clucked to the draft animal pulling the wagon, who slowly bestirred himself. The wheels rattled over the cobbles, and the bound prisoners grunted as every violent jolt tossed them about on the hard, rough boards of the wagon bed. With Blair leading in the wagon, Gerard and Vercleese followed at a leisurely pace on their horses, watching to make sure the pair didn't try to escape.

They went through the heart of town, passing the Town Square, the smithy, and the stables. The traffic had thinned by now, though many people were still out on foot. On some street corners, clerics exhorted folk to observe the forthcoming temple dedication with more propriety. But the citizens of Solace were proud of their new temple, which promised to be one of the preeminent structures in all Ansalon, and they were determined to celebrate the occasion.

At the Town Square, Blair veered onto a well-to-do residential street running westward, toward Crystalmir

Lake. He drew up to one imposing edifice. Behind him, Gerard and Vercleese reined in.

"Are you sure this is such a good idea?" Vercleese muttered.

"Oh, I think it's an ideal solution," Gerard said with a grin. "Wait here." He tossed his reins to his deputy and dismounted. He stepped briskly up the gravel walk to the front door, where he pounded hard enough, with the pommel of his sword, to rouse the heaviest sleeper. After a few minutes, a bleary-eyed butler opened the door. "Yes, who is it?" the servant demanded imperiously. "Who dares to wake the household at such an hour?"

Gerard moved so that the light from the man's candle shone on his face. "It's Gerard uth Mondar, the sheriff of Solace. And I have urgent need of Nyland's services for the night."

"The young master is asleep," the butler droned. "As is anyone," he added with a scornful look, "not engaged in scurrilous endeavors of one sort or another."

"You'd best hope I overlook your disrespectful comments," Gerard warned. "Now go wake up Nyland and bring him here, before I come in and roust him out of bed myself."

"You wouldn't dare," the butler said, although a slight tremor in his voice betrayed his uncertainty.

"Try me."

The butler tried to stare Gerard down but failed abjectly. "Hmph! I'll go see what I can do," he muttered at last. "Please wait here." He started to shut the door.

Gerard stuck his booted foot in the doorway. "I think I'll wait inside, if it's all the same to you."

The butler's glare told Gerard that it wasn't all the

same, but he acquiesced to the inevitable with poor grace and stepped aside. "If this is suitable," the butler said with a mocking tone, indicating the entryway, "I'll leave you here while I go rouse the young master."

Gerard nodded and the man marched off with a stiff, unhurried gait.

When someone appeared a few minutes later, it wasn't Nyland at all, but Lady Drebble. "What's the meaning of this?" she demanded. "What are you doing, banging on doors in the middle of the night and demanding that solid, upstanding citizens be rousted from their beds?"

"My dear lady, I have sore need of Nyland for the night," Gerard said diplomatically. "I'm afraid I'm going to have to impress him into duty serving as one of my deputies."

Lady Drebble began to wring her hands. "My little Nyland, occupied in such a . . . *common* undertaking? How remarkable! What could you possibly want him to do?"

"Guard a couple of prisoners."

"Guard prisoners!" cried Lady Drebble fanning herself desperately. "My little Nyland, associating with such rabble? Why, I won't hear of it! He might fall asleep, and then they'd cut his throat."

"If he's on guard duty, he won't be sleeping," Gerard observed dryly. "And of course the prisoners will be safely locked up."

"I insist upon speaking to the mayor," Lady Drebble said. She stamped a pudgy foot. "Right now!"

"Mother, what is it?" asked a young man's voice behind her. Moments later, the pale face of Nyland Drebble materialized in the little sphere of candlelight.

Gerard knew from Vercleese that Nyland was at least eighteen, although he was kept under so tight a rein by his mother's apron strings that he was treated as though he were twelve. "What are these men doing here?"

"Nothing, Nyland. It has nothing to do with you," Lady Drebble said. "Go back to bed."

"Nyland, get dressed," Gerard interjected. "You're coming with us."

The lad's eyes grew wide. "Am I under arrest?" He looked more delighted than dismayed.

"No, not at all." Gerard smiled, touched in spite of himself by the young man's innocence. "We badly need you to guard some prisoners for tonight."

Nyland's mouth fell open. "Are they dangerous ones?" he asked when he remembered to close it again.

"Not at all," his mother said hurriedly. "They're quite ordinary criminals, I'm sure. And I'm sure the sheriff can find someone else more suited for such a menial job."

"Oh, yes," Gerard said to Nyland, as though his mother hadn't spoken. "A couple of very dangerous sorts, indeed."

"But I'm unarmed." The young man looked embarrassed. "And I don't possess a weapon. Mother won't permi— that is, I have yet to select and purchase a suitable weapon."

"Well, that's easily remedied. I'll loan you my sword," Gerard said.

"Oooh!" Nyland breathed. He turned to his mother. "I-I really think I should go. After all, it's my, uh, civic duty."

"It's your patriotic duty," Gerard offered.

"It's my patriotic duty," Nyland echoed eagerly.

"Nyland, I won't hear of it! Now obey me and return to bed." When the lad didn't respond quickly enough to suit her, she stamped her foot again. "Right now, Nyland!"

"I'm sorry, Nyland, but this is man's work, or I wouldn't have asked you. You really must come with us," Gerard said. He looked the lad in the eyes. "That's an order."

"You hear that, Mother? My duty to my community calls me. I really must go." Nyland disappeared into the house before his mother could object, presumably to dress.

Lady Drebble turned on Gerard, her face purple with rage. "I'm going to protest to the mayor!" she cried. "I'm going to put a stop to this nonsense at once!"

"You might want to put on some proper clothes, first," Gerard said when it appeared she might launch herself into the street, still in her nightdress and robe.

"Hmph!" she snorted and spun away, slamming the door.

Gerard waited.

"Do you really think he'll come?" Vercleese asked, having slipped up behind Gerard sometime during the discussion.

"Oh, he'll come all right. He wouldn't miss this for all the world."

Sure enough, moments later Nyland bounded out of the house, still lacing up his breeches and tucking in his shirt. He glanced fearfully over his shoulder. "We should hurry," he said. As if to set an example, he raced down the walk and hopped onto the back of the wagon. "Come on. Let's go!"

Gerard and Vercleese grinned at each other, promptly complying. The lad's misgivings seemed well grounded, for no sooner were they under way, drawing away from the house, than Lady Drebble appeared again at the doorway, gesticulating hysterically. "Be brave, my boy!" she cried to the departing entourage. "I'll get you out of there! I promise!"

"Not before the night's out, I hope," Nyland muttered, just loud enough for Gerard to overhear.

At the jail, the two prisoners were tossed into an empty cell. They struggled against their bonds and attempted to speak, but all that emerged from their gagged mouths were sounds suggestive of the worst possible threats and curses. Nyland stood outside the cell, watching them with fascination.

"Here," Gerard said loudly, handing over his sword to the youthful jailer. "Keep a firm grip. Don't stab them unless you have to. But, uh, if you are forced to run them through, go for the vital organs. Try to keep the bloodshed down to a minimum. Cleaning up the jail can be such a mess."

Nyland held the sword, staring at it with wide eyes. Copper Mustache and his accomplice moaned into their gags and struggled harder against the ropes that held them.

"What if they try to escape?" Nyland asked eagerly.

"Then skewer them like the rats they are," Gerard said, speaking mainly for the benefit of the prisoners. He leaned close to Nyland and whispered, "But see that it doesn't come to that, will you? I'm counting on you; keep them frightened, but alive. I really do need them alive."

"All right," Nyland said, sounding disappointed.

"What are you going to charge them with?" Blair asked, ready to write something down in the official logbook.

"Hmm, they're under suspicion," Gerard said.

"Of what?" asked Blair, hesitating and looking doubtful.

"I'm thinking on it," Gerard said with a grin, watching the prisoners squirm.

"And where are you two headed without your blades?" asked Blair, seeing Vercleese unbuckle his sword as well and place it on the jail guard's desk.

"Someplace you'd rather not be," Vercleese replied glumly as he and Gerard returned to their horses. They mounted again and headed off into the dark, directing their way back past The Trough, where business as usual sounded well under way again, and on out of town.

They rode as far as Jutlin's mill, but instead of continuing across the bridge and down the road that ran alongside Solace Stream to Gateway, they turned their horses up into the mountains. Vercleese led the way. Gerard rode contentedly behind, listening to the wind sigh through the tops of the pine trees that began to grow thicker around them as they climbed.

Even at night, it was hot at this time of year. Gerard would have found it stifling were it not for Thunderbolt parting the air like a ship cleaving water, creating the illusion of a breeze.

After a while, however, the ground, merely hilly at first, rose more steeply, and the night air grew chilly. Gerard began to regret not bringing a cloak. He huddled inside his light cotton shirt as best he could and hoped they were getting close to their destination.

But Vercleese led on inexorably as the hour grew late. Finally, they reached a high mountain meadow and Vercleese stopped. "Here?" Gerard asked as his deputy dismounted.

Instead of answering, Vercleese began gathering wood for a fire. Seeing what the man was doing, Gerard made haste to help, for the one-armed knight was clearly hampered in such activity. Soon they had a good-sized blaze going, alerting anyone within miles to their presence. Stealth wasn't called for on this particular adventure, Gerard reflected wryly.

He tossed a dry branch as thick as his arm onto the fire. The smoke stung his eyes as a vagrant breeze picked it up for a moment; then the air fell still again. The wood sizzled and popped. Flames nibbled tentatively at one end of the branch before enveloping the whole piece with a voracious appetite. Gerard hugged himself, feeling warm again at last, and wearily flung himself down on the ground. Vercleese was already lying back, studying the stars. Something hopped through the underbrush near them then veered away from their presence, bounding deeper into the woods.

"Are you sure we'll find him here?" Gerard asked, propping himself up on one elbow to look at the older man.

Vercleese yawned, reminding Gerard how long a day it had been. In a moment, both were fighting to keep their eyes open.

"Don't worry," Vercleese said after a moment. "If he's around, he'll find us."

"How did you get a message to him?" Gerard asked.

The only answer that came was a soft snore from Vercleese.

Gerard settled back comfortably. He watched the moons sail by silently overhead. He wasn't even aware of falling asleep.

He was aware of waking up, however, for he became cognizant of the lean, sharp features of an elf leaning over him, leering into his face. It was Kirrit Bitterleaf.

Gerard jerked upright, not entirely surprised to see that he and Vercleese were surrounded by elves, their arrows nocked and bowstrings taut. Slowly, Gerard started to get to his feet.

"Sit," Bitterleaf said harshly, pushing Gerard back down. Gerard glanced at Vercleese, who gave him a look. Gerard sat.

"I believe you have requested an audience with me," Bitterleaf said in an unfriendly tone. He waved to the embers of their fire, still glowing in a great, ashy heap. "Either that, or you are the most stupid humans I've ever met. I'd have known you were here even without advance word."

Gerard examined the man by the dim light of the moons and dying embers. He understood with some sympathy, as he looked into that ravaged face, that Kirrit Bitterleaf had seen his people displaced and devastated. Likely, the elf didn't trust anyone, and certainly not a pair of humans who held positions of authority.

"You! I remember you from that encounter in town," Bitterleaf said after a moment, studying Gerard. "I don't normally have anything to do with sheriffs and knights."

"Ex-knights," said Vercleese dryly, drawing a sharp

look from Bitterleaf, which warned him to keep out of the conversation.

Gerard recalled with a twinge of shame how the Knights of Solamnia had failed the elven nation. If the knights had lived up to their responsibilities, the elves might not have lost their rightful lands. If Bitterleaf made no distinction between present and former knights, he had cause to despise Gerard and Vercleese, no matter that the ties between them and the knighthood were severed.

"To you, however, I owe a personal debt," Bitterleaf said, addressing Gerard and sounding reluctant to admit the fact. "Speak your piece, and to the best of my ability I will answer."

Gerard steeled himself, feeling he had but one chance with this elf and he had best make the most of it. "I wanted to meet with you and ask, what do you know about Sheriff Joyner's murder?"

Bitterleaf spat. "That Sheriff Joyner was a fool. He thought he could play Samuval like a piece on a game board. But that was none of my business. Most humans are fools." He stared meaningfully at Gerard, making Gerard flush. "Humans, however, are not my concern, or should I say the least of my concerns. I scarcely knew Sheriff Joyner and know nothing of how he died."

Whispers and tension rippled through the other elves as Bitterleaf spoke, as though their antagonism toward Gerard and Vercleese were being held barely in check by the elf leader.

"Do you know anything about the accident at the temple?" Gerard asked.

Bitterleaf barked with harsh laughter. "I don't care a fig about anything involving human religions, which have no real understanding of the holiness of nature and the true aspect of the gods."

"Would that belief lead you to murder a human?" Gerard asked evenly, doing his best to ignore the arrowheads pointed at his heart.

"No," Bitterleaf spat again. "Not as a matter of principle, anyway. For other reasons, however . . . perhaps." He shrugged.

"What about the rumors that elves steal from farms and the folk around Solace?"

"We steal when we have to," Bitterleaf said between clenched teeth. "We kill when we have to as well. I don't pretend otherwise."

"But we pay when we're able," one of the elves offered angrily.

Bitterleaf looked askance at the speaker. Gerard was sure there would be retribution later for his talking out of turn.

"If you are innocent of any wrongdoing," said Gerard, "then you won't mind showing me your knife."

Out of the corner of his eye, Gerard saw Vercleese staring at him, disbelieving his audacity.

"My knife? Why?" Bitterleaf, too, stared at him, with barely restrained fury. With one sudden, swift movement he whipped the knife out of the sheath at his belt and raised it up to press against Gerard's throat. "Here it is," he said, abruptly reversing his grip and offering the weapon to Gerard, hilt first. Gingerly, Gerard accepted it and examined the unusual curved shape of the blade.

Bitterleaf erupted into another smooth motion, producing a similarly curved sword from its scabbard strapped on his back. "And here's my sword, too, human!" he said. "And my bow and arrows, and the dagger I keep in my boot." With each new item he mentioned, another weapon landed at Gerard's feet. Bitterleaf shook with fury, waiting for Gerard's reaction.

The other elves chuckled scornfully among themselves.

Meeting Bitterleaf's eyes, Gerard picked up the sword and peered at the sweep of the blade. He liked the heft of the weapon. Whoever had forged the sword knew his craft.

"Satisfied, human?" Bitterleaf demanded, grabbing the sword from him as if Gerard's mere touch might contaminate it.

"Yes. Thank you, Kirrit Bitterleaf."

The elf captain scooped up his other weapons and made them disappear to their respective places about his person as swiftly as he had produced them. "Now we are even," Bitterleaf said. "You helped me once, and I have returned the favor. Next time we meet, we start out anew, with no debts to be repaid."

He backed slowly into the darkness, whirled, and vanished without a sound.

Gerard looked around, but the other elves had disappeared the same way. He and Vercleese were alone in the clearing, staring at each other and shivering in the predawn chill.

CHAPTER

19

"So did you find what you were looking for?" Vercleese asked as he and Gerard rode back toward town the next morning.

Gerard, half asleep in the saddle after a long, exhausting night, roused himself. "Hmm? What's that?"

"I said, was that worthwhile?" Vercleese said, sounding irritable. "Did you learn anything?'

Gerard frowned, forcing his fuzzy mind to focus. "Maybe. I don't know. I'll have to think on it."

"That sounds vague enough," Vercleese grumbled under his breath.

The horses picked their way down the steep slope of the mountain. The refreshing, pine-scented breeze soon gave way to the oppressive heat of the lower levels, making it even more difficult for Gerard to stay awake. He swayed and rocked in the saddle, giving Thunderbolt his rein.

There had been little sleep after the visit from the elves. The night seemed too full of eyes, too full

243

of arrows eager to sate their points in human blood. Gerard wasn't sure how much of a distinction the elves made between Knights of Solamnia, past as well as current, who had failed to live up to their duty to help restore elves' land, and Samuval, himself a former dark knight, who had seized the majority of that land and displaced its occupants.

Pine trees gave way to aspen and birch as the men descended. The upper leaves of the trees rustled listlessly at ground level, where the day had already grown hot and still. Gerard and Vercleese reached Solace Stream at last, turning toward Solace and passing Jutlin Wykirk's mill. The mill wheel turning indolently, but the place had a strangely deserted look.

By the time they reached town, many of the stalls were already closed in the marketplace, attesting to the lateness of the hour. Discarded cabbage leaves, onion skins, and carrot tops littered the ground. They rode on past Stephen's Grocery, where a large, flatbed farm wagon stood being loaded with enormous crates and boxes marked with such contents as horse feed and flaxseed. Three men were hoisting the boxes onto the wagon. One was Stephen; the second was probably his helper in the store, Gerard thought; the third was Jutlin Wykirk.

"So that's why the mill looked deserted this morning," Vercleese commented. "He's in town picking up supplies."

Gerard's gaze started to drift disinterestedly past the miller, then snapped back. There was something about the man's face . . . what was it? Gerard was prodded by some buried memory. Somewhere else he had seen that face, perhaps? At last he shrugged. If it were important, it would come to him in time.

The crates and boxes were evidently heavy, for the three men strained under their weight, barely acknowledging Gerard and Vercleese with nods as they worked.

Gerard and Vercleese stopped at the communal well near the town square. Vercleese slid from the saddle and gratefully splashed cooling water over his face. Nearby, the brutal hammering of the smith rang out in the still air.

"I'll be right back," Gerard said, turning toward the smith's shop.

Vercleese grunted and splashed more water on his face.

Gerard stepped into the dim interior of the smithy, where the heat assaulted him. Torren Soljack looked up from his hammering. "Is there something wrong with your sword?" he asked, challengingly.

"No," Gerard said, mopping his brow and wondering how the smith could stand the heat of the forge added to the already sweltering summer day. "It's an excellent weapon, most satisfactory. I wanted to come by and tell you as much."

"Then where is it, if it's so excellent?"

"We ran into a bit of trouble last night, and I loaned it to one of my deputies. But never fear, it's safe and sound and doing its job well over at the jail." As he spoke, Gerard wondered whether things were indeed safe and sound over at the jail. He hoped he wouldn't have any bloodstains to mop up when he got over there.

"Hmph!" Soljack snorted. He resumed hammering as if Gerard was no longer there, hinting he wished that were the case.

Gerard ignored the hint, although he felt awkward, knowing his next words would probably offend the man. Still, he had to ask. "You know," Gerard said between hammer blows, "I've seen some fine, unusually shaped swords on some folks around here lately. Baron Samuval for one."

Soljack paused, hammer upraised, cocking an eyebrow.

"And Kirrit Bitterleaf, a leader of the exiled elves, for another," Gerard said in a rush, pushing on. "Nice swords. Similar, in many respects."

Soljack glowered, becoming visibly angry. Still he waited without uttering a word.

"Did you make those swords for them?" Gerard finally blurted.

Soljack flung his hammer and tongs down and turned from the anvil, busying himself with the bellows that heated the forge, as if making it even hotter could somehow assuage his anger. "Folks are always blaming me for things, just because I got into some trouble once, long ago," he nearly shouted. "But I'm a changed man, I believe in Paladine these days. As for elves and the like, I've got nothing against any of 'em, but I draw the line at making swords for rebels and outlaws."

It was the longest speech Gerard had ever heard the man make, and he was taken aback by the extent of the smith's fury, which seemed to swell with the pumping of the bellows, as if the real forge he was heating was the one deep in his own soul. Then the smith ceased working the long bellows handle and slumped down on a nearby barrel, his head in his hands.

"I suppose you're going to persecute me. I'll have to pull up stakes and leave Solace, the same as everywhere else. And just when I was starting to like it here," he muttered.

"I'm sorry," Gerard said, after the man had fallen silent. "I didn't think it was your work, but I had to ask. As for the rest, I really don't know what you're talking about." Truthfully, he was grateful for, if a little puzzled by, the smith's answer, and was more preoccupied by the weapons he had seen at Samuval's fortress and then again in the mountains the previous night. "I wonder if you have any idea who might have made them," Gerard said as diplomatically as possible. "They did have a very distinctive look."

With effort, the smith roused himself. "In what way?" he asked miserably.

"They all had curving blades."

Soljack frowned then nodded. "I've heard of a technique for forging blades that results in such a shape. It's supposed to impart greater strength and an ability to hold an edge longer than more traditional methods, although I've yet to hear anyone complain of the more traditional weapons I make. I don't know of anyone who uses such a technique, at least not in these parts."

"Well, it was worth my asking," Gerard said. He started to leave the smithy, then turned back again. "I hope you will rethink your decision to leave Solace," he said. "I know you are highly valued here."

Soljack raised his head, his face an expression of abject misery. He appeared to consider Gerard's words, like a drowning man offered a saving rope.

"And as far as whatever you've done, I'm content to let that rest in the past, where it belongs. No one in Solace needs to know anything about it unless you choose to bring up the matter." He waited, but when Soljack seemed unlikely to respond, started from the shop once more.

"Sheriff," the smith said, his voice barely audible.

Gerard turned.

"Jutlin Wykirk . . . he has a brother," the smith said.

"What?"

Soljack nodded. "Jutlin has a brother, that's about all I can say. Lives across the sea somewhere. Comes to town every few months. I saw him once by chance, early one morning, heading out to Jutlin's place, driving Jutlin's wagon, which was stacked full of big boxes and crates. One of the boxes had broken open." He hesitated, uncertain. "I can't say for sure, but I thought I saw something gleaming inside." Soljack shrugged. "That really is all I know."

Gerard gave the smith a quick salute and ran out.

Vercleese was lounging beside the well, feeling somewhat refreshed, when he saw Gerard rush from the blacksmith's shop toward the grocery. In the street nearby, Jutlin was just starting to drive off. "Hey, Jutlin!" Gerard called out, running over to him.

Looking puzzled, the miller hauled back on the reins. The wagon creaked to a stop, evidently heavily laden.

Mystified, Vercleese watched Gerard run up to Jutlin. Looking wary now, Jutlin leaned down to hear Gerard whisper something to him. Jutlin pulled away, eyes flashing. Gerard yanked him back, whispered something more in his ear, then turned and strode over to where Vercleese was now rising to his feet. Jutlin drove off, looking back over his shoulder and scowling.

"What was that all about?" Vercleese asked when Gerard reached him.

"Come on," Gerard said, giving Vercleese a hand the rest of the way up. "Let's take these horses to the stable then head over to the jail. I'll fill you in as we go."

◆ ◆ ◆ ◆ ◆

"Tell you what," Nyland was taunting the prisoners, "I'll set the keys over here near the cell door, as if I'd accidentally dropped them, then I'll go back to the desk, put my feet up, and maybe take a little nap. That is when you should try to escape. If I'm really asleep, you'll be able to make your getaway." He grinned wickedly. "But if I'm only pretending, I get to run at least one of you through. What do you say? You won't get a better offer than that."

Neither prisoner spoke, contenting themselves with glaring at him contemptuously. Nyland sighed. This guard duty business was turning out to be far more boring than he could have conceived, and these prisoners weren't doing their part to liven things up. He eyed the distance to the cell and set the keys on the floor then hurried back to the desk. "Now just give me a few minutes to get ready," he said and closed his eyes, the sheriff's sword lying casually across his lap.

Just then, someone lifted the latch on the outer door of the jail. Nyland's eyes flew open. He looked over at the cell. But no, the prisoners were just then slowly reaching for the keys on the floor.

When the door creaked open, Gerard and Vercleese walked in, looking dusty and smelling of wood smoke. "Interesting! I'd love to know what went through

Jutlin's mind when you whispered that in his ear," Vercleese was saying. "It certainly must have caught him off guard."

Gerard waved him to silence and motioned toward the cell then stopped, frowning at the sight of the two prisoners crouched on the floor and frozen in the act of reaching for the keys. He shook his head in dismay and retrieved the keys as the prisoners slunk back to the far corner of the cell.

"Nyland, you've got to be more careful," Gerard said, coming over to the desk. "Those two might have escaped, cutting your throat on their way out the door." He swept Nyland's feet off the desktop and grabbed his sword. "I'd never hear the end of it from your mother if that happened."

Nyland decided it might be best if he didn't mention the little game he had been playing with the prisoners. Somehow, he didn't think the sheriff would approve.

The sheriff yanked Nyland out of his chair. "And speaking of your mother, you'd probably head on home and let her know you're all right. We'll take over with these two now."

"Wait," Nyland said as the sheriff nudged him toward the door. "What about my report?"

"Report?"

Nyland drew himself up to attention. "Deputy Drebble advises the sheriff that the night progressed without undue incident," he proclaimed. Under his breath, he added, "Unfortunately."

"Ah, yes. Well, I'm glad to hear it, uh, Deputy Drebble." The sheriff pushed him out the door. "Thank you. Now go on home. You've earned a good rest after your, ah, dangerous endeavor."

Blinking in the light outside, Nyland yawned and wished the night could have proved more exciting. Then he brightened. His mother wouldn't know any different. In fact, she'd likely be the first to believe he had enjoyed a harrowing experience. He could embellish the story he told her.

He hurried off, thinking up exciting details with which to regale his mother.

Once Nyland had gone, Gerard shut the door and turned to find Vercleese rummaging through the desk. Gerard frowned. "What are you looking for?" he asked.

"I know we put it in here somewhere," Vercleese muttered. "Ah, here it is!" He stood up, holding Copper Mustache's cudgel.

Gerard flinched. "I'm sure there's really no need for that."

Vercleese's only answer was to whack the top of the desk a couple of times, testing the heft of the weapon.

"Really, we should try questioning them first," Gerard said. "There may be no need to resort to violence, at least not right away."

Vercleese grinned mischievously. "I can always hope, can't I?"

"But what if you accidentally kill one of them?" Gerard asked.

"Why does it have to be an accident?" Vercleese responded. "Besides, the way I figure it, that's the advantage of having the pair of them. That way, if I get careless with one"—he whacked the desktop again, causing Gerard to jump—"we've always got the second as a spare."

In the cell, Copper Mustache merely stared at the two law officers, his eyes betraying little emotion, but an expression of horror spread across the face of his accomplice.

Gerard ran a hand through his hair, then tugged at his beard. "Still, I don't know. It doesn't seem quite right, beating them and all."

"Ah, you're too tenderhearted," Vercleese growled. "That's always been the trouble with you. I haven't gotten to conduct a good interrogation in months. It'll be good to get myself in practice again. I only hope I haven't grown too rusty." *Whack, whack.*

"What do you want to know? We'll tell," cried the accomplice.

"Shut up, Grudge!" snarled Copper Mustache.

"Grudge?" Vercleese said, peering at the cell. "Well, it's good to have a name, even if it's a strange kind of name. What kind of name is Grudge?"

"Everyone used to complain to my mother that she was always bearing a grudge, so when she had me. . . ." He shrugged helplessly. "It seemed like a good idea . . . to my mother."

Vercleese turned to Gerard. "Well, I think we should start with our friend Grudge. What do you say?"

"Randolph!" Grudge wailed to his companion.

"I told you, shut up!" Randolph with the copper mustache hissed.

"But they're going to hurt me!" Grudge was blubbering now.

"They're not going to hurt you, stupid." Randolph grinned fiercely at Gerard. "Are you, Sheriff?"

"Oh, I won't, but I can't be sure about my deputy," Gerard said. "He's a real loose cannon. Please, you'd better tell us what we want to know. I'm not sure I can stand to watch him go through another interrogation. The last time he nearly kicked a prisoner to death. Seemed to enjoy himself, too."

Gerard waited. Grudge huddled in the far corner of the cell, his hands over his head, sobbing. Randolph, however, stared back at Gerard, unmoved.

Gerard sighed, letting his shoulders sag. "All right," he said to Vercleese, his voice scarcely above a whisper. "You can have Grudge. I'll see if I can talk some sense into this one." Gerard shuddered. "But take him out back. I can't stand to watch you going about your work."

Vercleese grinned and walked over to the cell. He motioned Randolph away from the door, unlocked it, and hustled Grudge out, locking the door behind him.

"Randolph!" Grudge whined. "For pity's sake, tell the sheriff!"

"Tell me what?" Gerard asked, a hand up to restrain Vercleese. But when Randolph stared silently back at him, Gerard nodded to Vercleese, who shoved Grudge out the door. Gerard could mark their progress as they went around to the back of the jailhouse by the pitiable crying of Grudge. For a long moment, there was silence; then Grudge let out a blood-curdling scream.

"You're next," Gerard said to Randolph. "That is, unless you start talking.

253

Behind the jail, Vercleese held the cudgel aloft. "Again," he said softly. "Put your lungs into it."

"Or what?" demanded Grudge. "You'll really start hitting me?"

"Just give me an excuse," Vercleese said grimly.

Grudge stared fearfully at the upraised hand and obliged with another terrified scream.

"So how about it?" Gerard asked after the screaming had died down.

"Oh, I could tell you a few things, all right," Randolph said. "Starting off with your parents."

"Uh-huh. No, thank you. I mean, do you have anything you want to tell me about Sheriff Joyner's death?" Gerard asked, cutting short any crudeness Randolph intended.

"Sheriff Joyner?" Randolph snorted. "I don't know anything about any Sheriff Joyner. Not that I'd tell you if I did."

"Next thing you know, you'll be trying to convince me you don't know Jutlin Wykirk either."

Randolph grinned, almost with relief. "Who? Am I supposed to have killed him, too?"

That evening, Gerard sat in the inn, staring morosely at a plate of untouched food—not, thank all the gods, spiced potatoes. He was tired and discouraged. Their charade had failed miserably, and they hadn't gotten any useful information out of Randolph or Grudge.

Now Gerard sat, ignoring the strains of music from the same trio as a few nights earlier. He felt no closer to solving the murder of Sheriff Joyner, the mysterious death of Salamon Beach, or the fumbled attempt on his own life. He had to admit it was possible neither prisoner knew anything about any of the ominous events. It was just possible, he told himself, they were both innocent.

But he didn't believe it for a moment.

His musing was interrupted when someone came to stand beside his table. "I'm sorry, Laura, I'm just not hungry tonight," he apologized, before looking up into the face of—not Laura—Kaleen. "Oh," he said. Then, feeling his greeting had been inadequate, he added, "Hello."

"And good evening to you, too, Lord Porridge." Her laughter dispelled some of the weariness evidenced in her face. "Why so morose? You look as though you just lost your best friend."

"Nothing like that," Gerard said quickly, shaking his head. "It's just . . . business," he concluded lamely, unwilling to confide his thoughts or confess his failure.

"May I?" she said, pointing to an empty chair across the table.

"Of course."

Just then, the trio struck up a lively tune. Gerard looked around the room. There, right on cue, was Blair, sitting nearby and treating him to an icy stare.

"That is unless"—he said, a smile slowly spreading across his face—"you'd care to dance."

"Why, your lordship, a reprise?" she said with a curtsy. "I'd be honored."

He led her to the center of the floor, where the

tables had again been pushed back, right past—quite by chance, of course!—the table where Blair sat. Once out in the dance area, Gerard proceeded to demonstrate all the flourishes his instructor had been at such pains to teach him.

CHAPTER

20

Gerard had in mind to sleep late the following day. Unfortunately, that goal wasn't shared by the rest of Solace. He was awakened early in the morning by a polite, ladylike tapping on his door. Gerard rolled over, trying to ignore the noise. The tapping continued, not nearly as subtle as before. This time it came accompanied by Lady Drebble's voice. "Sheriff? I must speak to you at once about a matter of the utmost urgency. Sheriff, are you in there? Open up. I really must insist."

Gerard groaned and rolled out of bed, being careful not to stand too erect and bang his head on the rafters. "Just a minute," he growled. He pulled on his doublet and hose and opened the door.

Lady Drebble stood on his doorstep, looking disheveled. Her hair stuck out in every direction, having come loose from its normally elaborate coiffure. She wore an old robe that appeared to be reserved for household use; it was frayed at the cuffs and elbows. As soon as Gerard opened the door, she barged in.

"Why don't you come in?" Gerard said sarcastically, addressing the now-empty air before him.

"Sheriff, something terrible has happened, and I really must blame you," she said from her place in the room behind him. "This is all your fault. Nothing like this would have happened had it not been for your heavy-handed constabulary tactics the other night."

"Slow down," he said. "Nothing like what would have happened?"

Lady Drebble looked around for a place to sit and took the only chair, leaving Gerard standing. "Oh, it's just horrible. Horrible! You've introduced my little Nyland to these dangerous ideas, and now he's gone out shopping for a sword."

"A what?"

"A sword! He's even talking about joining the town guard. My little Nyland, associating with riffraff and common rabble." Lady Drebble sniffed loudly and began blubbering.

"Lady Drebble, the town guard ordinarily doesn't have all that much to do with handling prisoners," Gerard said, stretching the truth a little. "Really, most of their work is in more of an, um, peacekeeping nature. So Nyland wouldn't really have that much association with, as you called them, riffraff and common rabble."

"Prisoners! Who said anything about prisoners?" Lady Drebble drew herself upright where she sat. "I'm talking about the members of the town guard. A ragtag bunch if I ever saw one! Now you tell me he might have a regular association with prisoners as well?"

"Ah," Gerard said, finding no other words suitable for the occasion. He stood there a moment, trying to collect his patience. "Well, you know, serving in the town guard is a most honorable endeavor and might prove to be just the sort of discipline Nyland needs—"

"Discipline! My little boy doesn't need any over-bearing, dictatorial discipline by the likes of such ... such. . . ." She foundered, at a loss for words.

"Hmm, how about if I talk to Nyland?" Gerard suggested, unsure the boy would be a suitable candidate for the guard in the first place. "Perhaps I can convince him to undertake some other, more befitting pursuit."

"Yes, I think you should," said Lady Drebble, rising. "And talk him out of the ridiculous notion of buying a sword."

Gerard thought about the danger to society of having someone like Nyland going around armed with a sword and tended to agree. "Oh, believe me, Lady Drebble, I will certainly do my best," he promised. He added to himself, "Even if I have to break it over his thick head."

Lady Drebble nodded but made no effort to leave. She just stood there, glaring. Gerard wondered momentarily about Nyland's father, whether the man had actually passed away or simply slipped away—silently, in the night. "Well, then," she huffed. "Well. . . ."

Gerard gently eased her toward the door. "I'll get right on it, Lady Drebble. You have my word. As if the very welfare of Solace was at stake." As soon as I get enough sleep, he amended to himself.

Lady Drebble allowed herself to be nudged toward the door, although at the threshold she turned, as if needing to assert that any exit she made was of her own volition. "Very well, then, Sheriff, I leave the matter in your capable hands. But be advised, I'll be watching you." She wagged a plump finger under his nose. "Yes, Sheriff, I will be watching you very carefully indeed!" With that, she wrapped her frayed robe tighter around her and left in a swirl of tattered elegance.

Gerard let out a deep breath of relief, pulled off his doublet and hose, and fell back into bed. With a satisfied groan, he found a comfortable position. Hardly had he fallen asleep again, however, than another knock sounded on his door, this one more tentative than Lady Drebble's.

"What?" he demanded.

"Sheriff?" came a man's hesitant voice from the corridor. It sounded as though the man had his lips pressed to the wood of the door and was whispering. "Might I have a word with you? I'm sorry to disturb you, but it's . . . it's . . . a delicate matter of the utmost urgency."

Gerard's shoulders sagged. But he got up, put on his doublet and hose again, and opened the door. Outside stood Bartholomew Tucker. His hands fidgeted at his sides, then he tried interlacing his fingers in front of him, and finally he clasped his hands behind his back. He glanced about the corridor warily, as if afraid of being recognized, although Gerard's attic was the only door the narrow corridor led to. "Might I come in?" Tucker asked, leaning close and keeping his voice down. "I believe an element of delicacy is called for in this matter."

Gerard stepped aside and let the man into his room. As soon as Gerard closed the door, Tucker adopted an affected, blustering manner. "Sheriff, I must confess to a certain degree of embarrassment at being seen down at that . . . that lowlife establishment the other night."

"The Trough," Gerard said.

"Yes, ahem." Tucker forced an awkward laugh. "That place. Well, it wouldn't do for a man in my position to be thought a frequenter of such a place. I hardly ever go there, you know, it was just an unfortunate coincidence I was there." He tried to laugh again, but it came out as a choking sound. "Anyway, Sheriff, I thought perhaps we could come to some sort of arrangement with regard to the other night." He gave a broad wink, no doubt intended to be conspiratorial.

"An arrangement?" Gerard said.

"Yes, you know, in return for certain funds changing hands. . . ." Tucker fished out a purse and began rummaging through it. "I'm not sure how much would be appropriate, having little experience in such matters, but I'm certain we could come to some kind of understanding."

"Master Tucker, are you trying to bribe me?"

Tucker's laugh this time was high-pitched and brittle. "A bribe? Why, no. Whatever made you call it that?" His hands came forward to trace vague, anxious designs in the air. "No, I'm only offering a certain inducement, as it were, as a means of showing my gratitude for any service you might see fit to render me. . . ." He wound to a stop, like some kind of fantastical gnome device running out of steam. His hands fluttered uselessly in the air before dropping to his sides.

"Master Tucker, I think you should leave now," Gerard said as seriously as he could manage.

"But what of the other night?" Tucker asked, the wind having emptied out of him like a punctured air bladder.

"I assure you, I have no interest in revealing your indiscretions to anyone," Gerard answered. "I am a guardian of public morals and do not care a whit about your private behavior."

"Thank you!" Tucker swelled up again, trying to regain some of his earlier dignity. "Oh, thank you, sir!"

"Think nothing of it," Gerard said, showing him the door.

He closed the door firmly behind Tucker's receding back and returned to bed. A few minutes later, just as he drifted off to sleep, someone else knocked on the door.

"What!" Gerard demanded.

"Gerard, is that you?" It was Palin's voice. "You sound upset about something."

Grumbling, Gerard got out of bed and donned his clothes once again. He opened the door, letting his head hang wearily. "Hello, Palin."

"Good morning! May I come in?"

With a feeling of déjà vu all over again, Gerard opened the door and let his latest guest enter.

"Is something wrong?" Palin asked. "You look terrible."

"This is the way I always look when I don't get enough sleep."

Palin's face looked quizzical "What? Aren't you getting enough sleep lately?"

"Never mind." Gerard sank down onto the bed, indicating the chair for Palin. "What can I do for you?"

"A delegation from the town council has raised concerns about the lack of success on the criminal investigations. They're demanding some kind of progress

report, what with the town fair today and the temple
dedication tomorrow. I think they just need a little
reassurance."

Gerard nodded. "Fine. I'll be glad to reassure them."

"Good. They're down at the jail now, waiting for
you." Palin rose.

Gerard didn't move. "Now?" he repeated.

Palin nodded, already halfway to the door.

"Couldn't this wait until later?" Gerard pleaded.

"Gerard, I'm sorry. The matter simply needs a little
diplomacy."

Gerard thought about saying he was deathly ill and
wouldn't be able to meet with the councilors for at least
another hour. Instead, he pushed himself to his feet.
"All right, let's go."

Palin clapped him on the back. "That's the spirit!"

Outside, people were already streaming toward the
grounds for the fair, set up on the outskirts of town.
Most everyone was dressed in finery, although a few
sported costumes—owlbears and hell beasts and the
like. Gerard spotted an exceptional minotaur mask,
then realized it really *was* a minotaur, which was a bit
unnerving. He and Palin worked their way against the
flow of carriage and foot traffic, for the jail lay in the
opposite direction. Gerard couldn't help glancing at
the many strangers, wondering about the numerous
pickpockets and petty thieves—not to mention light-
fingered kender—undoubtedly drawn to Solace just
for this occasion.

When he and Palin reached the jail, they found four
town councilmen shuffling nervously, casting worried
eyes at the two prisoners in their cell, as though the
dangerous-looking pair might at any moment pull

off some daring escape attempt, killing or taking the councilmen hostage in the process. To Gerard's eyes, the pair merely looked bored. They believed they would soon be released.

Behind the desk, Blair sat waiting to be relieved of duty, having guarded the prisoners during the night. He yawned, affecting an uninterested look, although he awarded Gerard a baleful glance. Gerard nodded to him, and he rose stiffly to his feet. "They're all yours," he said to Gerard as he left, though whether he meant the prisoners or the councilmen, Gerard wasn't sure.

Upon seeing Gerard and Palin, Cardjaf Duhar stepped forward, taking it upon himself to speak for the group. "Sheriff, please pardon the intrusion into your daily duties, but we're wondering whether any progress has been made in the investigation in Sheriff Joyner's murder or the strange accident which killed architect Beach. Some merchants in town are fretting. They're feeling especially vulnerable during this time, when so many strangers are in town. We would hate to see the fair or, even worse, the temple dedication marred by any additional, ah, untoward events."

Gerard made an effort to project more optimism than he felt. "I can assure you, we're on the verge of a breakthrough," he said in a voice that sounded artificial in his own ears. "We should have all the necessary writs signed and warrants certified by midnight tonight."

"By midnight?" Duhar looked startled to hear such a bulletin. Even the prisoners sat up and took note, Gerard thought, although they kept their gaze sleepily neutral. The councilmen looked from one to another, then waited for Gerard to expand on the good news.

Gerard shuffled some papers on his desk, looking around elaborately, not meeting their eyes.

"Well," Duhar said at last, filling the awkward silence, "don't wake me at midnight, if it happens at an odd hour." He forced a chuckle. "Pleasantly surprise me in the morning."

Just then, the voice of Tangletoe Snakeweed rang out just on the other side of the jailhouse window. "Investigation on the verge of a breakthrough . . ." he cried.

Gerard flung open the door and yanked the kender inside by the topknot. He was still wearing his extravagant brocade coat, despite the heat. A most ridiculous uniform for a town crier, Gerard told himself. Gerard thought fast, sitting the kender down in the chair behind the desk. He immediately began peering at him from various angles, drawing down his brows as he pretended to think things over, and making sounds of approval in his throat with each new angle.

"Tangletoe, how would you like the job of sheriff's deputy for the day?" Gerard asked.

"What!" Duhar said, mirroring the astonishment on the other councilmen's faces. Palin looked especially skeptical. "Sheriff," Duhar went on, "perhaps we should discuss this—"

Gerard waved him off, his attention still on Tangletoe, whose eyes grew wide with delight . . . until they narrowed suspiciously. "Now what exactly would that entail?"

"You'd have to stay here and guard these two dangerous criminals for the day," Gerard said, indicating the glowering pair in the cell.

"Dangerous, you say?" Tangletoe mused, looking at

the prisoners with interest and rubbing his chin.

"Oh, very."

"Well, I don't know. How dangerous? They'd have to be pretty dangerous to interest me. Guarding them would mean I'd miss most of the town fair, after all," he ended sullenly.

"Yes, but you'd be an official sheriff's deputy," said Gerard encouragingly. "And someone trustworthy has to watch over these two, who are mighty, mighty dangerous. They might try to escape on this day of all days. I wish I could be here myself. Oh, I only wish! But as you know, since you're the town crier, I'm neck-deep in this important investigation."

Behind the bars, Randolph rolled his eyes and Grudge snickered.

"What's more," Gerard added, "you're the perfect candidate, having already proved yourself as a crier. If you do a good job, I'll reward you accordingly. Why, I'll . . . I'll let you march in tomorrow's ceremonial procession before the opening of the temple."

"Hey!" Duhar said. "Wait a minute—"

"Of course if the job doesn't interest you," said Palin, joining in, "perhaps I could volunteer—"

"Hey, wait! Don't be so hasty. I didn't say no, did I? I was just considering my options. I know what I could do! I could play some music for these two," Tangletoe said eagerly. He glanced at the cell, looking tempted. "As you probably know, I'm very musically inclined. Beautiful music ought to keep them calm and manageable. And besides, I know two or three really piercing notes if they get out of line." He glowered menacingly at the prisoners.

Still Tangletoe hesitated. Gerard added one more

incentive. "Here, I'll tell you what, you can even hold onto my sword for me. You won't have to use it, of course," he added hastily, "but just the fact that you're in possession of such a magnificent weapon will cow these villains."

Tangletoe's eyes went wide. "Wow! I can't believe what a good day I'm having so far."

"Wonderful! Then it's a done deal!" exclaimed Gerard, acting as though the matter were thoroughly decided. He clapped the kender on his bony shoulder. "You practice your music, watch over these two ruthless villains, and I'll be back to check on you a few times during the day."

"Oh, you don't have to worry about me," Tangletoe said, stroking the sword lovingly. "I've tangled with villains before. Many, many villains. Why, as my Uncle Trapspringer used to say, 'When it comes to villains, Tangleknot'—he always used to call me Tangleknot, getting me confused with a distant cousin on my mother's side of the family whose name was Snarlknot. You see, if you take the 'Tangle' part of my name and the 'knot' part of my cousin's, you get—"

"That's great," Gerard said, ushering the councilmen and Palin out the door and slamming it behind himself.

As soon as the door closed, the kender's flute started up, sounding loud and shrill even through the muffling effect of the stout jailhouse walls. Cardjaf Duhar shook his head irritably and strode quickly away, accompanied by the other councilmen, who whispered together out of earshot.

"Palin—" Gerard began.

Palin clapped Gerard on the shoulder, looked him

in the eye, chuckled, and said, "Whatever you're up to, I don't want to know the details. I trust you. Good luck."

Then he, too, hurried beyond range of the kender's flute.

Inside the jailhouse, Gerard heard the two prisoners already calling for him to come back.

CHAPTER

21

The day was perfect for a town fair: hot, clear, and with the midsummer prospect of lasting just short of forever. Even before Gerard reached the field where the celebration was being held, he felt the town's collective air of feverish anticipation. Barrels were trundled down the cobbled streets of Solace toward the field, thundering their proclamation of wine and spirits to be dispensed at the fair. As Gerard got closer to the field itself, the dusty air grew thick with the aromas of a dozen different kinds of savory meats being baked, boiled, fried, and roasted, along with the lighter smells of fresh breads and creamy pastries hot from the ovens. Musicians could be heard warming up on pipes and tabors, trumpets and harps.

But if the smells and sounds promised much from afar, the actual fair, as Gerard saw when he arrived, exceeded even a child's most unrestrained expectations. Merchants and vendors had set up bunting-draped stalls all around the edges of the field in a rough circle. Already, the festive mood was leading to lowered sales resistance and open purses as revelers, many in masks and costumes, bought trinkets and baubles they might otherwise conclude they had little need for. Food and drink flowed in abundance from many of the stalls. Others offered beaded and feathered masks to anyone who regretted not having thought to come with their own. Here and there, jugglers and magicians, sword swallowers and tumblers passed through the crowd, receiving applause and coins for their efforts.

From somewhere on the field, the musicians began to play. Evidently, however, no one had informed them what tune they were to perform, or at any rate not all had paid attention when told, for they launched into enthusiastic renditions of at least half a dozen different melodies, with each person trying to bring his fellows round to his choice by sheer volume. Gerard grinned, finding even this cacophony preferable to Tangletoe Snakeweed's flute playing back at the jail.

He spotted Odila and Kaleen, arm in arm and looking for all the world like mother and daughter, coming through the crowd toward him.

"Hello there, Cornbread," Odila said with a smile.

"Lord Porridge," Kaleen said, blushing a little. Or maybe it was just the day's warmth, Gerard told himself.

He nodded, grinning unabashedly despite himself. "I would have thought you'd be busy at the temple until late into the night, getting ready for tomorrow," he said to Odila.

Odila and Kaleen exchanged a glance. "The day is young," Odila said. "Even hard-pressed clerics deserve a break once in a while. Meanwhile, Stonegate is there with his workmen even now, seeing to the finishing touches. There isn't much we can do now until they're done with the interior."

"Will it all be ready in time?" Gerard asked.

For a moment Odila looked drawn. With effort, she brightened. "It had better be, or there will be an awful lot of disappointed people coming for the inaugural service tomorrow morning. But Stonegate assures us everything will be in order before then."

"He seems a good man," Gerard said. "I'm sure if he tells you everything will be all right, you can be assured it will be." He turned to Kaleen. "And what about you? What will you be doing later, while Odila's over at the temple?"

"Oh, I'll be busy as well," she said vaguely. "Lots to do."

Gerard shuffled for a moment, self-conscious because he didn't quite know where he was leading the conversation, or how to end it either. "Well, I suppose I'd better be . . ." he offered after a moment.

Odila smiled broadly, as if aware of his uncertainty. "Yes," she said, taking pity on his plight. "We had best be on our way as well."

Gerard nodded to each of them again, but before he could move away, Kaleen abruptly leaned forward on her tiptoes and kissed him lightly on the cheek. Then she and Odila strolled away, chattering conspiratorially, their heads together and laughing. Over her shoulder, Odila gave Gerard a teasing wink.

Gerard found himself suddenly warmer than the day alone could account for.

As Gerard walked on, he came upon Torren Soljack, away from his forge for once, standing in line to buy a skewer of meat from a vendor. Soljack reached the head of the line and pulled out his purse to count out the necessary coins. Before he could do so, however, Gerard stepped forward and pressed coins from his own purse into the vendor's hand. Soljack turned, surprised. "Thanks," he said gruffly upon seeing Gerard. His eyes flicked over the sheriff, taking his full measure. His expression, if possible, became more dour. "Still not wearing your sword, I see," he added. "You didn't happen to leave it with a deputy again, did you?"

"Yes, but only because doing so made him the best-armed man in Solace," Gerard said expansively, trying to stoke the smith's pride.

Soljack said nothing but went off chewing his meat, apparently satisfied.

One booth was attracting particular attention as Gerard drew near. A small target, hardly bigger than the bottom of an ale mug, had been mounted about heart-high on a post. The target was connected, by means of a system of levers and pulleys any gnome would envy, to a seat mounted above a large tub brimming with water. Cardjaf Duhar occupied the target seat in all his usual finery, looking a little embarrassed at being found in such an undignified situation.

For a modest sum, onlookers received three small bags filled with sand to hurl at the target. A long line of people eager to test their skill wound from the booth and out into the field. So far, no one had been able to hit the target. Cardjaf Duhar sat secure and dry, for all his chagrin.

"Excuse me," someone was saying as Gerard approached. "Excuse me, please."

The people waiting their turn parted to allow a very determined-looking Gatrice Duhar to step the front of the line. She smiled her apologies at those she had displaced, who appeared to accept her right to pre-eminence in this matter, and paid her sum to the man working the booth. When she had received her bags of sand, she hefted one, considering its weight.

"This is for uprooting me against my will from my home in Palanthas," she cried loudly, and lobbed the first bag.

It missed by a wide margin, sending a chuckle rippling through the crowd of onlookers. Duhar shifted nervously on his seat.

"This is for bringing me to such a"—she hesitated, considering the people around her—"such a bucolic paragon of social distinction."

As onlookers looked questioningly at their neighbors, trying to decipher her words, she threw the second bag. It too missed, though by a narrower margin.

"And this," she announced, hefting the final bag, "well, this one, Cardjaf Duhar, is simply because. After twenty-five years of marriage, I'm sure I must owe it to you for something."

She hurled the bag, putting her whole body into the effort. The bag smacked into the target, setting levers and pulleys in motion and dumping Duhar into the tub. He landed with a splash that sent onlookers scurrying back from the spray. For a moment, he disappeared beneath the surface. Almost immediately, he burst forth again, sputtering and gasping at the shock of cold water. The onlookers laughed and hooted. Gatrice Duhar beamed at her success.

"And try not to track water all through the house when you come home!" she warned her husband as he struggled to clamber over the side of the tub. "I just had the floors cleaned and would hate to have the work all undone so soon."

With a haughty toss of her chin, she turned and strode away. The revelers doffed their caps and parted before her as if making way for a queen, which in a way is exactly what she felt herself to be. Gerard grinned and went to help Duhar as he sloshed and squished the short distance from the tub to a ladder. As Gerard held the ladder steady, Duhar climbed with injured pride back into his seat, where he awaited the next onlooker eager to try his skill.

Gerard was about to wander on, when someone tapped him on the shoulder. "Excuse me, sir," said a boy, who looked nervous at addressing the sheriff, "but they sent me to say it's time for the swordplay demonstration."

Gerard nodded and followed the lad to a square ring marked off with ropes. The boy hung back as Gerard climbed over the ropes and into the ring. Vercleese was already waiting, a crimson sash around his waist designating him as the referee. He pointed to a pile of armor in one corner of the ring, and Gerard put it on, strapping and buckling the burnished plates in place. When Gerard had everything arranged to his satisfaction, including a serviceable, blunted sword at his waist, he turned, cradling the helmet under one arm, and faced his opponent in the opposite corner. Blair Windholm stood similarly attired, a deep scowl on his face as he studied Gerard.

Vercleese motioned them forward into the center of the ring. "No thrusting with points, no blows with the sharp of the blade," the knight told the two contestants. "They're dulled but still dangerous. We want to give the citizens an exhibition of skill, not a bloodbath."

Gerard nodded his agreement. So did Blair, though his expression suggested he would have preferred to have done otherwise.

"Then let the competition begin," Vercleese announced, stepping aside from the two combatants. They settled their helmets into place and squared off, feinting and circling at first to feel out their opponent's weaknesses. Blair roared and charged, slamming into Gerard and catching him a stiff blow with the flat of his sword. Gerard careened away, momentarily off balance.

The ferocity of the charge startled Gerard. He quickly resumed his stance on the balls of his feet and shifted his weight from side to side, letting his body remember the feel of armor, rediscovering the moves the armor permitted. When Blair again charged, foolishly attempting the same maneuver, Gerard was ready. He deftly sidestepped and sent Blair sprawling by slipping his sword between the sergeant's frantically churning legs. Then he waited for Blair to regain his feet.

Blair was more wary after that, although his style continued to rely more on brute force than on technique. After the initial attack, Gerard easily parried most of his blows, treating Blair as he would have treated a raw initiate into the knighthood who still possessed more enthusiasm than polish. Frequently, he sent Blair reeling across the ring, howling with frustrated rage. Gerard wondered at the vehemence of the sergeant's attacks, and several times Vercleese had to hiss a reminder not to use the sharp of the blade as Blair hacked away furiously at Gerard.

Finally, Vercleese called the match, awarding it to Gerard. Gerard wrenched off his helmet and drew in deep lungfuls of the breeze that blew across his face, keeping his eyes on Blair. The sergeant leaned heavily on his knees, head hanging as he gasped for air. Each gasp tore from his chest and throat, sounding more like a sob than a breath. His own helmet lay abandoned on the ground.

Gerard began unbuckling the armor, still keeping a watchful eye on Blair. The sergeant also began stripping off the steel plates, avoiding Gerard's eyes. His head hung as if in shame. As soon as he was finished, he climbed from the ring and shouldered his way through the crowd that had gathered to watch, ignoring the hisses and catcalls directed at him for failing to congratulate the winner. Gerard let him go, recalling the expression of fury on Blair's face when Gerard had danced with Kaleen. Clearly Blair was jealous, and that was an issue he and the sergeant had yet to resolve.

After thanking Vercleese, Gerard again wandered through the fair. He watched an egg toss for a time, where two lines of paired contestants faced each other across an open space, each pair tossing an egg back and forth across the ever-widening distance separating the two. The crowd hooted and laughed whenever an egg broke, splattering the would-be receiver with its contents and disqualifying the pair from winning the competition. When only one duo remained, the judge held their egg aloft, then hurled it to the ground, where it too burst, ensuring the winners hadn't somehow switched a boiled egg for the raw one they had been given. The crowd applauded, and the next round of contestants hurriedly took their places, lining up along the field.

In another area, a tug-of-war was under way, with

two teams of burly men straining and heaving at the rope. Between the teams, a yawning mud pit, specially dug for the purpose, awaited the losers. Occasionally, a small boy or young woman would dart from the crowd to lend his or her questionable strength to a favored team, only to be chased away, laughing, by the referees.

The happy day wore on. Gerard bought a midday meal of roast chicken from one of the vendors and munched on it as he strolled through the fair. He watched a kender win the greased-pole climb, and Gerard was as amazed as everyone else in the crowd when the kender somehow managed to alight from his task with clothes unsmudged, grinning and holding the prize purse aloft. Gerard shook his head amazedly. Apparently, the creatures were immune even to ordinary assaults of nature, if one could manage that climb without getting smeared with grease.

At the dunking booth, someone new had replaced Cardjaf Duhar, who had undoubtedly gone home to change. His replacement, still in dry clothes, jeered and taunted the contestants who took their turns trying to hit the target and dunk him. If his intention was to rile them and disrupt their aim, his efforts were proving successful, for most throws flew well wide of their target.

A little farther on, Gerard came to a cleared area where contestants demonstrated their prowess at another kind of throwing. But instead of three bags of sand, for a fee contestants were given three balanced throwing knives, which they aimed at a series of small blocks of wood some fifty yards away. Each block sported a quill feather, stuck into the block as a target. Gerard, who had to squint even to see the targets adequately from this distance, oohed and aahed with the rest of the onlookers as contestants occasionally landed a knife in one of the blocks with a resounding *thunk*, severing the quill. But so far, no one had managed to hit all three targets successfully.

Then, as Gerard peered down the range, a knife sailed into one of the blocks, cutting the feather cleanly at the quill. Almost immediately, a second knife followed the first, and a second quill drifted to the ground while the knife quivered, its point buried deep in the block of wood. There was a pause, before the third knife flew the length of the course, again sinking into its target, and the third feather floated away. A cry of admiration rose from the onlookers.

Gerard turned to see who the successful contestant might be.

It was Blair, who even now was accepting the prize purse from the judge. Gerard's eyes narrowed in thought. This was a skill of Blair's that Gerard hadn't known the man possessed.

Finally, with the afternoon beginning to wane, Gerard came to an area of the field that had been cordoned off, limiting access to several rows of benches lined up in front of a rickety raised stage. At the rear of the stage, a tawdry canvas backdrop depicted mountains and trees. Otherwise, the stage was bare. In the field beyond the backdrop, a cluster of gaudily painted wagons stood, grouped in casual disorder. No two of the wagons were the same, with some short and squat, and others considerably larger. They were all decorated with extravagant carvings of scrollwork and exotic figures and strange, half-threatening faces. Gerard was handed a playbill as he joined the throng streaming into the makeshift theater and found a vacant seat on one of the benches. Seeking only to pass the time, he read the playbill without much interest.

THE TRUE AND TRAGICAL HISTORY OF HUMA
A Play in Three Acts
Performed by the
Traveling Players of Gilean
Under the Direction of Sebastius
Written by Sebastius
Costumes, Sets, Backdrops
Designed by Sebastius
All Rights Owned by Sebastius

Gerard snorted. Evidently, this Sebastius was a very humble fellow. With talents extending to so many disciplines, it was a wonder he hadn't found employment in one of the larger, more fashionable theater companies of Palanthas instead of roaming the back country with his motley entourage. Could it be that Sebastius's appraisal of himself exceeded the estimation granted him by others?

Still, Gerard was glad to be sitting for a change, and he did have a couple of hours to kill before nightfall. He settled as comfortably on the bench as the hard, rough-hewn boards allowed and crossed his arms, daring the traveling players to entertain him.

The doors of the wagons banged open in quick succession, and the players emerged. The crowd gasped, for the troupe was a highly mixed lot that included an elf, a kender, and even a minotaur. Yet the reaction from the crowd was not as strong as Gerard would have expected even a year earlier, before Solace's rapid growth brought representatives from these same races and more into town. A large human with a face as pliable as bread dough took the stage and addressed the crowd, holding up his hands for silence.

"Good citizens of Solace, you do indeed see individuals from several of the races of Krynn among our number." He went on to extol the virtues of his troupe, as opposed to all others, for using elves to play the parts of elves, kender for kender, and even at times ogres for ogres. Gerard paid scant attention, assuming the real reason for the motley assortment of players was that these had been the only individuals whom Sebastius (who was apparently none other than dough-face himself) had been able to recruit.

At length, the performance got going. A man in pasteboard armor strode to the center of the stage and knelt. When the crowd grew sufficiently hushed, he began pouring out a supplication to Paladine, praying for the means of countering the desolation being wreaked across Krynn by terrible dragons. And here, some magic occurred. At least, that was the only way Gerard was able to explain it to himself afterward, for all at once the man before him was not some itinerant player spouting his lines on a makeshift stage, but it was the great and noble Huma himself, praying for aid in the midst of a real forest. In answer to his prayer, a white stag stepped onto the stage. Some part of Gerard knew this had to be only a person wearing antlers and a robe of white fur, but what he saw and heard was a real stag. Huma, exhausted and hungry, drew his bow to kill the stag but was unable to do so, so affected was he by its grace and beauty. Huma threw down his weapon, and to his surprise the stag beckoned him to follow.

With that began the true and tragic adventures of Huma, during the course of which he met and fell in love with a strange woman in a grove in Ergoth, a woman who turned out to be a silver dragon in human form. In the end, Huma and his dragon love stood together to battle the Queen of Darkness and her evil dragons. Though the Dark Queen and her minions were driven from the land, the battle cost Huma and his silver companion their lives.

The play ended, and silence fell upon the theater-goers. The stage became merely a stage again, and the players only players, who lined up to take their bows. The crowd erupted in wild applause. Gerard sniffed and wiped impatiently at his eyes as he, too, joined in the adulation, for he realized part of himself would always belong to the knighthood he had thought to leave behind.

He looked up, startled at how late the hour was. The sun was going down. With a glance over his shoulder to assure himself the stage really was only that and nothing more, Gerard hurried from the improvised theater and into the gathering gloom.

CHAPTER

22

Gerard's first stop was at the jail, where he heard Tangletoe's flute wailing long before he got to the door. The kender could probably walk the length of Darken Wood unmolested if he were playing that thing, Gerard thought. He flung the door wide and hurriedly motioned for Tangletoe to stop.

"But I was just coming to the good part," Tangletoe protested, pausing. "Don't you want to hear it?" He raised his flute to his lips threateningly.

"Maybe another time," Gerard said hastily. "Right now, I, ah, I've come to consult with you about important sheriff's deputy matters."

Tangletoe brightened. "Oh, I've been very diligent about my duties." He looked toward the cell. "Haven't I?" he asked the two prisoners.

A glance told Gerard the prisoners were beyond answering, at least for the moment. Grudge lay in a heap in one corner, moaning, his arms thrown ineffectually over his ears. Randolph crouched in another corner, whimpering. When he saw Gerard, he shuffled toward the cell door on his hands and knees. "Please," he begged. "We'll confess to anything. Only please make him stop playing that accursed flute."

"All right, I've asked you this before, and I'll ask you again. What about Salamon Beach's death?" Gerard asked. "Did you two arrange for the accident that killed him? Tell me the truth, and be convincing, or I may have to take a trip out of town for a few days, leaving Tangletoe here in charge."

"Yes, oh yes, we did! We're guilty. Hang us, please."

"And Sheriff Joyner's murder?"

"Oh, we're behind that one as well," Randolph said, hope glimmering in his eyes. "Yes, and we should hang for that one, too. Hang us twice, only make him stop." He waved toward the kender.

"And the theft of Mora Skein's prize carrots?"

"Who?"

"The seamstress."

"Oh. Uh, yes, I'm sure we're responsible for that crime as well. Probably premeditated." He looked up pleadingly at Gerard. "Is it a hanging offense?"

"Hmm," Gerard said, his face scrunched up in thought. He approached the cell. "Turn around."

With a look of confusion, Randolph did as he was told.

"Now lift the hair on the nape of your neck," Gerard told him.

Randolph hesitated. "Why? What are you looking for?"

"Do I have to tell the kender to start playing again?"

"No, no!" Randolph said, hurrying to comply. He lifted his lank, dirty, collar-length hair, exposing the base of his neck. There, at the hairline, Gerard saw what he was looking for: the tattoo of the secret gambling society. Things were finally beginning to make some sense.

"What about him?" Gerard asked, gesturing to where Grudge still huddled and moaned miserably.

"Oh, yes, him too!" Randolph said. "Him especially. He was the mastermind of the whole operation, the ringleader." He wrinkled his brow, wondering if this might exonerate him from responsibility. "But I was a very enthusiastic accomplice," he said quickly. "I should still hang for it! Get me out of here, please. There must be another waiting spot for the condemned."

Gerard thought he was probably telling the truth about the architect, at least. However, he had his own notions of who had done what, and who was whose accomplice.

He turned to the kender. "Tangletoe, I just remembered. I've got to go on a delicate and most dangerous mission, and I'll need my sword back."

Tangletoe looked crestfallen. "But . . . but. . . ."

"I'll tell you what," Gerard said, fishing around in the desk for the knife that had been thrown at him in the woods. "I'll leave you with this instead. This, um, this is a quite rare and valuable assassin's throwing knife. In the hands of an expert, it can bring a man down at fifty paces. So, if you're a good aim, it's an extremely deadly weapon. Are you a good aim?"

Tangletoe looked hungrily at the knife. "Oh, I'm a very, very good aim!"

"Fine, fine," Gerard said. He peered more closely at the kender. "You aren't exaggerating now, are you?"

"What, me?" Tangletoe exclaimed. "Of course

not! Why, my Uncle Trapspringer used to say, 'Thumblethumb'—that being another name he called me sometimes, you see—'Thumblethumb,' he used to say, 'there's no finer knife thrower in these parts than you—' "

"Good, good," Gerard interrupted swiftly, exchanging the knife for his sword, which he belted at his waist. "Now I'm going to entrust these two vicious criminals into your care once more—"

"What!" Randolph roared. "Sheriff, you promised! You can't! Why, it's inhumane." He looked ready to weep. "I've already confessed to everything, even the theft of the cabbages."

"Carrots," Gerard corrected, then studied the man more closely. "Unless there were cabbages involved as well."

"Oh, there were, undoubtedly!" Randolph told him. "I'm sure we stole some cabbages, too, at one time or another. Probably eggplants and cucumbers as well. Anything we can steal, we just steal, steal, steal! Believe me! Only please don't let him play that flute again."

Gerard turned to Tangletoe. "I'll tell you what, you guard these two, but don't play the flute anymore unless they try to escape. You need to spend some time, uh, sharpening the knife."

Tangletoe's shoulders slumped and his head drooped. "All right." Then he brightened. "But if they try to escape?"

"Then you have my permission to play your most piercing notes."

"What if I suspect they're *thinking* about trying to escape?" Tangletoe asked, studying the cell pensively.

"I leave the matter to your judgment," Gerard said and hurried away before the two prisoners could protest.

From the jail, he went to Palin and Usha's house, where Usha opened the door. "I'm sorry, Gerard," she said, "Palin's not here. He's still at the fair." She wrinkled her nose. "He complains about his mayoral duties, but I think in truth he loves every minute of the job."

Golden-eyed and silver-haired, she appeared, as always, exquisitely beautiful, despite the wisps of hair escaping from where she had bound it up on her head, or the twin smudges of paint dotting one cheek. "Uh, actually, I came hoping to see you," Gerard said, struck shy in her presence. He glanced toward the back of the house. "I gather, since you're out and answering the door, the painting is finished?"

She smiled. "Yes. Just in time, too."

"Might I see it?" Gerard asked.

Her expression clouded. "Well, I didn't intend to show it to anyone until the temple dedication tomorrow—"

"Please," he said. "It's a matter of some urgency, involving the temple."

"In that case, of course." She held the door open and motioned for him to enter then led the way to her studio. The room was alight with candles. "I had just finished applying the finishing touches," Usha explained as Gerard's eyes swept the room, taking in the abundance of light.

Gerard nodded and stepped to the center of the studio, where the painting of Odila in front of the temple sat on an easel. In the picture, Odila looked radiant, adorned in the finest white-robed apparel of a cleric of Mishakal. Usha had even captured the pale spray of freckles that spilled across the bridge of her nose and onto her cheeks. In her hand, she carried the Staff of Mishakal. But it wasn't Odila that Gerard stared at. "The portents?" he asked, peering closer at the architectural details of the temple, where the images of death and destruction had been before.

"As you see," Usha said, beaming.

Gerard nodded once again and stepped back. "It's beautiful," he said.

Usha looked at her hands, appearing for all the world like a bashful girl. "Thank you."

"And now, I must be going," Gerard said.

Usha indicated the painting. "Did you find what you were looking for?"

Gerard thought the matter over before replying. "Yes, I think so," he said at last. "At least I know what I'm no longer looking for, and that's valuable too, after all.

"If Palin asks," she said at the door, "where shall I tell him you've gone?"

"Tell him I went to see a man about some seed and grain," Gerard said, hurrying into the deepening night.

"Where have you been?" Vercleese growled irritably when Gerard finally made it to the stable, where the knight already had both their horses saddled and ready.

"What's the matter? Were you worried about me?" Gerard asked, his voice honeyed with innocence.

"I, ah . . . oh, let's go!" Vercleese grunted.

Gerard grinned and accepted Thunderbolt's reins.

They rode to the checkpoint Gerard had set up on the road to Gateway. The young guardsman on duty looked bored and sleepy until he saw who his visitors were; then he snapped to attention.

"That's all right, ah . . ." Gerard began.

"Thomas, sir."

"Thomas, yes. Well, Thomas, there is something I want you to do. We"—Gerard indicated himself and Vercleese—"should be back by midnight, when your shift ends. But if we haven't returned by then, I want you to go straight to Blair and give him this message. Will you do that?"

Thomas nodded eagerly, accepting the sealed scroll Gerard handed him.

"Excellent," Gerard said. "Then I leave the matter in your capable hands."

With that, he and Vercleese rode on toward Solace Stream.

"Did the message tell him where to search for our bodies?" Vercleese growled. But he spurred his horse forward, keeping up with Gerard, evidently not expecting an answer.

Half an hour later, they arrived within sight of Jutlin's mill, just barely visible in the starlight. Gerard halted Thunderbolt. "I told him that I would come alone," Gerard reminded the knight. "So leave your horse here and go the rest of the way on foot."

"Are you sure about your strategy?" Vercleese asked, but Gerard hushed him and prodded Thunderbolt to a walk again, heading for the mill.

In the mill yard, Gerard got down briefly and studied the deep wagon ruts worn into the packed dirt, tracks that led to Jutlin's spacious barn. He strode over and banged on the door with the pommel of his sword. "Jutlin? It's me. Open up."

Gerard heard the heavy bar slide back; then Jutlin opened the door and peered out, holding a lantern up to examine Gerard's face. "You come here with your weapon drawn?" he asked, trying to affect a laugh. "Sheriff, what must you think of me?!"

Gerard sheathed the sword and stepped into the barn. Jutlin followed with the lantern, scurrying to keep up. When Gerard paused to examine a stack of crates and boxes labeled with different kinds of seed and grain, Jutlin set the lantern down on a nearby box and moved behind him.

"What exactly is it you looking for, Sheriff?" he asked. "Your message was a little vague."

Gerard stooped and picked up some of the straw that was strewn ankle deep on the floor of the barn. Idly, he let it sift through his fingers. Then he walked up to one of the crates marked "Flaxseed" and began to pry open the lid, using his sword.

"This is a lot of seed and grain," he said casually as he worked.

Jutlin chuckled nervously. "Well, I am, after all, a miller," he said. "That's what I do, grind seed and grain."

"Don't they have millers where these crates and boxes come from?" Gerard asked, pulling out a handful of flaxseed and letting it, too, trail through his open fingers.

Jutlin scowled but said nothing.

Gerard straightened, again sheathing his sword. "Well, it just seems a bit strange," he said.

"What's strange?" Jutlin asked. "What are you going on about?"

"Hmm? Oh, just that when Vercleese was here before, he said he recalled seeing stacks of crates and boxes as well, and those, too, were marked as seed and grain."

"I told you, I'm a miller," Jutlin growled. He hesitated. "Besides, those blasted elves are always coming here and stealing stuff. I have to get new supplies all the time."

Gerard laughed.

"Well, they are!" Jutlin said hotly, flushing with anger.

"Come on, Jutlin, we're wasting time," Gerard said. "You and I both know that. Where is your brother? I'd love to meet the rascal."

Jutlin backed away. "I told you in town, I ain't got no brother."

"That's all right, Jutlin," said a voice from the depths of the barn. "No use pretending any longer."

A man stepped out of the shadows, the man Gerard had first seen aboard *The Merwitch* wearing his peculiar dun-colored robe and cowl. The man with the familiar face Gerard had seen at the gaming table at The Trough. A face that looked familiar partly because it bore such an obvious resemblance to Jutlin's, although in the case of the brother, the face was more muscled, hardened. The brother came forward now, his cowl thrown back to reveal that menacing face.

"I'm the one you want to do business with, Sheriff," the newcomer said easily. "Aren't I?" He paused, considering. "You do want to do business, don't you?"

"That's what he told me back in town, Garth," whined Jutlin, backing farther away as if he might just slip out the door and escape.

"Shut up, Jutlin," Garth said, the command sounding casual on his lips, as if he'd spent a lifetime perfecting just the right tone with which to dismiss his brother. "Let me do the talking." He turned back to Gerard. "My brother says you want a cut of our little action, is that right?"

"You're selling arms and swords to all comers around here, am I right?" Gerard asked. Drawing his sword, he plunged it dramatically deep into the crate of flaxseed he had opened earlier. Feeling around down in the depths of grain, he drew out one of the distinctive, curved-bladed swords. "The elves and Samuval's band and Paladine knows who else. Anyone who can pay, right?"

"That's right," said Garth without moving, his eyes narrowed and hard. "And why shouldn't you have a cut of the action in order to look the other way, isn't that right?"

"The other sheriff, he wasn't smart that way, so—" Jutlin began.

"I told you to shut up!" Garth barked, more vehemently this time.

Jutlin, obviously afraid of his brother, let his sentence hang unfinished. His back was now against the barn door, and he looked distressed at being unable to edge away any farther.

There was a tense silence. "Lay your weapon down," Garth said at last.

Gerard looked at his hand as if surprised to find he was still holding his sword. "Now why would I do that?"

"Because we're all friends here, just doing a little friendly business together," Garth answered tersely.

"All friends," Jutlin repeated, sounding nervous.

"You, sir, are no friend of mine," Gerard said, brandishing his sword before him. "And you and your brother are under arrest."

"What?" said Garth, chuckling. He stepped fully out of the shadows at last, revealing one of the curved swords at his belt. "Oh my, are you trying to arrest me? That could spoil a beautiful friendship before it even gets going." He drew his own sword. The curved blade gleamed wickedly in the lantern light. "Besides, I think you miscalculate the odds here. After all, there are two of us, and only one of you." He gestured for Jutlin to come around from behind Gerard.

"Count again," said Vercleese, stepping out from behind a stack of crates, his own sword drawn.

So swiftly that it surprised everyone, Jutlin gave a shout and kicked over the lantern. The fire burst out and spilled rapidly over the straw-covered floor. Gerard, momentarily distracted by the flames, heard a groan and turned. Vercleese was slumped over, a knife protruding from his armless left shoulder. The knight clutched the knife hilt with his right hand and wrenched it free. But when he grabbed up his sword, he staggered, unable to keep his footing. He crumpled.

"Villain!" Gerard shouted. He charged Garth, and their swords met with the ring of clashing metal. The fire, meanwhile, was spreading through the barn, licking at the crates and boxes. Smoke filled the air, burning Gerard's eyes and throat. The heat scorched his entire body. The flames lit the scene garishly as he and Garth fought, matching each other blow for blow.

"Gerard, behind you. Watch out!" Vercleese cried from his crumpled position.

Gerard dodged another stroke from Garth and whirled just in time to catch Jutlin sneaking up behind him, one of the curved daggers in his hand. Jutlin froze, coughed on the heavy smoke, then dropped the dagger and ran for the barn door, flinging it open and disappearing into the night.

Through the open door, fresh air poured into the barn, fanning the flames into an inferno. The fire crackled and roared, climbing the walls and dancing along the overhead beams.

Gerard was clearly the more skilled fighter, but he was also fatigued from his long day at the fair, including the swordplay demonstration. Garth's violent style of attack pressed him hard. At one point, Garth's blade cut a wild swath through the air, slicing into Gerard's sword arm. Gerard grimaced and followed up on the stroke, finding a momentary advantage as Garth recovered his balance. Slashing downward, Gerard sent the arms dealer's weapon skittering across the floor. Garth lunged for it desperately just as part of the roof collapsed, engulfing him in flames.

Gerard rushed over to Vercleese and heaved him to his feet. With the knight leaning on him heavily, Gerard guided their path through the open barn door and into the night, where they coughed and wheezed in the clean air. But Gerard paused only long enough to see Vercleese safely away from the burning building; then he dashed back inside, holding his breath as long as he could against the thickening smoke. He found Garth's booted foot protruding from a heap of debris. The charred boot seared Gerard's fingers, but he pulled the man free, dragging him out of the barn.

The villain was still alive, though he labored for every breath. Gerard rushed over to a water trough and filled a bucket, splashing Garth with the contents to put out his smoldering clothes. Garth gasped at the shock of the water, groaned, and lost consciousness. Gerard, still retching from the smoke, collapsed beside him. Together, he and Vercleese watched the building burn to the ground.

CHAPTER

23

Fortunately, Thomas saw the blaze from the checkpoint and delivered the message to Blair right away instead of waiting until midnight. Garth might not have survived otherwise. When Blair arrived, he promptly took charge, summoning a wagon to carry Garth to Mistress Hulsey's shop, and insisting that Gerard and Vercleese accompany them there as well, despite their grumbled protests that they didn't need the aid of a healer for their wounds.

Argyle Hulsey bound Gerard's wound with salve and supported his arm in a sling. He grimaced each time she poked or prodded him.

"And you," Mistress Hulsey went on, turning to Vercleese, "surely you should know better by now, getting into trouble, having already lost an arm."

"Aw, what more could happen?" the knight asked sullenly. "You can't cut the thing off twice, after all." He winced at her roughness as she wrapped his wounded shoulder in linen strips soaked in pungent ointment.

"Go, the both of you," Mistress Hulsey said when she was finished. "Let me see to this other one." She indicated Garth, whom she had already treated sufficiently to keep him from dying. "Maybe he'll be grateful for my services."

"Will he live?" Gerard asked.

With her birdlike manner, Mistress Hulsey cocked her head and considered Garth, who moaned and tossed, still in an unconscious state. "Well, he's badly burned, and he won't ever be quite the same, but yes, I think he'll live. Not that he'll thank you for it, is my guess. Now go. Leave me be in peace."

She shooed them out the door. Gerard arranged to meet in a few hours with Blair and Palin, who had learned of the fire and met them on their way to Argyle Hulsey's shop, then stumbled up to his room at the inn for some much-needed sleep.

He awoke shortly after sunrise, stiff and sore, with burning eyes and a rasping throat. Still, he considered himself fortunate to be alive. He dressed awkwardly, hampered by his injured arm, which hurt more than he cared to admit, and made his way to the jail, where he was to meet the others.

He relieved Tangletoe, who had insisted on guarding the prisoners through the night, and separated the knife and miscellaneous office items from the kender's pockets before sending him on his way. Then he sat down to engage the two by-now-stupefied prisoners in a conversation while he waited for Palin and Blair.

It proved a most fruitful discussion. Threatening to bring back Tangletoe was incentive enough for finally loosening Randolph's and Grudge's tongues.

"So Garth was selling arms to the elves and Samuval, and somehow Sheriff Joyner got suspicious," Palin summarized Gerard's findings a short time later, "and when he went out to Jutlin's place, they killed him and hid the body in that field."

"Yes," agreed Gerard. "Something like that. We'll get all the details once we track down Jutlin. But that shouldn't be too hard to do. Jutlin'll be lost without his brother helping him out with every decision he has to make."

"And those two in the back?" Palin asked, jerking his head in the direction of the prisoners.

"That's a funny thing," Gerard said, tugging on his singed beard. "The architect's death had nothing to do with Sheriff Joyner's demise, not at all. The architect owed those two—and a couple of others I hope to catch up with later—lots of coin. It seems Beach had been gambling every night, desperate to win, but he kept on losing big. He was in way over his head. This pair warned him, then threatened him, and finally they rigged an accident. I think they only intended to give him a scare, but the situation got out of hand. One way or another, these two are responsible for Beach getting killed and injuring the others."

Palin shook his head in amazement. "How did you get them to confess?"

"Oh, that." Gerard chuckled. "That wasn't me really; it was Tangletoe. Apparently, our two friends back there aren't very musically inclined. Or at any rate, they didn't much care for Tangletoe's flute-playing. In fact, they got a little tired of his company in general.

He's rather talkative, as you know. Anyway I've never seen two criminals happier to see the sheriff get back to the office."

Just then, Cardjaf Duhar burst through the door. "I just heard!" he exclaimed excitedly. "This is marvelous! I hear you've got everyone under arrest and all the cases solved."

"Well, not quite yet," Gerard said modestly. "Not all."

Palin waved several rolled sheets of paper in the air. "Nonsense! False humility! I've got all the writs and warrants made out right here."

"Marvelous! Marvelous!" Duhar went on, looking none the worse for his repeated dunking the day before. "What an excellent sheriff you've turned out to be!"

"Temporary sheriff," Gerard said modestly. "Just temporary."

"Please, no! Not temporary!" said Duhar. "You're the right man for the responsibility. Don't leave Solace. Everyone's always leaving Solace." His tone on the last statement was abruptly rueful. "Give me your word you'll stay on the job!"

"Well . . ." Gerard said, considering the offer as he looked around the room. Blair looked away, down at his shoes. Palin's eyes were twinkling. Finally, Gerard's gaze returned to Duhar, and he nodded. "Uh, yes. Thank you. I accept your kind offer and will be happy to stay on the job as sheriff of Solace."

In a flurry of mutual admiration, everyone began congratulating everyone else. The mini celebration was interrupted by the sounds of musicians tuning up and crowds gathering outside somewhere in the distance.

"Well, it's a grand day!" Palin exclaimed. "A grand day for Solace!"

"Yes," said Duhar, choking with emotion. He took out a kerchief and blubbered into it, blew his nose, and wiped away a tear. "Though it's a sad day, too, for some of us." He looked up and saw Gerard staring at him, uncomprehending. "Oh my goodness, the procession! I have to run!" He dashed out the door.

"What did he mean?" Gerard asked.

Blair shrugged, looking bewildered as well.

Palin was heading toward the door, leaving the scrolls he had signed on the desk. He stopped at the door, pausing just long enough to turn and address Gerard and Blair. "Oh, you two don't know, do you? Of course you don't! Well, you'll find out sooner or later. His beloved daughter Kaleen has joined the holy orders and will leave Solace after the dedication ceremony today, as an acolyte to Odila."

"What?" exclaimed Gerard and Blair together. While both were astonished, Gerard couldn't suppress a grin, while Blair looked crushed.

Palin was already out the doorway, in a hurry to get to the procession, where he was expected to lead the march in his official capacity as mayor.

"Well!" said Gerard, at a loss for words.

"Huh!" said Blair. He stood, shoulders sagging. "I guess I'd best be off as well.

"Not so fast!" Gerard said, waving him back to his chair.

"But—"

"But, nothing. You're staying right here. We have a few things to discuss."

"But—"

Gerard waved his objection away. Awkwardly, he got to his feet and came around the desk to stand in front of Blair. "As you well know, one of the crimes hasn't been solved yet. The knife that someone threw at me"—he fished around and produced the weapon he had liberated from Tangletoe's pouch—"evidently it was intended to scare me into leaving town. Well, it took me a long time to figure out the culprit. I've gone to the bother of having Palin prepare an arrest warrant, with the name of the suspect. I'd like you to deliver this warrant for me."

He handed one of the scrolls to Blair, who was shuffling uncomfortably.

"Take it. There, now open it up," Gerard told the sergeant. "Go ahead. Now read me the name."

With shaking hands, Blair unrolled the scroll, read it silently, and turned pale. His head drooped and he slumped to a chair, letting the scroll tumble to the floor.

Gerard pulled a chair over and sat next to him. "I found out something I didn't know at the fair the other day. You're an expert knife thrower, Blair. You could easily have hit me with that knife if you really wanted to, couldn't you?"

Blair just hung his head lower in shame.

"You were trying to get me to leave town because you thought I was in love with Kaleen, weren't you?"

Blair nodded with a barely perceptible motion.

"Well," Gerard said, retrieving the scroll from the floor and crumpling it up, "we'll let that be our little secret. Kaleen is leaving town, I'm staying as sheriff, and I was never in love with her anyway. At least, I don't think I was!"

Blair looked up, a flicker of hope in his eyes.

"I'm a man who believes in second chances," Gerard

went on. "Here's yours. Your job today will be to stay here at the jail and guard these two miscreants, and to make sure everything stays safe and peaceful in town."

"But the procession—" Blair began.

"And if all goes well," Gerard continued as if the man hadn't spoken, "you'll still have your job and reputation at the end of the day. Now, if you'll excuse me, I have a procession to catch." He hurried out the door.

The procession was being organized (if a term suggesting that much coordination could be applied to the confused milling around Gerard found taking place behind the town hall) by Palin's clerk, a nervous young man driven to distraction. He looked ready to take to his bed for a tenday once this task was complete. Gerard hoped Palin would give him the necessary time off to recover.

Gerard saw the Ostermans talking to Brynn Ragulf, speckled with flour even on this august occasion, and his tiny, earnest-looking wife. Kedrick Tos and Tyburn Price were having an animated conversation, punctuated by considerable laughter, with Cardjaf and Gatrice Duhar. Bartholomew Tucker, his wife on his arm, gave Gerard a guarded nod and went to greet Palin and Usha. Nyland Drebble swaggered about, wearing a little toad-sticker of a sword. Even the explosive smith, Torren Soljack, was there. He spotted Gerard, quickly checked to see whether this time the sheriff was wearing his sword, and gave out a rare smile.

The harried clerk managed to separate Palin and

Usha and directed them to climb aboard a heavily decorated wagon that would be drawn at the head of the procession. Behind the wagon marched the visiting dignitaries and members of the town council, followed by the town guard, all of them dressed in their finest uniforms. To the rear of the guardsmen came the musicians, presumably the same ones whose cacophony had assaulted Gerard's ears at the fair the day before. Given that Tangletoe Snakeweed had sweet-talked his way in as one of their number, blowing on his flute like mad, Gerard didn't hold out high hopes for hearing much in the way of melody. But there would be an abundance of enthusiasm. As Gerard watched, the clerk dragged a protesting Torren Soljack over to where the musicians were grouped, gave him a huge drum with which to mark the beat, and scurried off to see to other preparations. Soljack caught Gerard's eyes, grinned and shrugged, giving the drum a few trial thumps.

A squabble broke out as the members of two guilds argued over which group should take precedence in line. The argument ended in a coin toss, and the threat that if the two groups continued to argue, they would both be banned from the procession altogether, a threat that quickly silenced all concerned.

The clerk materialized at Gerard's side. "Sheriff Joyner always used to carry the town banner," he said, thrusting a pole at Gerard. The pole was topped by a white silk banner, onto which a majestic vallenwood was embroidered.

Gerard indicated his right arm, still dangling in its sling. "I don't know. That's my good arm," he explained. "But there"—he scanned the crowd and sighted Vercleese—"there's the man who should carry the banner today."

The clerk looked doubtful, but handed the banner over to Vercleese, who beamed with pride. "But what about you?" Vercleese asked when Gerard drew near. "What will you do? Folks will be expecting the sheriff to do something."

"I'm sure I can buy a couple of bags of candy from one of these vendors." Gerard indicated the enterprising sellers who were just beginning to hawk their wares, as they threaded their way through the throngs gathered to watch the procession. "I'll hand the candies out to the children as we pass."

"Capital idea!" beamed Vercleese.

"Quiet!" Palin's clerk shrieked above the hubbub just then, and Gerard realized the man had been calling for silence for some while. Amazingly, a hush descended on the officials and dignitaries, perhaps one borne of shock that a mere underling would dare to address them so. The clerk was by now too distraught to notice their censure, however. "Now, is everybody ready?" he asked. When no one dared answer in the negative, he said, "Musicians, begin playing!"

The musicians did so with gusto, most of them mercifully in tune. With the steady beat of Soljack's drum to measure everyone's steps, the procession got under way.

Gerard had never felt prouder.

The procession followed a serpentine route that took it through much of Solace. Everywhere along the way, people lined the streets and peered from bridge-walks, greeting members of the entourage and cheering. Gerard saw Laura on the deck outside the main room of the inn and Argyle Hulsey in front of her shop. Brentwood and Dorla Gibbs had come into town, as well as Biggin Styles from his pig farm (the smell of which, clinging to Biggin, kept the area around him relatively clear, despite the otherwise crowded street), Corly Ames, and Trent Linden and his wife. Even Gerard's dancing instructor had turned out for the occasion, tall and haughty as she dabbed self-consciously at a tear.

At one point, the procession wound past the Tomb of the Last Heroes, and Gerard felt a peculiar sense of having come full circle in his journey. He had reached a suitable ending to this stage of his path in life, yet it was also a new beginning. He felt the medallion of office hanging around his neck, a weight now grown familiar and comfortable, and grinned. It was time to update those letters home with a new one relating how things had turned out. This time, however, he felt at ease with where he was and what he was doing. This time, he would actually send the letters to his parents and let them know he would be staying on in Solace.

He saluted his fallen friends as he passed the tomb, thinking especially of Caramon, thanking him for his sage advice when Gerard had first returned to Solace.

They marched all the way to the new temple, where the civic, secular portion of the day's observances concluded. As they drew up in the temple grounds before the glistening, newly completed structure, the religious aspect took over. The musicians ceased playing, and a hush fell over the multitude. A reverential awe took hold, replacing the more boisterous procession. Quietly, the town officials and visiting dignitaries led the way up the steps, through the huge double doors, and into the temple entrance hall. On ordinary occa-

sions, worshipers would then file into one of the two
worship rooms on either side of the entrance hall, but
for such a major ceremony as this, with so many people
in attendance, the crowd continued instead through a
second set of double doors and into the central chamber
of Mishakal.

Pungent incense filled the air, mixing with the
smells of new plaster and freshly applied whitewash.
Gerard stifled a sneeze that felt too profane for the
surroundings. The statue of the goddess dominated
the chamber, looking out over her followers with a
benevolence that transcended the mere marble of the
sculptor's art. Gerard felt a moment of disorientation,
remembering the dream he had had of the statue holding the bloody body of Salamon Beach. But all hint
of Mishakal's ominous tidings had vanished, and the
goddess gazed at him serenely.

Once in the chamber, the worshipers sat on temporary wooden benches constructed just for the
dedication, for normally the spacious hall with its
domed roof high overhead would be kept free of such
ordinary furniture. When the crowd was seated and a
hush had descended like a palpable presence over the
room, an acolyte sounded a great bronze gong three
times. The deep, bass rumble reverberated in Gerard's
chest long after the gong was struck.

This was followed by a formal procession of clerics
and acolytes from the entrance hall to the foot of the
statue of Mishakal. This was a more solemn procession than its civic counterpart. Odila led the grave
assembly, dressed in a blazing white robe and bearing
a five-foot long blue crystal staff. Of course, it wasn't
the Blue Crystal Staff, the one given to Riverwind by

a manifestation of Mishakal, but rather a replica, a symbol of the healing power of the goddess. Similarly, the disks Kaleen bore in sober majesty weren't *the* Disks of Mishakal, those one hundred sixty platinum repositories of sacred learning now housed in Palanthas, but smaller reproductions, crafted just for such occasions of worship as this.

Kaleen looked lovely dressed in her acolyte's robes, Gerard thought. He swallowed past a lump in his throat, realizing how much he would miss her. Still, he realized she had been seeking something all along that Solace couldn't provide, and he was glad she had found what she apparently was looking for. Perhaps in time Kaleen would return, and he would still be there and would see her again.

He felt content to let the future bring what it would in its own good time.

EPILOGUE

That night, Gerard sat in the inn, his earlier elation having slowly evaporated during the long day. The room seemed more crowded than ever, and the chairs and tables were being pushed back to allow room for dancing. In one corner, a lone fiddle player tuned his instrument. From snatches of overheard conversation, Gerard could tell that the temple dedication had gone off gloriously. Solace was justifiably proud of itself.

Late in the day, Gerard had found a merchant bound for Southern Ergoth who had agreed to deliver Gerard's letters for him. The crimes had been solved. He had a job he enjoyed. All in all, he had nothing to complain about.

So why, he wondered, did he feel so low?

People kept stopping by his table, clapping him on the shoulder and congratulating him on solving both murders. They were glad, they said, to have him for their sheriff. Each time, Gerard mustered a smile, thanking his well-wishers for their thoughts. People were even sending over fresh tankards of ale, until

Gerard had a veritable wall of them lined up in front of him—far more ale than he dared to drink in one evening. He still got a queasy feeling in his stomach when he recalled the last time he had overindulged in ale.

The first night he had danced with Kaleen.

Someone came to stand by his elbow. Another well-wisher, he thought, and turned with a forced smile to hear what this person had to say. To his surprise, a pretty young woman with fiery red hair hovered there. She smiled nervously. "Will you be having some of Otik's fine spiced potatoes this evening, sir?" she asked.

"Huh?"

"Otik's potatoes, sir. Will you be wanting some?"

Slowly, Gerard realized she must be the new serving maid Laura had hired to replace Kaleen. "Oh, no, thank you." He considered a moment. "But is there some of Laura's chicken and dumplings, by any chance?"

"I believe so."

"I'll have some of that instead."

"Very well. I'll have it right out." The girl curtsied prettily and hurried away.

Gerard watched her go. She seemed very capable, especially given that this was her first night on the job and the inn was as busy as Gerard had ever seen. And she certainly wasn't hard on the eyes.

Gerard found himself looking forward to the upcoming days, when he would make a point of taking his meals at the inn. Things were looking up in Solace, he decided. Yes, things were certainly looking up, indeed!

THE LINSHA TRILOGY COMES TO ITS THRILLING CONCLUSION!

CITY OF THE LOST
Volume One
MARY H. HERBERT

Linsha Majere, the granddaughter of Caramon Majere, a hero
of the War of the Lance, has been entrusted with a terrible
secret. When the precarious order of Ansalon is shattered, she
must embark on a desperate quest to save the city from an
unstoppable enemy.

FLIGHT OF THE FALLEN
Volume Two
MARY H. HERBERT

As the Plains of Dust are torn asunder by invading barbarian
forces, Rose Knight Linsha Majere is torn between two vows—
her pledge to the Knighthood, and her pledge to guard the eggs
of the dragon overlord Iyesta. To keep her honor, Linsha will
have to make the ultimate sacrifice.

RETURN OF THE EXILE
Volume Three
NANCY VARIAN BERBERICK

Linsha has been taken prisoner, and the only chance she has to
keep her vow and save the dragon eggs is to marry the feared
leader of the Tarmak invaders. On the far-away island home of
the Tarmak, she finds hope in the most unexpected place of all—
among her enemies.

www.wizards.com

THE MINOTAUR WARS
RICHARD A. KNAAK

*A new trilogy featuring the minotaur race that
continues the story from the New York Times best-
selling War of Souls trilogy!*

NIGHT OF BLOOD
Volume One

As the War of Souls spreads, a terrible, bloody coup led by
the ambitious General Hotak and his wife, the High Priestess
Nephera, overtakes the minotaur empire. With legions of
soldiers and the unearthly magic of the Forerunners at his
command, the new emperor turns his sights towards Ansalon.
But not all his enemies lie dead...

TIDES OF BLOOD
Volume Two

Making a bold pact with the ogres, and with the assurances of
the mysterious warrior-woman Mina sweetly ringing in his
ears, the minotaur emperor Hotak decides to invade Ansalon.
But betrayal comes from the least expected quarters, and an
escaped slave called Faros, the last of the blood of the lawful
emperor, stirs up a fresh, vengeance-driven rebellion.

EMPIRE OF BLOOD
Volume Three

A new emperor sits on the throne in Nethosak, supported by
fanatical Protectors and the dark magic of the Forerunners.
Faros leads the rebellion to the capital and the temple, to a
showdown with the usurpers—and destiny.

www.wizards.com

THE KNIGHTS OF SOLAMNIA RISE TO POWER AGAIN!

The Rise of Solamnia

DOUGLAS NILES

LORD OF THE ROSE
Volume One

From the chaos of the War of Souls emerges a mysterious stranger who unites the knighthood and leads the feuding factions of Solamnia into war against barbarian invaders.

THE CROWN AND THE SWORD
Volume Two

The Lord of the Rose leads his army against the barbarians, wielding revolutionary new weapons. But his most deadly enemy awaits him not on the field of war, but in the halls and courts of the ancient Solamnic kings.

THE ELVEN NATIONS TRILOGY GIFT SET

FIRSTBORN
Volume One

PAUL B. THOMPSON & TONYA C. COOK

In moments, the fate of two leaders is decided. Sithas, firstborn
son of the elf monarch Sithel, is destined to inherit the crown
and kingdom from his father. His twin brother Kith-Kanan,
born just a few heartbeats later, must make his own destiny.
Together—and apart—the princes will see their world torn
asunder for the sake of power, freedom, and love.

THE KINSLAYER WARS
Volume Two

DOUGLAS NILES

Timeless and elegant, the elven realm seems unchanging. But
when the dynamic human nation of Ergoth presses on the
frontiers of the Silvanesti realm, the elves must awaken—and
unite—to turn back the tide of human conquest. Prince Kith-
Kanan, returned from exile, holds the key to victory.

THE QUALINESTI
Volume Three

PAUL B. TOMPSON & TONYA C. COOK

Wars done, the weary nations of Krynn turn to rebuilding their
exhausted lands. In the mountains, a city devoted to peace, Pax
Tharkas, is carved from living stone by elf and dwarf hands. In
the new nation of Qualinesti corruption seeks to undermine this
new beginning. A new generation of elves and humans must band
together if the noble experiment of Kith-Kanan is to be preserved.

www.wizards.com

COLLECT THE TALES OF THE
HEROES OF THE LANCE!
NEW EDITIONS AVAILABLE!

THE MAGIC OF KRYNN
Volume One
In these ten tales of adventure and daring, the original
companions of the War of the Lance are together again. The
tales tell of sea monsters, dark elves, ice bears and loathsome
draconian troops.

KENDER, GULLY DWARVES, AND GNOMES
Volume Two
Nine short stories by superlative writers tell the tales of the
well-loved companions as they confront danger, beauty, magic,
friendship, and their destinies.

LOVE AND WAR
Volume Three
Finally, the legend of Raistlin's daughter is revealed. This story,
in addition to ten other compelling stories of chivalry, heroism,
and villainy fill the pages of this stirring addition to the
DRAGONLANCE canon.

THE TALES OF
THE HEROES OF THE LANCE CONTINUE!
NEW EDITIONS AVAILABLE!

THE REIGN OF ISTAR
Volume Four
Before the Cataclysm, in the wondrous days of the Kingpriest,
marvels abounded. A kender becomes a Solamnic Knight
(almost), an ogre saves the dwarven race, and gladiators
compete in the bloodsport of Istar.

THE CATACLYSM
Volume Five
The Kingpriest's arrogance brings the wrath of the gods upon
Krynn. The result is the Cataclysm—chaos and anarchy, despair
and villainy...and inspiring heroism.

THE WAR OF THE LANCE
Volume Six
The world of Krynn is caught in a terrible war between the
minions of Takhisis and the followers of Paladine. Dragons clash
in the skies and a small band of friends, who would one day
be known as the Heroes of the Lance, strive for freedom and
honor.